KAY

## *"I'm attracted to you,"*

Jesse Breen said softly. "And you're attracted to me. And feelings like this are gifts not to be wasted."

Marnie Raines's beautiful eyes took on a dark glint. "You do assume too much if you believe I play around."

"I never meant to imply that you do. I'm not trying to seduce you, Marnie. I'd just very much enjoy seeing the fair with you, and since you are technically a single woman, I didn't think I was steppin' on anyone's toes."

"I've never quite trusted a man who was both a blunt talker *and* a charmer."

"I'm generally a forthright man."

"Are you always this overbearing?"

"I think of it as masterful. Besides, you like it."

"That attitude is way behind the times."

"And that's a shame, isn't it? I guess I'm about the last of the good guys."

"Either that, or a man who's a bit too big for his britches...."

Dear Reader,

Each month, Silhouette **Special Edition** publishes six novels with you in mind—stories of love and life, tales that you can identify with—romance with that little "something special" added in.

August is a month for dreams . . . for hot, sunny days and warm, sultry nights. And with that in mind, don't miss these six sizzling Silhouette **Special Edition** novels! Curtiss Ann Matlock has given us *Last of the Good Guys*—Jesse Breen's story. You met him in *Annie in the Morning* (SE#695). And the duo BEYOND THE THRESHOLD from Linda Lael Miller continues with the book *Here and Then*—Rue's story.

Rounding out this month are more stories by some of your favorite authors: Laurey Bright, Ada Steward, Pamela Toth and Pat Warren.

In each Silhouette **Special Edition** novel, we're dedicated to bringing you stories that will delight as well as bring a tear to the eye. For me, good romance novels have always contained an element of hope, of optimism that life can be, and often is, very beautiful. I find a great deal of inspiration in that thought.

What do you consider essential in a good romance? I'd really like to hear your opinions on the books that we publish and on the romance genre in general. Please write to me c/o Silhouette Books, 300 East 42nd Street, 6th floor, New York, NY 10017.

I hope that you enjoy this book and all of the stories to come. I'm looking forward to hearing from you!

Sincerely,

Tara Gavin
Senior Editor
Silhouette Books

# CURTISS ANN MATLOCK
## Last of the Good Guys

*Silhouette Special Edition*

Published by Silhouette Books New York

**America's Publisher of Contemporary Romance**

A new broom sweeps better,
but an old broom knows the corners.
— Karen's Grandmom Anderson
(a very wise lady)

My gratitude to Tara and Leslie for their valuable insights.

SILHOUETTE BOOKS
300 East 42nd St., New York, N.Y. 10017

LAST OF THE GOOD GUYS

ISBN: 0-373-09757-3

First Silhouette Books printing August 1992

Printed in the U.S.A.

**Books by Curtiss Ann Matlock**

Silhouette Special Edition

*A Time and a Season* #275
*Lindsey's Rainbow* #333
*A Time to Keep* #384
*Last Chance Cafe* #426
*Wellspring* #454
*Intimate Circle* #589
*Love Finds Yancey Cordell* #601
*Heaven in Texas* #668
*Annie in the Morning* #695
*Last of the Good Guys* #757

Silhouette Romance

*Crosswinds* #422
*For Each Tomorrow* #482
*Good Vibrations* #605

Silhouette Books

*Silhouette Christmas Stories* 1988
"Miracle on I-40"
*To Mother with Love* '92
"More Than a Mother"

## CURTISS ANN MATLOCK,

a self-avowed bibliophile, says, "I was probably born with a book in my hand." When not reading or writing—which she does almost constantly—she enjoys gardening, canning, crocheting and motorcycling with her husband and son. Married to her high school sweetheart, the author is a navy wife who has lived in eight different states within a sixteen-year period. The nomadic Matlocks finally settled in Oklahoma, where Curtiss Ann is busy juggling two full-time careers—as homemaker and writer.

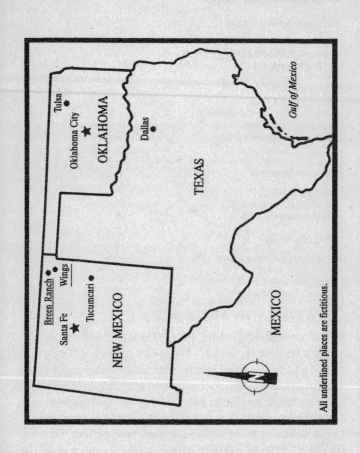

All underlined places are fictitious.

## New Year's Day

*Jesse Breen...*

That he'd lived a full five decades slipped up and hit Jesse full in the face on New Year's Day, when Celeste Mendoza decided to turn her back on their six-year affair in favor of marriage with a hardware store owner up in Trinidad.

"Charlie Hayward is serious," Celeste told him that fateful morning, right after a nice, warm night, while sitting across from him at the linen-covered breakfast table, sipping coffee from her gold-trimmed bone china, wearing a ruffled and laced gown that showed the mounds of her breasts such as only women over forty were given to having—breasts as creamy rich as the butter Jesse was spreading on his toast.

The hairs prickled on the back of Jesse's neck. "*I'm* serious," he said and quietly set his knife to the plate. He *had* thought of marrying her...someday. And he hadn't known that Celeste had seen any more of Charlie Hayward than when she needed nails for hanging pictures.

She faced him squarely. "Have you been serious for these goin' on seven years, or are you simply workin' up to it?"

Jesse stared into her knowing, dark eyes.

"If Charlie asks me to marry him, I'm going to," she said.

Jesse knew what she wanted him to say but was unable to say it.

Celeste carefully set down her china cup, reached to the counter and snatched up a newspaper. She smacked it down right on top of his buttered toast, saying, "Here, you had better start lookin' for another woman to cozy up to."

Feeling struck by a stiff winter wind, Jesse watched her flounce from the room, her lacy gown billowing out behind her. Looking downward, he saw the paper she'd give him was the *Lonely Hearts Newsletter.*

As he found his boots and put them on, he thought how he wouldn't be coming to the comfort of this homey cottage anymore, to the comfort of this warmhearted woman. He took up his hat and coat. He left the *Lonely Hearts Newsletter* on the table. He'd just opened the front door when Celeste came back into the room. They gazed for long seconds at each other.

"You love Charlie?" he had to ask, supremely sorry that he hadn't come around to wanting to marry her and knowing he was losing one of the best friends of his life because of it.

"Yes." Her eyes held a reservation, but she spoke quite firmly. "You and I, Jesse…we've been a comfort to each other, but I want more now."

"I wish you the best," he managed to say.

Hat pulled low against the bright sunlight of a new year, he drove away in his pickup truck. Alone in the sole vehicle on the black line of a New Mexico state highway snaking out across the high, rolling, snow-covered plain, Jesse came face-to-face with what he'd been trying to ignore for the past year—that twenty-one had turned to fifty-one, and there was no going back, ever. He'd been a widower for some sixteen years now, was the father of three grown sons and a grandfather, too. He had strands of gray in his thinning brown hair, lines around his eyes, age on the backs of his hands.

Lately he'd taken to surveying himself, naked, in the long mirror in his bathroom. He was only a bit thicker around the middle than his sons, and due to a lifetime of hard, physical work his muscles were still rock hard. He was just shy of six feet in his boots, broad across the shoulders, thick in the biceps and tight in the thighs. He could still ride all day and take a turn or two around the dance floor that night.

In his modest estimation, his features couldn't be termed pretty: his nose had been broken twice, his cheekbones stuck out like those of an outlaw, and he had enough lines running out from his eyes to make feet for some half-dozen crows. Still and all, he knew he had appeal; he never lacked for feminine attention from young girls on up to matron ladies, whether it be at a tavern or a church supper or a café.

Common sense told him there would be many more sojourns on horseback into the mountains, as many trips to New York City as he wished, still time yet to learn to fly a plane or anything else for that matter, and hopefully, God willing, a number of times yet to make love to a woman in the sunshine.

But for the first time in his life he'd lost the great desire for doing any of those things. Somewhere along the way, Jesse Breen's passion had gone exceedingly dim.

*Marnie Raines...*

It was Marnie's birthday—her thirty-sixth—but none of the fifty-some people who'd gathered for the sumptuous New Year's Day party in Patrick Vinsand's spacious penthouse apartment on the fifteenth floor knew it. And Patrick had forgotten.

From the time she'd awakened that morning, Marnie had waited hopefully for Patrick to surprise her in some intimate and private way. She had romantic visions of him pulling out a velvet case containing a pearl necklace, or handing her a card with diamond earrings tucked inside, or perhaps presenting her with a single red rose and telling her it couldn't compare with her beauty.

She still clung to expectant hope, but it was afternoon now, and that hope was fading fast. She would have her tongue cut out before she reminded him; having to remind someone wasn't at all the same as him thinking of it on his own.

Feeling a growing sense of suffocation creep across her shoulders, Marnie slipped away from the crowd of people, most of whom were veritable strangers, and closed herself in the black-and-white tile bathroom off of Patrick's bedroom. Beyond the closed door she could hear the clink of crystal and china, the drone of voices and occasional bursts of laughter and soft music underlying it all. Drinking in the solitude, she carefully pressed a cool damp cloth to her face for moisture and then renewed her lipstick. Spying a single gray hair among the rich auburn ones, she plucked it out. She was vain about her hair, she thought.

In all honesty, Marnie knew she could pass for twenty-five. Well, at least twenty-eight. Of course, everyone looked younger these days with bran diets and high-style exercise clothes women could wear to the grocery store. However, not everyone had led the physically wearing life Marnie had.

For a slice of time she gazed into the mirror and saw again the young girl with long auburn braids who'd begun working alongside her father and brother in the fields, chopping cotton, at the age of eight. She'd picked the cotton, too, from dawn to dusk, and strawberries, beans, and just about everything else that could be picked or dug or chopped.

Chills ran down her spine as she looked around the sparkling room. Her family had often lived in a one-room shack smaller than this bathroom—when they weren't living in their old '49 Buick Roadmaster—where their toilet had been a chipped enamel bowl.

She stared into the mirror and searched the image there, finding no resemblance to the girl who'd lived in a Buick.

Her body was femininely filled out in the right places with firm flesh, instead of sharply bony all over. Her skin was very pale because she deliberately kept it protected. Where once her hands had been scabbed and callused, they were now soft and smooth. Even the long scar on her stomach from that cut that had given her a case of tetanus had faded almost clean away.

Suddenly her father's face and voice filled her mind. He used to laugh and say, ''Little sugar, anyone born on New Year's

Day is born into a special life." Poor Daddy. He'd lived on dreams that had never come true.

A knock sounded at the door. "Marnie? Are you in there?" It was Patrick.

Hope that maybe he'd remembered her birthday surged through her. She whipped open the door. "Yes... I was just taking a bit of a breather."

He smiled and bent to kiss her neck. "Aren't you having a good time?" he whispered.

"The hostess isn't expected to have a good time," she answered blithely, telling herself she was being a silly child over this birthday business.

"Everything is going great—you can relax." He grinned. "It's a super New Year's party, baby. Your arrangements are perfect, as always, and I admit you were right about having a day party instead of a New Year's Eve bash. No one can talk seriously at those night bashes. Come on out—Herb Wallis just got here and asked for you."

He took her arm. She took several steps, then stopped, and he cast her a questioning look.

She threw her arms around him, pressed her cheek to his. More slowly, his arms came around her.

"What is it, baby?"

*Do you love me?* Her heart cried out with the anguish she couldn't voice.

She shook her head and smiled at him. "Oh, nothin'—just happy New Year."

He kissed her lightly and escorted her around the penthouse, accepting compliments on the party and giving Marnie total credit for it all, while his handsome hazel eyes danced with appreciation when they lit on her. Patrick was like that, always giving appreciation when it was due; he said it brought out the best in employees.

As she moved with him, nestled in the crook of his arm, Marnie told herself that she wasn't his employee. She received a number of admiring glances, a number of curious and envious ones, too. She paid no heed but smiled and said all the niceties, assuming well the appointed roll of glamorous mistress to the wealthy and dynamic Patrick Vinsand. When she clinked her champagne glass with Patrick's in a merry new year toast, she silently wished herself happy birthday.

And she experienced the odd, sharp sensation of her life dribbling away like sand down a bottomless hole, never to be had again.

## Chapter One

As Jesse directed his one-ton dually pickup truck and stock trailer through the thick, slow moving Oklahoma City traffic, a hulking camper cut over in front of him and bumped up over the curb of the entry into McDonald's, the driver obviously intent on getting a hamburger or to die trying. Jesse slammed on his brakes and hissed a few good expletives.

He was hot and tired, having driven from Wings, New Mexico, that day—all the way across the endless prairie of the Oklahoma panhandle, then down here to OKC to the state fair.

With the window down, he breathed in the warm September air and exhaust fumes and patted his fingers on the steering wheel in rhythm to a Don Williams tune coming from the compact disk player in the dash. His best lizard boots still shone but were pinching his toes, the sharp creases had faded from his denim jeans, his once crisp shirt now stuck to his back and his hair was damp beneath his silver belly Stetson. In the opposite seat Ham slept curled in a ball, the same position the dog had started out in at six o'clock that morning.

Jesse had the depressing thought that he'd made this same drive many a time in his younger years, and he couldn't remember feeling so tired from it. Years made a lot of changes in a man, he guessed. A man gained patience and understanding and lost stamina; at this point, he didn't care for the exchange.

He turned east, and the traffic thinned a bit and made him feel that at last he could draw a good, deep breath.

A flashy Cadillac convertible, top down, came around him, pulling over in front of him in the left lane in order to pass a green clunker of a pickup in the right. At the wheel was a woman wearing giant black sunglasses and a white scarf wound tightly around her head and neck. Her shoulders were bare, and at first glance he thought *she* was bare. Then he saw she wore a red sweater that hung off her shoulders.

Picking up speed, he stayed right behind the Cadillac. Gazing down at the back of it, he mused over the color—a cross between pink and brown. He finally decided he would call it pink. The interior was white.

Only people who lived in the city could have white interiors. Jesse at times had longed for a vehicle with white seats but hadn't ever been able to bring himself to be so foolish. What with living on a ranch and raising three sons, white seats were as practical as a black velvet bed for a collie. He looked at the woman's head swathed in that white scarf, its ends whipping in the wind, and imagined the type of woman who drove a pink Cadillac with white seats. And wore a sweater hanging off her shoulders.

Then, in one of those crazy, uncontrollable instances where everything happens in the blink of an eye and there's not a single thing a person can do other than go with the flow, the pink Cadillac stopped, and Jesse ran smack into it. He had only a split second's reaction time in which to stomp on his brakes, when he saw the brownish-pink trunk growing before him.

His body slammed into the seat belt stretching across his chest. As his head bounced around, he saw Ham fly up into the air like a black-and-white hawk feather carried on the wind, and then saw Ham hit the floor at about the same time a crashing blow came from behind. Screech, wham, honk and bang, and in two seconds Jesse found himself sitting there, the hiss of steam from somewhere and Don Williams still singing from the CD player. He blinked and stared at Ham, who stared bug-eyed and accusingly at him from the floor.

He hadn't only run into the Cadillac, but someone had hit him from behind. A glance in the right side mirror confirmed this—a blue pickup stuck out from the rear corner of the trailer.

*The sheep!*

He unsnapped his seat belt and had the door open before the belt whirred away.

*Oh, man, hope the sheep aren't hurt.... Oh, man, oh man....*

He hit the ground.

*The woman!* He spun around and ran for the Cadillac. The sporty vehicle now appeared to be an appendage to the taller, red front end of his truck. The woman was getting out, slowly, as if dazed.

"Are you all right, ma'am?"

Running his gaze over her, he took her elbow to help her stand. He didn't see any blood on her and swept his gaze over the Cadillac, looking for clues to damage he might have missed. The windshield was smooth; no head had cracked it. In fact, everything from the seat forward appeared perfectly intact.

Her face came up, and those big black sunglasses gazed at him, like fly eyes, he thought.

"Are you all right?" he asked again. He brought his hand up to snatch off her glasses, then decided against it. "Maybe you should sit back down and wait for a medic."

She took off her sunglasses and looked at her car, horror blooming across her pale features, like June cactus blossoms in a morning sun.

"What have you done? Oh, my...oh! *You've smashed my car!*"

She gazed at the sight with eyes the size of saucers, and her voice rose with each word until it reached a peak that could almost shatter glass. She apparently didn't have a concussion.

"Yes, ma'am," he said and turned, running toward his trailer. It had been pushed onto the side of the road by the force of the impact.

The sheep—*the sheep!* he thought, hunkering down and popping up to peer through the aluminum slats of the sixteen-foot stock trailer as he ran. He couldn't see any fleecy bulky beings, though he could hear bleating. It seemed to come from several directions.

He rounded the end of the trailer to see the tailgate lying cockeyed on the hood of the blue pickup, which had its front end shoved into the right rear of the trailer.

Suddenly a four-legged, woolly ball sprang from the trailer with a loud bleat. Jesse made a grab for it but missed, and it—Fancy, his best lamb—scurried off, apparently like the five other companions she'd been traveling with, running crazed between the cars. Jesse, not quite wanting to believe it, took another look into the trailer. Yes, it was empty, leaving him clean out of breath.

"Aw, jeez . . . *jeez!*"

This from a young man with California blond hair and a bright green cap that he kept slapping against his baggy black pants as he danced around in misery, looking from the trailer to the pickup truck, a neon blue souped-up job with the words The Hulkster emblazoned in gold along its side.

"Man, did you have to stop like that? Aw, jeez. . . ." He was near tears, no doubt seeing his car insurance bill approach the size of the national debt. At least he, too, appeared physically unharmed.

For the brief minute Jesse allowed himself to look at the mess, the dismal facts ran through his mind: nine-month-old, top-of-the-line Ford 350 crew cab dually, with the perfect seat for his behind, and a brand-new Aluminum-Lite trailer, purchased three days ago for the express use of his sheep. And this trip was the first time his sheep had been in it. His prize-winning Rambouillets, which were now running around loose out there among the cars and pickups and campers. And all because he'd been preoccupied with a bare-shouldered woman driving a pink Cadillac with white seats, who had decided to stop in the middle of the road.

People were beginning to gather. Above the noise of engines and the babble of voices came the sound of a police siren growing louder. Ham was barking out there somewhere, already on the job rounding up his charges. Jesse spied one of his yearlings, Elsie, cruising down into the deeply ditched grassy median.

Then he heard distinct bleating joined by a woman screaming.

"Aaahhhh! No! *No . . . no!*"

He rounded the trailer to see the white-scarfed woman waving at a white woolly—Sadie, a yearling ewe—standing smackdab in the middle of the Cadillac. And just when he thought he'd seen everything there was to see in this world, Jesse thought. Something had to have scared Sadie there, and in all the melee, it couldn't have been too hard.

"Get . . . *get!*" The woman yelled and waved—without much effect, because another woolly—Irma—went clopping over the crunched trunk of the pink car, pushed Sadie and squeezed into the area behind the driver's seat, one sheep following another as was their nature.

"Oh . . . !" Sobbing, the woman gestured frantically at Jesse. "Get them out! Oh, no . . . go, you . . . get!" Ripping the white scarf from her head, she waved it and yelled at Sadie as the bulky ewe moved into the driver's seat.

"They won't hurt you," Jesse said, running to calm her. "They're safe from the traffic there, and if you'll be quiet, they will, too."

"Safe? In my car! On my *leather* seats! You idiot!"

Taking into account her experience, Jesse let the insult pass. "Yes, ma'am. I'll get them into the trailer as soon as I can gather the others."

The woman turned on him like a viper.

"You don't intend to leave them here? You've already massacred the back of my Cadillac—must you trash the rest, too? Look! *Look what you did!*" Her arm was the wrath of God pointing at his sin.

"Me?" Ire, like lava in a simmering volcano, rose up in Jesse. "Ma'am, I'm sorry, but *I* wasn't the one to slam on the brakes in the middle of two lanes of traffic."

"I didn't stop!" She stamped her foot. "I slowed to avoid hitting the little old lady who decided to drift over into my lane!"

"What little old lady?" Jesse said with a wave of his hand, indicating that obviously there was no little old lady in sight.

"Well..." She looked down the road and gestured with great disgust. "She's gone on. But she was there! And if you hadn't been ridin' my bumper, you would've been able to stop and avoid demolishin' the back end of my car!"

"If you wouldn't have *stopped* in the middle of a thoroughfare, none of this would've happened. And if it makes you feel any better," Jesse pointed at his truck, "the front of my pickup isn't in such good shape, either!"

They stood glaring at each other.

Suddenly a reflection of light flitted across the woman's face, and Jesse realized the eyes he stared into were large and a striking blue—and filled with angry tears. Her hair curled to her shoulders and was dark against her starkly pale skin. Large gold loops dangled from each ear and waved in the breeze. And her lips were glistening pink. It came to him that she was a real beauty at the same time that she turned away and wiped at her cheeks.

Then he thought he was pretty stupid standing there arguing with a bawling woman while his sheep were running around loose. He straightened and turned away.

"Ham—" he commanded the dog that had appeared, panting happily "—get Elsie." He pointed to the ewe chomping grass down in the ditch; then he moved away to look around for the two missing sheep—Billy and Fancy—while trying to keep an eye on those in the Cadillac. Since he'd forgotten to tell Ham he wanted Elsie in the trailer, the dog naturally brought the ewe to where the others were corralled—into the pink Cadillac, Jesse saw, when he heard the woman begin ranting again.

"No! Oh, not another one! Get out of my car!" She jerked open the door and took hold of Sadie by the neck and tugged.

Jesse leapt over and pulled her off. "Stop it! Leave her be!" Sadie started to jump out, and Jesse pushed her back in and slammed the door, all the while holding the woman at arm's length.

"That is leather, I tell you! *Italian* leather!"

"And it's dead, but that sheep is alive and worth damn near seven thousand dollars!" he roared, having reached his limit for taking nonsense.

The woman blinked and shut her mouth as if he'd slapped her, which Jesse felt on the verge of doing. Stepping back, she crossed her arms. "At least let me get my purse before they stomp all over it."

Jesse looked over and saw a white bag that Irma was now straddling. He stretched over, jerked it out, thrust it at the woman, then stalked away.

Two policemen arrived and set to sorting out traffic. By that time calling the paramedics seemed unnecessary, though Jesse thought the woman from the Cadillac should have been checked over. She was greatly unsettled, to say the least. Billy, the big ram, was found. He was pretty worked up and had dented a few cars with his rolled horns. Two giggling teenage girls brought up little Fancy. Jesse managed to get Billy back to the trailer, and Ham succeeded in bringing the rest of the flock and holding them corralled inside until the cockeyed tailgate could be set into its cockeyed space. Jesse, with help from the young driver of the neon blue wreck, who identified himself as Jimmy Pollard, worked on securing it there with some grunting, some expletives and some good old trusty baling wire.

At last, all parties involved—which included the three drivers of the wrecked vehicles, two people who claimed to have seen it all, and four people who claimed Jesse's ram had dented their cars—grouped around the police car to give their names and stories. In the interest of getting rid of people, the officer in charge first took the names of the owners of the ram-damaged cars. Jesse thought a number of these people were seizing the opportunity to make a little money by blaming Billy for damage he had nothing to do with. Jesse certainly wouldn't want to be the insurance adjuster on this one. And he didn't want to see his next insurance premium, either.

Then it was time for the details of the wreck. After several group starts, the officer pointed at Jesse. "You. Give me your story—starting with your name."

Jesse pushed back his hat, gave his name and told what had happened from his viewpoint in four concise sentences, not sparing himself from blame, but not taking it all, either.

"He's leaving out about the old woman in the green car," Cadillac Woman said, with a hand on her hip. Cadillac Woman was the mental name Jesse had given her. Actually, his full mental description was: Beautiful Cadillac Woman with top cream skin and heavenly legs. He added to it as he went along.

"I didn't see any old woman or a green car," Jesse said matter-of-factly.

"That's obvious—just as it's obvious that you should have," Cadillac Woman said with a superior look. Jesse added "smart ass" to his mental description.

"I saw the wreck from start to finish." This was put in by a woman with big red hair, who for some reason felt a vested interest in all this. "I saw the old woman in the green car."

"No, it was gray," someone else added.

And Jimmy Pollard put in helpfully, "There was a green pickup truck up ahead of me."

Jesse said, "The old woman in the green car doesn't have a thing to do with any of this." He pointed his finger at Cadillac Woman. "Old woman or no, you still stopped in the middle of a thoroughfare."

"I didn't stop!" She stomped her foot. "I just slowed down—then had to stop when you smacked into me!"

"I'm not disputin' that I smacked into you. But I couldn't help it when you stopped."

"That's exactly what happened to me!" Jimmy Pollard said, and waved his baseball cap.

"You should have been prepared," the woman with the big red hair said. "You should always be prepared to stop."

Jesse was warming up to tell Big Red Hair what she should be prepared to do when the police officer's voice cut across the furor.

*"Hold it!"*

Silence reigned. Anyone with a lick of sense knew to give way to a man in uniform who stood six and a half feet and carried a gun. The officer pointed his pencil at Jesse and read aloud what he'd written, confirming name, address and details. When

Jesse confirmed the report's accuracy, the officer tore off a slip of paper and thrust it at Jesse. "You can go," he ordered, and Jesse went—for all the reasons just stated above.

He didn't pause until he reached his trailer, where he looked at the slip of paper the officer had given him. It was a healthy ticket for improper driving.

Folding it away into his pocket, he looked at his sheep. They were fine, munching sweet alfalfa hay as if nothing had ever disturbed them and as if they'd never eaten in their lives, exactly as sheep were supposed to behave. Propping a hand on the trailer, he took off his hat and ran a hand through his wet hair. It was hot as August, which was two weeks gone. He looked forward to the Cadillac. Jimmy Pollard and a couple of passersby had freed it from the front end of Jesse's pickup truck in order to move both vehicles off to the side of the road, but the Cadillac, its back end smashed into its rear tires, still couldn't be driven.

With a sigh, Jesse pushed himself away from the trailer, got a rag from the tool box of his truck and walked to the Caddie. Beautiful Smart Ass Cadillac Woman with top cream skin and heavenly legs was still talking over at the police car.

He saw now that her hair was more red than brown, which had been his earlier impression. A deep sorrel color that shone in the bright sunlight. It curled to her shoulders and waved in the wind. The bright red sweater that hung across her shoulders flowed over her curves to her thighs, and below that, black pants fitted her heavenly legs like a second skin. On another woman those clothes might have sort of screeched, but on her they spoke softly, alluringly, with class. Everything about her said class, pure wool and a yard wide—and Jesse was a man who knew his grades of wool.

Reluctantly he jerked his gaze back to the Caddie. He didn't really want to look at the white seats. Sheep stomp when they get agitated, and their hooves had undoubtedly cut the *Italian* leather, as Cadillac Woman had described it. Not to mention that about all any stock animal did was eat and go, and there was little chance those white seats had escaped staining. It did seem a bit silly to worry over them, though. With the rear end all smashed in like it was, the insurance adjusters would more than likely find the Caddie a total wreck. Still, Jesse felt the gesture of wiping them up was the polite thing to do.

Then he was amazed. He searched the interior, but by the grace of God there wasn't one tear in the leather seats, though there were a few good messes. And as he did his best to scrub them up, he smelled a very acrid scent wafting up from the carpet on the passenger side.


Marnie was not happy to have gotten a ticket for negligence; she'd gotten it because the police officer simply felt it his duty to hand everyone involved a ticket—can't figure out who's to blame, so just blame everyone! She, however, was intelligent enough to see the uselessness of arguing over it. Ordinarily she might have tried flirting her way out of it, and without guilt, either, because this was a tough world, a man's world, and a person had to live by what was, not by what a person wished could be. But she was too wrung out to flirt and cajole. And, though she wasn't about to say it, perhaps she was a *little* bit at fault.

She strode back across the double lanes to her car—her fifty-six-thousand-dollar Cadillac Allanté now sitting crippled on the side of the road. A Datsun speeding along honked angrily and whooshed past, and she ignored it. She was the pedestrian, after all, she thought. She saw that farmer bending over into her car. What was he doing to it now?

Hand on her hip, she stopped. "What are you doin'?"

His body straightened slowly, like the unfolding of a powerful machine. She noticed first his wide chest, then the way his hat sat on his head at a cocky angle—she'd noticed that before—but she hadn't noticed that his eyes were the palest, iridescent blue, like ice on a high mountain underneath the blue sky. He was at once handsome and homely. He was a rugged man, tall, solid, skin nearly as brown as his hair, and with a virile presence so strong it made her instantly aware of being a woman.

"I got most everything wiped clean," he said and gestured toward the seats, "but, uh, one of them peed on the carpet." He gazed at her, his eyes studying her intently, and she averted hers. "I'm sorry about crashin' into you," he said.

She looked back at him, gave a large sigh and an accepting nod and tossed her purse into the driver's seat. She stared glumly at the smashed rear end. What the hell did it matter that now her seats were clean, or that she had sheep pee on her carpet? Her car was ruined.

"The nice thing now would be for you to apologize for stoppin' in the middle of the road," he said.

She glared at him.

He noticed then the fine, tiny lines spreading from the outer corners of her deep blue eyes. Those and a certain presence about her that told him she wasn't a young thing like he'd first figured. At least in her thirties, he mused, again running his eyes over her hair and those absurdly large earrings that blew in the wind. She was accepting now of what had happened, though far from happy about it.

Oh, he was a cocky son of a gun, she thought, as she took in the glimmer in his eyes and the mocking set of his mustache. His attractiveness struck her again, too, when she wished it wouldn't. He wasn't a young man. Of middle age, and holding it very well, she thought as her body reacted. Irritated with herself, she turned back to the crumpled mess of her Cadillac.

"Could be they'll put a new rear end on it," he offered.

"I have some camera equipment in the trunk," she said in a small voice, and despite herself, her bottom lip quivered.

"Oh?" He looked again at the smashed metal. "How much equipment?"

"Not too much. Two cameras and two lenses, one rather large, all in a bag."

"Oh, well, there's plenty of room for that in there. It probably just got shoved forward. Let's take a look."

"I tried. The lid's stuck. The trunk area goes clear through under the folded top, and you can get to it from inside the car—but the inside door is stuck, too."

"Wait a minute."

He retrieved a crowbar from his toolbox and went to work, prying the crumpled trunk lid until it sprang up. They both peered inside. Of all the empty space in that surprisingly large trunk where the black bag could have been and remained perfectly safe, it had to be in the far left corner. Compressed there. She grabbed the bag's handles and jerked it free.

"How's it look?" Jesse asked as she took out the camera, then the lenses.

"Bent," she said. One camera, her newest and best, was unscathed. The old one, the one that was precious to her and could not be replaced, had been damaged at the lens connection. A fresh lump rose in her throat, and she hastily returned the camera and obviously compacted lens to the bag and stood. "Thank you," she said stiffly and slammed the trunk lid down. It promptly popped back open. "Oh!" She whirled away.

Jesse followed. Wanting to say something to make her feel better, he said, "The kid's or my insurance company will pay for your camera and lenses, too, if you make a claim. And your insurance rates won't go up." He motioned toward the kid, Jimmy Pollard, who stood in the parking lot across the road, watching as the tow truck hooked up his neon wreck. "His insurance will probably be pickin' up the bill for all three of us."

Her gaze swung over to the boy. "His will? Why?"

His eyes lingered on her bare shoulders. "Ah...third guy in a three-car pileup. The kid and I both got tickets for riding too close to the car ahead, and I imagine our insurance companies will be conferring, but the last guy's insurance usually has to pay. At least, that's what happened to my son when he was in a wreck like this."

"Oh," she said. Her gaze swung back to Jesse. "Will your truck run?"

He nodded. "The radiator has a leak, but it'll get me to a garage." In any case, the damage to his truck was nothing like what had happened to her car. It was his trailer that would never be the same. He pulled out his wallet. "Ah...let me give you my name and address." On the back of his business card, he wrote the name of the hotel where he was staying in the city and the name of his insurance company.

She got her purse and wrote down similar information for him, saying, "I already called my agent—from my car phone."

Her accent was striking, Southern, but different from Oklahoman, more stretched out, with the edges of her *L*s and *R*s rounded softly. Pushing back his hat, he gazed at the card she'd handed him. Her name, Marnie Raines, address and phone number were written in flowing blue ink on the back of a card for an insurance agent. *Marnie.* When he looked at her, he still thought Cadillac Woman.

"I'll call my agent as soon as I get my sheep taken care of," he said, tucking her card into his shirt pocket. "I'm from New Mexico, but I gave you the telephone number of the hotel I'll be stayin' at while I'm here—I'll be here through Thursday."

She nodded absently, her attention turning to the tow truck that had arrived for the Caddie.

Jesse remained with her as her car was hooked up from behind. He felt she needed someone standing there by her, a woman alone who'd just gone through a pretty good shock. He'd always been better than average at comforting women; he liked to comfort women. His Gina and Celeste used to say he only did it when *he* wanted to, though, not always when it was needed, proving he did it for himself. Perhaps he did.

She sniffed hard a few times and dug around in her purse— one of those great big affairs that could do as an overnight bag. After a minute, Jesse handed her his handkerchief.

"Thank you," she said, then dabbed at her eyes and nose.

When the tow truck was ready, Jesse asked if she had a ride— though he was uncertain as to how to help her, other than to call her a cab.

She shook her head at his offer. "I have a ride," she said, and pointed to a long black limousine he hadn't noticed before, sitting off to the right side of the road some hundred feet up ahead.

Jesse looked with wide eyes from the limo back to her. *The woman had called a limo?* Most people made do with a cab.

She was digging into her purse again. He ran his gaze over her hair, noting how the sun gleamed and glimmered on it, like copper leaves turning in the wind. Turning wildly, he thought in a second of romantic fancy.

He shifted his gaze and his stance, saying, "Guess that's it."

"Wait." She held out several bills. "Would you take these over to the boy?"

The top bill was a hundred. Puzzled, Jesse stared at the money. "Why?"

"Because his insurance payments are going to go sky-high, and none of this was really his fault." She shook the bills and sniffed again. "It's two hundred—all I have right now—but maybe it will help him some."

Jesse slowly took the money. "There's no need for you to feel responsible for any of this. What happened is called an *accident*—not an *on-purpose*."

She gave a small, dry smile. "I know *I'm* not responsible—but I imagine I have a bit more money to spare right now than he does. And I remember what it's like to be eighteen."

"Why don't you give it to him?"

She averted her face and shook her head, setting her earrings to bobbing. "Please?" She turned those glimmering wide eyes to him.

It wasn't the tears; tears never shook him. It was that he perceived and understood her shyness.

"Sure—and I'll add a bit to it, how about that?"

She swung her purse handles over her shoulder, saying sharply, "I think that's only fair, because if you'd been payin' attention and not ridin' my bumper, this entire *accident* probably wouldn't have happened."

Fire sparked inside Jesse. "I wasn't the one who stopped in the middle of the road—" He broke off.

They gazed at each other, each challenging the other. And then Jesse felt the stirring of something he hadn't felt in a long, long time.

"Ohh, I was payin' attention all right, ma'am. I saw all that was in front of me—but maybe your problem was that you were spendin' too long lookin' in your rearview mirror."

Her eyes flashed. "*I* was not the one who ran into someone," she snapped and thrust his handkerchief into his hand and stalked away across the road, not even bothering to check for cars, as if none would dare hit her.

For a second, Jesse stood there staring at the sad and humiliated pink Cadillac being towed away and the black limo that followed it. Then he looked over and saw Jimmy Pollard about to leave in another tow truck.

He called to him and hurried over, pulling out his wallet as he ran.

* * *

Sidney pulled the limousine to a rear door of the Vinsand Plaza Hotel. "You're sure you're all right, Miss Marnie?" he asked, his pale, wrinkled eyes full of concern as he took her hand to assist her from the rear seat.

Not wanting to concern him, Marnie managed a smile. "Yes, truly, Mr. Sidney. Thank you." For some reason Sidney always brought out her best Southern belle side, and since he always insisted on calling her Miss, she always called him Mr.

"Always a pleasure," he said grandly.

Her sneakers made no sound on the clay tile flooring as she hurried, clutching her purse and camera bag, toward the elevator. Sue Doherty, clerk of the gift shop, called and waved from behind the counter, and Barney Fisher, his mechanic's tool belt tugging his pants down on his hips, gave his usual salute. Marnie returned both greetings but continued on, feeling compelled to get home.

She pushed the combination of buttons that gave her access to the private elevator and rode to the top floor of the west tower, where the Vinsand penthouse suites were located. She held back her tears until she'd reached the safe privacy of her own apartment.

She stood for several seconds leaning against the door, as if holding out the world. Across the living room, the heavy, dusky blue drapes were flung wide, and two late-afternoon sunbeams streamed into the room, catching sparkling dust in the air and painting patterns on the mauve carpet and deep blue printed couch.

Her tears came then, brimming up and rolling down her cheeks. She knew she was emotional and considered it an irritating foible that should be controlled, something she'd learned to do to a certain extent but no further. She was proud that she rarely cried from physical pain, but ashamed that she still cried as easily from sadness as from joy, or even from seeing something especially beautiful, such as the sight of a dewdrop on a flower petal. At this moment her emotions rolled and swelled with terrifying force—fright from the unforgettable feeling of being hit, sorrow over her car and Miss Phoebe's camera and sharp joy that she and the two men were in one piece.

Pushing herself away from the door, she quickly crossed the room, dropped her purse and camera bag on the couch and snatched up a tissue. She struggled for some measure of composure. She didn't want Patrick to see her in such bad shape—wouldn't allow anyone to see her so out of control—and more than anything, in this moment she wanted to go to him, wanted his comforting.

The door that connected her smaller apartment to his penthouse was ajar, as usual. Marnie stepped through to his large and airy living area. The elegant room, with its modern, white leather sofa and chairs and fine Oriental-style tables and chests, was as quiet as the dead and equally as undisturbed, but from deep in the apartment Marnie heard Patrick's voice. *Oh, Patrick, please hold me.*

She continued on, white sneakers silent on the thick carpet, a certain panic rising as she followed Patrick's voice to his private offices.

"Patrick . . ."

She rounded the doorjamb of the outer office and saw him, shining with dynamic energy, standing in the middle of the room beyond with a phone to his ear. Her gaze fixed on him, she hurried forward, when her path and view of Patrick were suddenly blocked by a tall, looming figure.

"I'm sorry, but Mr. Vinsand wishes not to be disturbed."

Marnie stopped and stared into the grim features of Dorothy Hines, Patrick's private secretary. That Marnie had forgotten about the stern woman said a lot about her rattled state of mind.

"I called him on the private line, Dorothy. He's expecting me," she said, and shifted to pass the woman.

But Dorothy shifted, too, holding her ground as the reigning warden of her domain. "Mr. Vinsand is on a conference call right now and specifically left orders that he didn't wish to be disturbed."

Dorothy Hines was one of those people who had never appeared young. No one, not even Patrick, knew her exact age, but Marnie guessed it to be around forty. She was tall and straight up to about five feet nine inches, with straight, dull brown hair cut in a blunt bob at her earlobes, bangs straight across her forehead, straight pointy nose and straight, thin lips. A woman excellent at her job as private secretary to the CEO of the Vinsand luxury hotel chain and who had always made it clear that she not only thoroughly disapproved of Marnie's relationship with said CEO but generally disdained Marnie all the way around.

Marnie tried not to take it too personally, because Dorothy disdained a lot of people.

Now she drew herself up and still found her eye level somewhere around Dorothy's chin. "He *is* expecting me, Dorothy. I spoke to him half an hour ago." She went to step around the woman, but Dorothy again blocked her way.

Dorothy said, "He's on a long-distance call, and I have my orders, in which he didn't exclude you."

"He'll see *me*," Marnie ground out, and stepped firmly around the warden.

As she passed into Patrick's office, she shoved the door closed behind her.

## Chapter Two

Patrick motioned her to him. Quickly she ran to his side, and he absently draped an arm around her while continuing to speak into the telephone.

Marnie's heart squeezed, and she blinked furiously, fighting the insistent tears. She wrapped her arms about his taut waist, pressed her cheek to the hollow of his shoulder, absorbing his strength. His scent, that of laundry starch and Tabac cologne and his particular male warmth, was wonderful in its familiarity.

"I don't care what Johnson says, Clark," he said into the receiver. "Williams is on the edge of bankruptcy, and he's got to sell. The alternative is being flat broke, and he won't want that at his age."

"Patrick," she whispered.

"Stalworth doesn't know his head from a hole in the ground," Patrick said, managing to yell into the telephone without raising his low tone by even half a decibel. "We're going to have to get rid of him. I don't care what it costs—we'll save in the long run."

Marnie tugged on the placket of his shirt and gazed at him imploringly.

"Hold on, Clark," he said, and covered the receiver with his hand while his black eyes gave her a quick but intense study. "You're okay?"

She nodded and rubbed her collarbone. "The seat belt bruised me a little is all, but the..."

Patrick, nodding, took her hand. "Look, sit over there in my chair while I finish this with Clark. Go on—I'll be just a few more minutes." He stepped away and returned his attention to the telephone. "Okay, Clark...."

Marnie gazed at him as she slowly lowered herself to the edge of the tall-backed leather chair behind his desk. He paced and talked in strong, assured tones.

Sit in his chair, he'd said, and of course it was the practical thing to do. To wait her turn. After all, she wasn't dying. But she felt like a person bleeding to death after being told to wait her turn for the doctor.

She cautioned herself not to behave like an unreasonable child. Rising to gaze through the sheer curtains of the window, she battled conflicting emotions. It was wearing, the constant tug-of-war between the feelings inside of her. There she stood, quiet and calm, when what she wanted to do was cry and fling herself all over Patrick. Did everyone have to battle their feelings as much as she did? Patrick didn't seem to. He always seemed to do exactly what he wanted, in a cool, calm manner. She could count on one hand the times she'd seen him lose even a fraction of composure in all their years together. She folded her arms tight across her and thought how silly to be shaking now when she was safe and sound. Yet a strange anxiety grew in her bones.

The memory of her family's old Buick filled her mind. Their Betsy, they'd called it. Standing there, she relived it all, as fresh as if it had been yesterday, the fear and panic when the Buick had slipped off the wooden bridge into the rushing waters of a flooding creek. The screams of her mother and sisters; the water across her feet, up her legs; scrambling to get herself and the baby, little Lucy, from the water, and then staring in desolation at their sinking car. Seeing all their worldly belongings swallowed by the muddy water had been worse than the crash.

Patrick's hand on her arm and his words, "What happened, baby?" brought her back to the present.

She turned, looked into his dark, intense eyes and felt a sense of relief at having his attention at last. "I was coming from Beaver's Camera Shop. I'd dropped off five rolls of film I shot today so he could process them tonight. I should have come around instead of taking Reno, but I'd forgotten how sometimes the fair traffic..."

"Marnie...can you get to the important part?" Patrick urged, his eyebrows knotted slightly as he glanced at his desk.

She took a breath and searched frantically to express herself in fifteen words or less. "I saw this old woman weaving over into my lane, so I quickly slowed down. A pickup was following too close behind me, and he ran into me, and then another pickup ran into him. Oh, it was a mess..." She fought the rising tears again. "The entire rear end of the Cadillac was smashed up like an accordion, and my camera bag with it. I had Miss Phoebe's camera in it."

"Was anyone hurt?"

She shook her head.

"That's good. I'm assuming the police were called and proper reports made."

She nodded. "Yes, and insurance companies exchanged and all that." She left out the part about getting a ticket, feeling vaguely embarrassed and imperfect somehow. Patrick never did things like get tickets.

"Who'd you call for the Caddie?"

"The dealer—Bud Rodgers. I just thought—"

"You did fine," he soothed. "And since no one was hurt, there's really no problem. The insurance will cover either having the Cadillac repaired or getting a new one. Oh, hell, don't even worry about having the car repaired. Just go down tomorrow and get yourself a new one. I'll call Bud Rodgers about it this evening. All you'll need to do is tell him what color you want." Happily having settled the matter, he kissed her forehead.

A cold chill washed over Marnie. "But I don't want a new car."

Patrick's eyebrows rose.

"I like this one," she said. "I'm used to it."

His dark eyes flicked over hers, and then he swung away to his desk, chuckling lightly. "Always my frugal Marnie, and that's great, baby, but there's no need. That car is almost three years old. Get yourself a new one, and I promise that if the old one can be repaired, it won't go to waste. We can sell it—or give it to the Cancer Fund. They're always willing to take vehicles, and we get a good write-off while doing a generous act. I imagine someone down there would get a big kick out of driving around in a Cadillac Allanté."

She stared at him feeling crazy and helpless, and thinking, Get rid of it, just like that?

He gazed at her and tapped a pencil on the desk. "It should have been traded in last year, Marnie, and the frame's probably bent now. To get good as new, you're going to have to buy new."

She knew that. It wasn't that she didn't realize the car was gone. It was that she was saddened and disappointed and wanted to talk about it.

But in an instant of stark clarity, with one of those odd sensations of total detachment, as if she were standing over in the corner and looking on the scene, she saw Patrick's annoyance. His eyebrows and mouth were drawn into matching straight lines. She herself appeared to lean forward, while he appeared to lean backward, away from her. Annoyed and repulsed.

The cold, mortifying realization that she had broken an unspoken rule by getting emotional swept through her.

Instantly she grappled for the cool composure she'd learned by careful training. "You're right, Patrick. Sometimes I get such a silly attachment to objects."

His relief was immediate. He smiled. "Well, baby, I can understand that, with something that's rare and original—but as fine a car as that Cadillac is, it's simply one of many." He came around his desk, propped his buttocks against it and took her hands. "So what else did you do with your day, besides demolish an expensive car?"

"Oh, nothing special. Took pictures down the road here, where they're building that new fun park, and then I went to the fair. I got several good pictures of some carnies and children on the rides." She saw his attention waning and knew what she was speaking of was highly boring to him. It didn't sound captivating, even to herself. "Are you still going to be able to get away to go to the fair with me tomorrow?" she asked quickly. He'd promised her since the fair opened over a week ago that he would take her. And each day they had set, he'd ended up putting off.

He stood and again walked behind his desk. "I'm not sure, baby. I'll try."

"We don't have to go all day," she said. "A few hours in the afternoon or evening is plenty of time." She'd always loved fairs—big ones, small ones, in between ones. But it wasn't the same to go alone.

"I'm sure I should be able to manage that," he said pleasantly, then raised his eyebrows. "In all this picture taking and car wrecking, you didn't forget tonight's dinner, did you?"

She shook her head. "Of course not."

"And did Dorothy tell you this morning to change the time to eight?"

Business. Always business must go on. It paid the bills for her, too, after all.

"Have you ever known Dorothy not to carry out one of your orders?" she said, and if he noticed her sarcasm, he didn't show it. His gaze was already back on his desk, as he shifted through papers. "It's all arranged—eight o'clock, dinner party for six in the large alcove." The small private dining room would have done, but Patrick hated small anything, and he used atmosphere to his advantage. He'd chosen the open alcove in the hotel restaurant instead of his penthouse for this dinner because he wanted to convey a sense of unimportance to his business opponent, though the dinner was by no means unimportant to him.

"Good, because Hudson Williams and his advisers can't make it until then. Was Zach able to get the king crab flown in?" He raised his eyes to her.

"Yes, and in case anyone is allergic to shellfish or simply prefers something else, he's also preparing a specially roasted lamb. And Tony and Neil will both be serving." She'd done her work well, she thought, feeling again that oddly detached sensation of seeing them both from far off.

Patrick cast her his most handsome, appreciative grin. "Ah, baby, what would I do without you to handle all these things?"

"You would hire a social secretary," she said before thinking.

But he smiled, reached out and grabbed her to him, wrapping his arms around her. "Much easier said than done, believe me," he said huskily, then kissed her.

There had been a time when he could curl her toes with his kiss, until she'd come to find his kisses a little too perfect, calculated, like everything he did, to elicit a certain response.

He lifted his head and searched her with a dark, intense gaze. "I couldn't do without you, Marnie." And there was sincerity in his voice.

She threw herself against his chest and hugged him fiercely.

The buzzer sounded from his desk, and he tugged away, casting her a puzzled smile. Propping himself again on his desk, he said into the telephone receiver, "Yes, Dorothy. Good." Pushing another button, he said, "Ogden—could you get those figures? Great."

Marnie watched the look of deep concentration slip across his face. Her gaze slid to his shoulders, and she recalled how he felt in her arms. Thin, refined. In stark contrast to the way she imagined that farmer who'd run into her car would have felt, and she pictured the rugged, broad-shouldered man. Feeling disloyal, she pushed the thought away.

Bending into Patrick's line of vision, she traded waves with him, then quietly left.

Dorothy looked up over the rim of her glasses. Marnie met her gaze and had the impulse to stick out her tongue, thought better of it, then did it anyway. At least she got a deep frown out of the stern woman.

In the hallway she turned toward Patrick's bedroom. When she stepped into his black-and-white tiled bathroom, fresh fluffy towels were in place, toiletries waiting. Silly to check; the cleaning personnel did their job well or risked being fired, after all.

The bedroom was large and almost devoid of anything personal. Except that the furniture was original, teak from the Far East and leaned toward the Oriental in design, the room could have been one in any finer hotel. There were no pictures of family—Patrick's mother was nearly a stranger to him, he didn't get along with his father, he hated his two ex-wives and had no children, brothers or sisters. There weren't even snapshots of friends, nor even a photograph of Marnie beside his bed. He always said he didn't need a picture of her because he had the real thing. She'd given him pictures, had taken pictures of him and a few people closest to him and had put them in an album for him, which he kept shut away in a cabinet, along with a number of awards from business and civic groups and a couple of trophies from tennis tournaments and his horses. Patrick wasn't vain in any way. Marnie thought, not for the first time, that the bedroom *did* reflect Patrick: it was impersonal.

From within his long closet she pulled out two dinner jackets, one white, one charcoal. The white was her favorite; she thought it made Patrick look like Michael Douglas when he'd starred as that Wall Street tycoon. Patrick had laughed at that, but he wore the white more often. She hung three choices of slacks along with the jackets on his valet chair, buffed a pair of dress shoes, laid out a black belt and cummerbund, for him to choose, and a black silk bow tie. Either she or Dorothy always had to tie his ties. Leaving a lamp burning, she walked quietly back down the hall, past the offices where Dorothy sat typing. Patrick's back was turned to the door; he was still on the telephone.

When Marnie entered her own private suite, she held the doorknob for a long second. Then she pushed the door, which had always before remained slightly ajar, securely closed.

She had asked Patrick for her own apartment, and he'd complied, right down to allowing her to chose the paint, wallpaper and carpeting. Her small apartment was the direct opposite of Patrick's penthouse in that it was highly personal. It was her haven, her home, and it wasn't designer perfect, neither modern nor traditional but in every way cozy and comfortable.

Her living area was crowded, with a deep blue, stuffed, round-armed couch and matching chairs, cherrywood tables and bookcases and traditional brass lamps with wide shades. Scattered around were books and magazines on photography, women's magazines, and always library books needing returning and often a paperback novel or two. She made herself read several pages of something everyday in order to practice reading, something she'd mostly taught herself and still struggled with.

Her efficiency kitchen, though rarely used, had a homey air, too, with "country-charm" style towels and hot pads laid out, colorful teapots and vases that indicated she loved charm and the colors blue, brown and yellow.

In each room was a large vase of fresh flowers, delivered once a week from the hotel florist, and throughout the apartment, displaying her passion for photography, framed photographs hung on the walls. Most of them she had taken herself and many revealed a life she'd once lived, though she would never have admitted that to anyone. She and Patrick saw each other in his penthouse, slept together in his bedroom. He'd never slept in her bed. If he wanted to speak with her, he called her on the phone to come over to him. Dorothy had poked her head in once or twice, but the person who saw the apartment most was Cleo, who came twice a week to clean.

No friends came to this apartment for coffee or a game of cards or a night of watching movies on television. A woman in Marnie's position didn't have close friends, because she was expected to be at Patrick's beck and call. And Marnie simply never met any women she wanted to be friends with.

Now, passing through to her bedroom, she turned off the air conditioning. On the far side of her bedroom, she opened the sliding glass door that led out to the rooftop patio. She pulled the white sheer curtain and rich blue drape across so that they fluttered in the breeze, then removed her clothes, enjoying for a few seconds the fresh air on her bare skin, before donning a blue, cool silk robe. She had a lot of silk things and enjoyed feeling the fabric against her.

She brought her purse and camera bag from the living room, sat on the bed and took out the cameras and lenses. The lenses, glass cracked in one, the other long one long no more, she tossed aside. They were costly but easily replaceable. Carefully, lovingly, she picked up the broken camera, turned it over in her hand. A 35mm Yashica TL Electro X, nothing fancy, by today's standards outdated by twenty years, though it still took excellent pictures, and Marnie used it all the time. Its worth could not be seen with the eye but was felt in Marnie's heart. It had been given to her by her best friend in the whole world, Miss Phoebe. It had been Miss Phoebe's own camera, and she'd given it to Marnie the night before she died, the same night she gave Marnie the diamonds. Now the camera's lens sat at a decidedly awkward angle. Marnie wondered if she could have it repaired. Patrick always maintained that anything could be bought. Could money buy her a miracle for this camera?

Her gaze came up, and she looked at Miss Phoebe's portrait photograph, one she'd taken herself when Miss Phoebe was still able to stand in front of her mantel. Her eyes moved to more pictures, three black-and-white framed photographs displayed on the opposite wall, different views of the faces of migrant workers that she'd taken nearly eighteen years ago. The lighting on them wasn't the best—she'd just been learning then, and her camera had been one she'd found in the trash. But she kept these faces here in her bedroom to remind her of where she'd come from. Of where she never wanted to return.

Aching all over, she curled up in the middle of the wide bed, gazed at the draperies and thought how crazy Patrick would think her to discover that not only was she attached to the Cadillac but took great delight in watching the motion of curtains.

Thinking about the Caddie started her crying again, and she didn't know which was worse, the loss of her car, the damaged camera, or that Patrick couldn't begin to understand how she felt about any of it. He couldn't understand because she'd never told him—though, considering his high intellect, he should have figured out for himself what Miss Phoebe, and therefore her camera, had meant to her.

But there was just no way he could understand about the Cadillac, because he'd never had to live in a car—and he didn't know Marnie ever had, either. She and Patrick never talked of painful things. Marnie didn't talk of painful things to anyone; talking about them never changed them. A person faced her own pain and went on. That was all there was to it.

After several minutes she quit crying and lay still, her mind drifting back nearly seven years to when she'd met Patrick. It had been at one of Miss Phoebe's splendid parties. They'd dated, even though Marnie had been a nobody—nothing more than one of Miss Phoebe's servants, actually—and Patrick was heir to a small but prestigious hotel chain. Patrick was often an intellectual snob but never a social one.

He'd quickly begun trying to get her into bed. He'd nagged, had sent flowers and costly presents, had even asked her three times to come live with him. But Marnie had refused, even when Miss Phoebe had found out about Patrick's attentions and ordered her to go.

"He's a rare catch, honey," Miss Phoebe had said, her wizened eyes sparkling. "That man's goin' somewhere!"

"He only wants to sleep with me, Miss Phoebe." Marnie had had plenty of experience with men wanting that.

"Oh, phooey! Most men start out with only that idea, but end up fallin' in love—just like my Charlie did. And at the very least, child, you may end up with some very good jewelry. Patrick Vinsand isn't one to buy junk."

Miss Phoebe and Marnie had in common a respect for money, though they'd come by it in totally different ways. Where Marnie had been raised in a car and all around the rural South, Miss Phoebe had been raised in a pillared mansion in Atlanta, where her daddy had sat on the bench of a court, not a park. Miss Phoebe had been wild and headstrong and had infuriated her wealthy father by running away and trying for a career in "moving pictures." Completely disowned by her family, Miss Phoebe had found herself thrust into a life of poverty for which she was totally unprepared. Refusing to repent and still wanting to enjoy luxuries she was accustomed to,

Miss Phoebe had taken up with a train tycoon, her Charlie Magee. Because they'd ended up not only married but in love until Charlie's death, Miss Phoebe believed that life was a real joy and that love came to all.

Marnie had never explained to Miss Phoebe why she didn't believe that, about the number of times men, beginning with her own dear but no-account daddy, had shown her the truth of the world. She hadn't thought it needful, at Miss Phoebe's age, to cast shadows on the woman's faith.

And, though she agreed with Miss Phoebe's view that Patrick's offer was an opportunity, it had been her experience that a man's interest rarely lasted past the conquest. Besides, she couldn't bring herself to leave Miss Phoebe, who at eighty-nine had only one relative left, a brother-in-law who controlled her estate and was just waiting for her to die. Miss Phoebe needed her, and Miss Phoebe was the best friend she'd ever had and had given her the best home, the best life, she'd ever known. Marnie was happy with Miss Phoebe and wasn't going to leave until she had to.

But the very day Miss Phoebe had been laid in the ground, Patrick—who always claimed he won at business because he had great timing—had appeared in the doorway of the grand old apartment in Memphis and asked again.

"Come live with me, baby," he'd said.

Marnie had stood there and stared at him. He'd stared back, handsome and cocky as hell, which Marnie found at once irritating and terribly exciting. Around them moving men were hauling out the furniture: the Steinway piano, the rose-patterned lanterns dating from before the Civil War, the centuries-old tapestry from the dining room. Miss Phoebe's brother-in-law was feasting after his long wait.

"And do exactly what, Patrick? Sleep with you for a few nights?"

But Patrick only smiled slowly. "Oh, yes, I want that," he said. "I want that and more, Marnie. I'm damn tired of fluffy little babes tryin' to convince me they love me, while their eyes are shinin' with dollar signs. But you—you've got style and grace and see things straight. I want you to be my right hand, just like you've been for Miss Phoebe, doin' just what you did for her—take care of my apartment, my clothes, my private appointments. Watch my diet, remind me to take my vitamins, host my dinners and throw my parties. I can't promise you marriage—I've done that twice, and I'm not certain I'll ever want that again. But I'll provide for you just as if we were married. I'll even draw up a contract and stipulate any specific benefits if you want.''

Marnie had fingered the check in one sweater pocket, a severance of two-hundred-fifty dollars from the brother-in-law, who'd said when he'd given it to her, ''I don't in the least feel you are entitled to a penny more, because no doubt you and the others have been filching from Phoebe for years and have quite a nest egg set aside.''

To which Marnie had snapped sharply, ''There isn't much room for filchin' from a woman who's given a pittance of *her own money* on which to live.'' The remark hadn't seemed to bother his conscience any.

What she had gotten, unbeknownst to the brother-in-law, and which was then in her other sweater pocket, was Miss Phoebe's best diamond ring and necklace—the only two good pieces of jewelry Miss Phoebe had left, because over the past years she'd been forced to sell the rest in order to keep up the life-style she enjoyed so. She'd given the diamonds and the camera to Marnie the night before she'd passed, saying they were Marnie's insurance for her future. But Marnie had thought then, as she still did, that she would rather starve to death than sell Miss Phoebe's diamonds. There were some things—not many, but some—that money couldn't buy, such as the few good memories she had.

With the items in both pockets gripped tight in her hands, Marnie had said to Patrick, ''I want my own apartment,'' and walked away with him.

Forgetting the fluttering curtains, and rolling onto her back, she recalled with stark clarity taking up Miss Phoebe's camera case and one battered suitcase, while Patrick ordered his driver to put her larger cases, which had been Miss Phoebe's, too, into his car. She'd cried when they'd driven away, and Patrick had patted her hand while sitting two feet away, stiff and straight as a frosty tin man—or, in Patrick's case, a high-grade silver man.

They had not gone away together out of the fantasy of passionate love, but out of real emotions just the same: desire, need, mutual respect and a timid trust that each would never ask too much from the other.

Sitting up, she reached for the framed photograph on the table beside her bed and gazed down into Patrick's cocky grinning face. Six years they had been together now, and Marnie marveled at that. She had not given their union six months and knew perfectly well Patrick had never imagined it would continue for so long. He'd never known, either, because she never told him, that she'd fallen in love with him. If he'd guessed, he'd never acknowledged it in any way.

She sighed at her own foolishness. She knew now that unconsciously she had gone along with Patrick all those years ago because she'd hoped, dreamed, that maybe he would come to love her. She'd bought Miss Phoebe's fantasy dreams of life and had hoped it would turn out between herself and Patrick just as it had for Miss Phoebe and her Charlie. Only it hadn't. And she had to face the fact that she'd been as foolish as a turkey in a rainstorm.

For the past months she'd schooled herself to face the fact that Patrick was never going to love her, not the way she wished. And she didn't love him anymore, not the way she once had. Maybe she'd only been in love with the idea of love, but losing the idea was equally as hard.

It was a bitter pill—the loss of hope.

None of it was Patrick's fault, she thought in staunch defense. He'd never promised her love; he'd never even suggested that. And he *was* fond of her. And he made certain she had everything she could want.

She sat up and raked back her hair, thinking how there were a good many righteous souls, such as Dorothy, who would point a finger and condemn her as a prostitute, no matter how high-class. But none of them, as far as she knew, had ever felt hunger pangs—from no food, not simply a diet—nor had they ever called a car their home, nor watched their baby sister die because she couldn't get medical treatment. And heaven knew many a woman married a man—or stayed married to him, all the while despising him—for nothing more than the same security for which Marnie had bargained.

As she stalked to the bathroom and ran water into the tub, she thought that because she'd chosen to come with Patrick she was able to take a delicious soak in this very whirlpool bath. Because of choosing his offer, she lived in a lovely little apartment, wore silks, satins, diamonds and gold, and could drive a brand-new Cadillac convertible. Because of that one choice, not only had Marnie herself lived very well for six years, but her sister had been able to finish college and become a successful CPA.

Oh, yes, there was no denying it had turned out to be a very good choice. From the first, she and Patrick had enjoyed a good relationship, better than many married people. Patrick was often a cold man, but not unkind, and had always been a surprisingly considerate lover. And he was often terribly generous, especially with her. She knew what was expected of her, he knew what was expected of him and they each honored these expectations. She and Patrick had been very happy together.

*But they weren't any longer.*

Her gaze came up and she stared at her image in the wide mirror.

Patrick seemed happy. The disenchantment was inside herself. An aching that ate at her soul.

She had everything, she thought. There was nothing more. *Was there?*

As if to provide an answer, the telephone on the marble vanity rang. With the amusing thought that it was God calling to give her the answers she sought, Marnie picked up the receiver and said a hesitant, "Yes?"

"Is this Miss Raines?"

So much for whispered prayers, Marnie thought, because it was Dorothy, speaking as if someone else would answer Marnie's phone—or as if reminding Marnie there was a more correct way to answer.

"No, this is Miss Raines's secretary," Marnie said blithely, blinking away tears and grinning as she imagined Dorothy's frown. "May I take a message?"

There was a pause, then Dorothy spoke sarcastically. "You may please tell Miss Raines that Mr. Vinsand has a last-minute meeting over at Central Bank before dinner. His instructions are for her to meet him at the Top of the World restaurant at eight o'clock."

Marnie's heart dipped, and the spark of impishness vanished. "Thank you, Dorothy," she said and replaced the receiver.

She was to meet him at the hotel restaurant. Patrick couldn't even bother to escort her.

Jesse took his own bags up to his hotel room. He never liked bellhops hovering around him; it made him feel claustrophobic. His sons all told him it was more because he liked to be in control. Jesse believed it was because he didn't like a lot of fuss—he would use bellhops when he got too old to carry things...which had better be when he was dead. Setting his bags on the floor, he tossed his hat onto the desk and plopped on the bed to remove his boots.

He'd gotten the sheep and Ham settled in pens at the fairgrounds, then concentrated on taking care of his truck and trailer. The truck was in a garage recommended by Sam Teague, Jesse's insurance agent and an old friend, but the trailer remained over in the fairgrounds lot awaiting an adjuster. It had been one full day since he'd risen at 4:00 a.m., and Jesse felt about like that Cadillac had looked this afternoon.

Glancing around, he found his room was as to be expected in a first-rate hotel: carpet and drapes both thick enough to deaden the sound of a gunshot, bed large enough to accommodate a family, and all the other accoutrements neatly drawn together in an elegantly restful color scheme, necessary to create a home away from home that was far more luxurious than the home back home.

"Hell of a place for an old buckaroo," Jesse muttered. That was how he felt at that moment—like a seasoned rider who'd taken on one too many wild broncos. The buckaroo part was comforting; the old wasn't.

The telephone rang, surprising him.

"Dad—I've been worried. Thought you'd get in earlier than this." It was Rory, his middle son.

"Had a wreck just after I got in town." It was a bit embarrassing to admit a wreck to his son; seemed like fathers weren't supposed to be the ones to get in wrecks.

"You're okay?" Rory asked quickly, and the concern in his voice was gratifying.

"Sure . . . rig bent up a bit is all."

"That's good. How about meetin' me and the guys for supper and tellin' us all about it? We've got reservations in an hour up at that fancy place on the top floor."

Jesse said he would, even though he would rather have ordered in and spent the evening lying in bed, watching television. But he told himself it was such behavior that made old codgers.

He glanced around the room again and felt lonely. Though Rory was already here, in this same hotel, they'd skipped their usual routine of sharing a suite. It had been Rory's casually proposed suggestion, and Jesse had understood that his son wanted to enjoy his father's company but not feel fettered by parental presence. Rory either had or was hoping to get lucky. The arrangement suited Jesse fine. One thing a person's offspring never thought about: maybe ol' dad would prefer being free of his progeny's presence. Maybe ol' dad might get lucky, too.

Giving a doubtful grin, Jesse sighed. He wasn't the wild young man any longer, and in that moment he felt all of his fifty-two years. His chances of getting lucky were undoubtedly slim.

The sorrel-haired Cadillac Woman from that afternoon popped into memory. He recalled her pale shoulders above that red sweater and her graceful legs in those tight . . . well, tight whatever they were, because they hadn't been the pants he was used to seeing but more whatever those women in exercise shows wore. He mused that it might be very nice to share the company of a beautiful woman. Quick fantasies flashed across his mind—of looking at her over a candle-lit dinner table, holding her and waltzing her around a dance floor to a romantic Bellamy Brothers tune, kissing her white shoulders while he slipped off her clothes.

Then he came to his senses. He was, after all, the old buckaroo who'd wrecked her car and ruined the camera equipment in her trunk, and she was a sophisticated young woman who would undoubtedly take exception to all that.

His gaze lit on the large digital clock on the nightstand and set him into motion. With the expertise of a methodical man, Jesse quickly unpacked and stowed his clothes in the closet and drawers. Tucked into the corner of his suitcase, he found a new paperback Western and a copy of the *Lonely Hearts Newsletter*. His heart warming, he picked up the newsletter and chuckled. This was the work of his daughter-in-law, who'd obviously slipped the newsletter into his things while helping him pack. That Annie, she never gave up.

"Matt and I made out fine through that paper, Jesse," she'd reminded him at least a dozen times. "I wouldn't know you except for that paper. There's no reason why you shouldn't find a nice woman through it, too."

Annie had a very romantic nature, like his Gina used to have. Dreamers, both of them. He was awfully glad to have Annie in his life.

His eye lit on an ad in the newsletter, and slowly Jesse lowered himself to the edge of the bed and read, "Divorced white female, 49, nothing flashy, just a good old-fashioned woman in search of a good old-fashioned male...." The words blurred as his thoughts flitted back to Gina. Regina had been her full name, but he'd rarely used it. What would she think of him answering these ads? He hadn't told anyone, but he'd answered three ads, had met two nice ladies and one snooty biddy.

Regina. He thought he could hear her laugh.

He'd found himself thinking a lot about her these past months. They had shared a love hotter than the sun in July for all the seventeen years of their marriage. Between them they had created three good sons—Matt, Rory and Oren—and built a good, solid ranch. The pain washed over him. A large part of him had died with his Gina.

*God knew he was lonely.*

Suddenly Jesse realized his vision had blurred with tears, that he was sitting there with his memories and sorrow and none of it doing a bit of good while time ticked along. It was behavior like that that made old codgers, he reminded himself.

Setting the paper aside, he carried his gray sport coat on a hanger to the bathroom, where the steam from his shower could work on it. Within twenty minutes he'd showered and dressed, shined his snakeskin boots and was combing his hair. He leaned toward the bathroom mirror and adjusted the silver clasp of the bolo at his collar, then straightened and surveyed himself.

Not too bad for an old grandpa, he thought. Nope, not bad at all. Annie always said he was rakishly handsome. God love that Annie.

Slipping the key into his pocket, he closed the door to his room and walked down the hall to the elevators with a jaunty step.

He took the elevator to the lobby. It was filled with people, and his skin crawled a little. Living so much of his life far out in the country, he always had a considerable period of adjustment when he came to the city, though he liked cities—to visit, not to live. He especially liked fairs, just like some little kid. It never bothered Jesse to carry a pocket of childishness around with him; his mother had taught him that that was the road to living forever.

A bellman directed him to the elevator up to the restaurant. It seemed a waste to have a certain elevator that went only to one floor. He was whistling softly when he approached and saw there was a group of people waiting.

The whistle died on his lips as his gaze fell on a strikingly beautiful woman standing a little to one side, alone. It took about three full seconds to recall where he knew her from, and then it hit him like a splash of cold water.

*Cadillac Woman.*

With her deep sorrel-colored hair pulled on top her head and those creamy-white shoulders bare again. In a royal blue dress that clung to her curves and took a man's breath, diamonds sparkling around her neck and dangling from her ears.

Her gaze came around and met his. And her eyes filled with the same astonishment that thumped in his chest.

# Chapter Three

Her eyes were the shimmering deep blue of a high mountain lake on a clear winter morning, and they captivated him.

"Well, hello," he said.

"Hello," she answered coolly and turned away.

Jesse found that uncalled for, but he wasn't overly thin-skinned. Or easily discouraged.

The elevator doors opened, and the small group of people pressed forward, crowding up like sheep in a hurry to get through a gate. Cadillac Woman stepped forward, but took a look at the full elevator and hung back. The door swished closed, and she was left there, standing beside Jesse. She cast him a fleeting glance.

He rocked back on his heels. "Goin' to dinner?"

"Yes." She looked straight ahead, leaving him looking at her profile. High cheekbones, turned-up nose.

"You remember me, don't you?" he thought to say, when it suddenly occurred to him that maybe she was so cool because she thought he was some kind of masher. Maybe that hadn't been recognition he'd seen in her eyes at all. "I'm the one who's truck—" he winced "—ran into you this afternoon."

"Oh, yes, I remember you." Her eyes came round slowly. "How could I forget?"

"Pretty good coincidence, us runnin' into each other again like this, isn't it?"

"Yes, it is . . . but, I can hope, not nearly as disastrous."

"You have holdin' a grudge down to a science."

She cast him a wide-eyed look of surprise, then averted her eyes.

They stood in silence, and Jesse tried to place her rich, Southern accent. He was pleased that no one else joined them before the elevator doors opened once more. When they did, he politely gestured for her to enter first, then followed. The elevator doors swished together, closing them inside the walnut-paneled box. Alone.

He gazed at the graceful line of her neck. Her skin was a rich cream. She glanced at him, and he flashed her a grin. She didn't smile back.

Without trying to hide his interest, he swept his gaze down her graceful curves, then back up to linger again on her pale shoulders. The deep blue of her dress looked great against her skin.

"I understand this restaurant is top-notch."

She raked him with her gaze. "Considering the prices, it should be. And you'd better be prepared with a thick wallet."

"I'll manage," he said, then added, thoughtfully, "I suppose you're meetin' someone?"

"Yes."

But she certainly wasn't meeting her son as he was. Their eyes met and held.

"I take it you have no aftereffects from our run-in this afternoon," he said in a low voice.

She looked away. "No," she said with a shake of her head. The diamond earrings swung and caught the light. "And you?"

"Right as wash on Monday," he said.

A smile played over her lips, a smile she was trying hard to control. The lady preferred to remain cool. "I wish my car had been so lucky."

Jesse didn't have a reply for that.

The elevator stopped, and the doors swished open. Cadillac Woman stepped forward into the elegant, dimly lit restaurant lobby, and Jesse put a guiding hand to her back, an automatic, polite gesture he didn't even realize he'd made until heat rose on his palm. She moved away toward the restaurant.

Jesse stepped quickly beside her and grasped at something to say to keep contact with her now that fate had once again thrown them together. "Oh, I gave Jimmy Pollard your money and added some of my own. That suit you?" he added when she paused and faced him.

"That was generous of you, Mr....ah..."

"Jesse Breen. And you're Marnie Raines, right?" As he said it, her identity finally turned from Cadillac Woman to Marnie in his mind.

"Yes." Her expression was one of amused tolerance. He could see she knew he found her attractive, was used to men being attracted to her.

"What did the damage on your car turn out to be? Can it be repaired?"

"That hasn't been decided yet, though I'll be purchasing a new car as soon as possible. What about your truck and trailer?"

"The truck'll be fixed in a couple of days, but I don't know about the trailer, yet. I'm holdin' out for a brand-new one."

She looked around him toward the dim entry to the lounge then back at the elevator. Looking for the guy she was supposed to meet, Jesse thought.

"Ah..." He rocked back on his heels and hesitated, then decided what the hell. "May I say, ma'am, that I envy your date of the evenin' to be havin' dinner with such a beautiful woman as yourself."

Her eyes flashed upward, meeting his. She smiled with self-conscious pleasure and averted her gaze to look somewhere around his chin. "Thank you, Mr. Breen. And your date is equally as fortunate to be havin' dinner with so handsome a man." Her soft, Southern speech rippled over him as pleasantly as a brook in summer.

"Name's Jesse." He waited for her to look into his eyes again. "And I'm meetin' my son and a couple of his friends."

"Oh."

"I could change my plans. My son wouldn't mind if I stood him up. I don't suppose you could..." He'd gotten carried away with himself and wished he could sew his mouth shut as she shook her head.

"I'm sorry, I couldn't. I'm..."

"Marnie!"

A tall man strode forward from the lounge. Dark hair slicked back, white coat and black tie, he put Jesse in mind of F. Scott Fitzgerald's Gatsby fellow. The guy spared Jesse a swift glance, then focused on Marnie, took her hands and gave her a swift kiss on the cheek.

"The arrangements are perfect, as always. Thanks, sweetheart."

He raised his eyes to Jesse, and in an instant Jesse felt his measure being taken. It didn't bother him, because he was doing a little measuring of his own.

Marnie introduced them, and Jesse found himself shaking hands with *the* Vinsand for whom the hotel in which they stood was named, as well as quite a few others, luxurious all, across the South. His first impression was that Patrick Vinsand expected him to be impressed, and because of that, Jesse refused to let on that he was.

Patrick Vinsand's hand was smooth, yet his grip strong. He was somewhere around forty, had benefited from childhood braces and enjoyed not only a tailor-made tux but a top-of-the-line Rolex watch. He was handsome enough to make women faint and sharp enough to cut himself rolling over.

Keeping a proprietary hand on Marnie's elbow, Vinsand said politely, "Are you going to be staying with us long, Mr. Breen?"

"A few days—I'm showin' my sheep at the fair."

"I see. I hope everything is to your liking?" Vinsand asked, and Jesse thought the guy was slicker than oil on a baby's butt.

"Very comfortable, although you could probably do with usin' feather pillows on the beds."

"Call housekeeping. They'll bring you as many as you'd like." Vinsand inclined his head with a condescending smile. "And now, if you'll excuse us, we have guests waiting."

"Certainly," Jesse said, giving an equally cool and polite nod. Jesse Breen could be all dignity when the occasion required.

As he watched the two enter the restaurant, he stroked the back of his head and thought he should probably get a haircut. And then his eyes once again, for a fleeting second, met those of Marnie Raines. She'd paused to glance back at him.

Even though Vinsand had been as proprietary with her as a ram with one of his ewes, Jesse thought, there hadn't been a wedding band on her finger.

Patrick's hand tightened on Marnie's elbow as they made their way to the private alcove. "Who was that guy?" he asked in a low tone.

She replied in an equally low tone, "The gentleman who ran into the Cadillac today."

Patrick flashed her a quick glance with raised eyebrows. "I see," he said.

She wondered what he saw, glad there wasn't time to discuss it now. Undoubtedly he saw nothing more than a man paying her a minuscule bit of attention, she thought. It wasn't anything Patrick hadn't seen in the past, and he'd never been a jealous man. He had nothing to be jealous about. He owned her, lock, stock, and barrel.

Their guests were waiting at the table—four men in black ties and jackets, who all rose when Patrick and Marnie approached. Patrick quickly made the introductions between Marnie and Hudson Williams and Williams's two associates, and Marnie and everyone smiled cordially at each other, while behind the men's smiles Marnie suspected their feelings were much less than cordial. She immediately liked Hudson Williams, though. He was a gentleman of the old school.

The fourth man at their table was Ogden Turpin, a thirty-five-year-old business genius, as innocent as a ten year old and what was commonly referred to as a nerd, though he looked grand in his formal black-tie rig. Ogden was Patrick's right-hand man and one of the rare people Marnie considered a friend. Sitting on her left, he smiled encouragingly, his eyes twinkling behind thick, brown-rimmed glasses. She and Og bolstered each other at these social-business affairs.

Then Marnie's gaze strayed to the dim room beyond the alcove, skimming over a blur of bodies, tables, flickering candles, until she found herself looking directly at Jesse Breen. And he was gazing directly at her. She couldn't clearly see his luminous blue eyes, but she *felt* them. He smiled! Quickly she averted her gaze to her water glass and lifted it to her lips.

She tried to pay attention to the conversation at the table, she truly did, but it was all so boring. Offers and counteroffers and sideswiping, all done under the cloak of polite conversation. The men threw in discussion about golf and tennis and were careful to include her in all of it, but she answered automatically. Her mind couldn't seem to keep itself from that table across the room where Jesse Breen sat, the cocky son-of-a-gun farmer come to town. *Really, Marnie!* But, then, it was a diversion after all, she rationalized.

He sat with three younger men, cowboy types dressed in their Sunday best. Oklahoma City was awash with them on weekends and holidays, so she'd seen such men often. But Jesse somehow seemed to stand out, a man apart, she thought.

Twice more her gaze strayed to him, and each time he was looking her way! And smiling. They were covertly flirting, and it was quite fun. There was no way to deny it.

Jesse, Rory and two of Rory's friends, Kipp Stewart and Larry Young, sat at a table by the window with a great view of the city lights below.

Jesse, however, barely glanced out the window and pretty well ignored the conversation of the others. From where he sat he had a perfect view of Marnie Raines. His line of vision went straight across the low-lit room and right through the wide, high arched entry to the alcove where she sat at a table of men. One of the low-watt, recessed ceiling lights was directly above her head.

She saw him, too. Oh, her glances were quick, something no one was likely to notice, but they were there. He smiled at her a couple of times. They were most definitely flirting with each other.

It did enter his mind that quite possibly Rory and Kipp and Larry, men closer to her own age, all of them rough-and-handsome cowboy types, could be what drew her glance. Especially Rory, who'd drawn quite a bit of feminine attention when he'd walked through to the men's room. His son was a sight, Jesse thought proudly. No doubt about that. All his boys were.

However, he figured that if young and deathly handsome were all Marnie Raines wanted, she wouldn't be looking any farther than Vinsand on her right.

Rory broke off in the middle of whatever he was saying to ask, "What are you lookin' at?" He twisted around in his chair.

Marnie picked that moment to return Jesse's gaze. She paused with her wineglass in the air and looked right at him. He lifted his own glass in salute to her. A smiled flickered over her lips, and then she returned her attention to the men at her table.

Rory, his father's son and never one to miss a pretty face, didn't miss a thing. He turned wide eyes to Jesse. "You know her?"

"She's the one I ran into today."

"She is?" Rory's head swung around as if on a pivot. Kipp and Larry looked, too.

"I need to try crashin' into her car the next time I want to meet a woman," Kipp said. "New approach, Jesse?"

"A blessing that happens to a God-fearin' man," Jesse returned with good nature. Then, "Quit gawkin' at her. Didn't any of your mothers teach you it isn't polite to stare?"

"Seems as if Gramma forgot to teach you, Dad," Rory said. He swished his wine around and gazed at Jesse over the rim of the glass with a speculative, highly amused grin.

Feeling suddenly a tad foolish and not wanting to embarrass Marnie, Jesse pulled the other men's attention back by asking about the competition they faced in the team penning event at the fair. He strove to pay attention to the conversation. Still, his gaze wavered a number of times to the beautiful woman who glimmered like a rare jewel far across the room.

They didn't linger over the meal, because the younger men were eager for a night on the town. As Jesse rose, he looked over at Marnie's table. She was laughing, leaning close to the man on her left. She didn't look Jesse's way, and he figured he was pretty silly to think of her doing so.

Rory promised to check on Ham and the sheep when he checked on his horse stabled at the fairgrounds, so Jesse decided to return to his room.

"You sure you won't go with us, Dad?" Rory asked when they reached the lobby. "I'll pick up the tab."

Jesse shook his head. "Been a long day. I'll take you up on that some other night, though."

Rory waved as the three men headed away. For a moment Jesse stood there listening to their laughing voices fade. Then he walked to the elevator and went up to his room.

He stood there a minute while the emptiness closed around him.

Quickly he turned on the television for company. As he hung up his coat, his thoughts returned to Marnie Raines. She sure was a sight, he thought, and the two distinctly different meetings they'd shared flitted across his mind.

Wondering at the coincidence of running into her at the hotel, he pulled the card she'd given him from his wallet and gazed at her handwriting.

The address she'd written was the one for the Vinsand Plaza Hotel. She lived right here!

He thought of Vinsand greeting her with a kiss, the way the man had kept a close hold on her, like a dog guarding what was his. But Jesse also recalled that she hadn't been wearing a wedding band—or an engagement ring, either.

But she did live here—and this was Vinsand's place.

She could simply work for him, though she didn't look like any kind of secretary Jesse had ever seen.

And then he had to ask himself why any of it should matter to him. Marnie Raines was simply a pretty woman he'd run into. Whether she was married or in any way involved with someone wasn't any of his concern. Hell, she had to be close to twenty years younger than he was! And he was beyond any kind of a relationship with any woman—the past year had proved that to him.

He tossed the card onto the nightstand, then paused and picked it up again, checking the telephone number. He could call her, he thought.

*And say what, Breen?*

He tossed the paper aside again, swearing at his own foolishness.

It was nearly midnight when Marnie, wearing a flowing ivory robe buttoned demurely at the neck, prepared coffee in Patrick's kitchen. She softly hummed an old Dolly Parton tune that she'd heard on the radio when she'd been changing her clothes. She liked to listen to country music late at night. She didn't listen to it with Patrick; he listened to pop-rock or easy listening, considering country music low-class. That seemed quite a silly assumption to Marnie. She suspected that he didn't enjoy it because he couldn't relate to the deep emotions expressed in country songs.

Ogden appeared in the doorway. The black coat and bow tie he'd worn at dinner were gone, the top buttons of his crisp white shirt unfastened. Blinking behind his thick, dark-rimmed glasses, he shyly said, "Ah...need some help?"

Marnie shook her head. "Thank you, Og, but I've got it."

They shared a smile. Ogden slipped his hands into his pants pockets.

"Want some cookies with your coffee?" she asked.

Ogden gave a little jump, then bobbed his head. "Yeah. Sounds good."

She took a package of pecan sandies, Patrick's favorite, from the cabinet and began filling a plate. Ogden shifted from foot to foot.

At last he said, "Marnie, if I wanted to get a woman's notice, what would I do? I mean, what would make her want to go out with me?"

"Just your smile and askin' nicely would probably do the trick," Marnie replied, tenderly amused. Poor Ogden was so

shy. She, who'd suffered the same malady, understood only too
well.

"It hasn't," Ogden said sadly.

"Who is this silly woman? Do I know her?"

Gazing down at his feet, Ogden shifted them again. "I'd
rather not say."

"Have you tried flowers?" she asked gently.

He frowned. "I thought of it, but I didn't know which way
to go. I thought maybe I should send her some roses or some
candy, or maybe perfume would be better. But I don't know
what kind of perfume to buy—or even if she likes perfume.
And maybe she's allergic to roses, because I haven't ever seen
her have flowers or anything."

Marnie looked at Ogden's face and knew this was terribly
important to him.

"Flowers, most definitely. All women love flowers, and it
doesn't matter a whit if they happen to be allergic—we women
will suffer through it for a gift of flowers," she said and tried
to imagine the type of girl Ogden would be interested in. Shy,
demure, fresh as whole milk and pretty as a flower herself. "Go
get a bouquet of flowers. Not roses—they can be overwhelming, and this woman you want to cajole. Mums and daisies,
anything in gay colors. Just the bouquet wrapped in paper, not
in a vase, so they look almost like you picked them."

"My mom grows flowers in her greenhouse," Ogden said
quickly, picking up on the spirit. "I can get some from her."

"That would be perfect. Hand-deliver your bouquet in a casual way. Then let her think about them for a while—a day or
two. When you ask her out, make it for lunch, and call about
midmorning. That way she has time to think about it, but not
too much time to get frightened. And make certain you suggest a comfortable place—Mr. Joe's Café would be good. It's
a nice place to talk, but not intimate. Try that and see what
happens. If she says no, don't get upset. Simply repeat the
process. Persistence always wins in the end."

Ogden smiled broadly. "Gee, thanks, Marnie. I guess you
know more about people than anyone else I know."

Surprised and touched, Marnie turned to pick up the tray. "Oh, I don't know about that, Og, but I hope I've been a help."

"You have.... Here, let me take that tray."

He swept it out of her hands and followed her through the shadowy penthouse to where the lights shone brightly from Patrick's offices. As her gaze lit on Patrick, sitting on the edge of the couch with his crisp shirtsleeves rolled up, bow tie hanging undone and papers held up before his face, she wondered who the special woman was who'd pulled Ogden's attention from his beloved facts and figures. What did this woman have that could pull a man from his business?

Patrick cast her a preoccupied smile. Marnie motioned Ogden to set the tray on the desk, and she began to fill their cups with coffee. Patrick smiled absently at her and took his cup with one hand while reaching for another file with the other. "Thanks, baby. We'll be able to make our offer in a week," he said to Ogden.

Marnie brought Patrick his glasses from his desk and sat near him on the arm of the sofa.

"We could make it now," Ogden said. "If we wait, Williams may find the partner he wants. He's lookin' hard."

Marnie began massaging Patrick's shoulders as he shook his head at Ogden.

"There won't be another offer," Patrick said. "The old man is in too far, and no one wants to bail him out. Even his son won't help."

Ogden nodded. "If Williams's son follows through on his promise to sell his five percent, we'll have nearly forty-five percent anyway. We can force a merger."

The comment surprised and saddened Marnie. She'd found Hudson Williams a charming gentleman, and it hurt to think his son would sell what she knew meant a lot to the older man.

"I never count on anyone doin' what he says he'll do," Patrick said. "That stock would be nice, but what will turn the tide is Anderson calling in Williams's debt."

Marnie gazed at the coffee table strewn with papers and files and thought of Hudson Williams, a seventy-year-old man who had begun his chain of midpriced motels back in the sixties.

Like dandelions, they had flourished everywhere, becoming a symbol of the American family on vacation. They were successful for at least twenty years, before they began to decline. Today they were grossly out-of-date, inefficient and pushing Williams to bankruptcy unless he could find financing to revamp his operations.

"Must you take over Hudson Williams's motels?" she asked, speaking her thoughts aloud. "Mr. Williams doesn't want to sell, but he would like your help as a partner. Wouldn't that be good for both of you? And he seems such a nice man...."

"I'm a businessman, Marnie, not the head of a charity. And I don't become partners with anyone. He's an old man—he'll be paid enough to retire in style." He turned to gaze at her and softened his tone. "I'm not out to rook him, Marnie, just own his company. It'll be a blessing to a lot of people. The employees benefit by more secure jobs, higher pay and better benefits once we streamline the operation."

She nodded, knowing that once again she'd overstepped an unspoken boundary. After a moment, she stood. "It looks like you and Ogden will be a while. I think I'll go ahead and turn in."

Patrick looked fully at her then. "I'm sorry, baby, but we do need to see to a few things here yet. How about meeting me for breakfast in the morning?"

She extended her hand, and he took it. "I'll have Tacita order cinnamon rolls," she said and answered his smile with one of her own. Then she dared to remind him, "We have a date for the fair tomorrow."

"Yes. It's a date." He nodded and flashed her his charming grin, but it seemed a practiced thing.

It was on the tip of her tongue to offer to wait for him in his bedroom, but she simply kissed him quickly and murmured good-night. As she closed the door behind her, she felt terribly silly for her strong urge to cry.

Though she'd left several lamps burning and the evening was warm, the apartment seemed cold and empty. Passing quickly through the living room, she turned off the lamps. In the bedroom she switched on the television; the screen flickered with an old black-and-white show, one of her favorites—"Maverick," with a very young James Garner.

Settled in the bed against three plump pillows, she watched the show with the avidness of an old movie-and-television buff. Miss Phoebe had given her the interest and taught her the names of stars from the silent-movie era up through the sixties' big-screen epics and television comedies. Time had stopped there for Miss Phoebe, who insisted Marnie could have been another Loretta Young.

Marnie watched the screen and thought that they simply didn't make heroes the likes of James Garner anymore.

Jesse Breen popped into her mind.

*Where had that thought come from?*

She recalled him as he'd been that afternoon—tall, somewhat craggy, a bumpkin-come-to-town in his sharply creased denims, Sunday boots and hat. And, oh, but he'd been angry at her for shooing his sheep. She chuckled, recalling how they'd shouted at each other, their noses only inches apart. And she recalled, too, his definite aura of virility.

Then that memory merged with the one of him stepping into the elevator. How white his shirt had been against his tanned face. His handsomeness had come as quite a shock. His elegance had astonished her, yet it seemed to fit him every bit as well as plain cotton denim.

Was he staying in the hotel? Chances were...

For a long second she gazed at her purse beside her dressing table. Slipping from bed, she went over and brought it back, dumped everything out, searched and found the card Jesse Breen had given her. Jesse Breen, registered Rambouillet sheep, Wings, New Mexico. No box number or street address. Marnie had seen towns of that size before. On the back of the card he'd written an Oklahoma City phone number—the one for this hotel.

He was here, somewhere in this building, below her.

*She could call him.*

Her gaze cut to the clock. It was past midnight.

*No!* She couldn't and wouldn't be calling Jesse Breen, and not simply because it was midnight. How could she even consider such a thing?

She returned her attention to the television. But finding herself repeatedly seeing Jesse Breen's face and hearing his voice in place of James Garner's, she clicked off the set and resolutely went to sleep.

Marnie was not a morning person and had to drag herself from bed. But by eight-thirty she was perky, with a bit of makeup on and her hair combed. With her silk caftan fluttering out behind her, she breezed into the penthouse. The draperies were pulled, allowing bright light to flood the living room. The murmur of music from a Spanish radio station floated from the kitchen.

"Good morning, Miss Marnie," Tacita said and gestured toward the opened patio doors. "I set the breakfast table on the rooftop."

"Thank you, Tacita. Oh, what a pretty morning!" She and Tacita exchanged wide grins. "I promised Mr. Patrick that he would have cinnnamon rolls for breakfast. And order fruit, too." Tacita always ordered breakfast brought up from the hotel restaurant. About the only thing ever prepared in Patrick's wonderfully equipped kitchen was coffee.

Marnie hurried on toward Patrick's bedroom. He wasn't there or in his study, so she backtracked to his office, stiffening her spine in anticipation of Dorothy. Somehow, some small noise or scent, told her the secretary was already in place and working. Didn't that woman ever sleep?

"Good morning, Miss Raines." Dorothy turned from the file cabinet.

"Good morning, Miss Hines," Marnie replied as she continued across to Patrick's private office door. A splash of color caught her eye. There, seeming out of place in an office so orderly as to be cold, on the corner of Dorothy's desk sat a vase of wildly colorful flowers—yellow mums, white daisies, some purple things she didn't know the name of.

Pausing with her hand on the doorknob, Marnie looked from the flowers to the stern secretary and thought of her conversation with Ogden. Surely it couldn't be!

Then Dorothy shot all speculation about that from her mind by saying, "Mr. Vinsand isn't in."

Marnie stared at the woman, a cold chill sweeping across her.

Dorothy said crisply, "He instructed me to tell you he wouldn't be able to join you for breakfast. He had to fly to Memphis first thing this morning."

"Memphis?" Marnie said faintly.

"Yes. He left forty-five minutes ago."

She hated being the last to know; she was, after all, supposed to be closer to Patrick than his secretary. Still, she had to ask, "Did this trip just come up? Some problem with the hotel there?"

"Yes, Mr. Vinsand decided on going only this morning. As to the purpose of his trip, he didn't instruct me to comment. He did say he didn't want to wake you." Dorothy definitely loved being in the know when Marnie wasn't. "He also said to remind you to visit the Cadillac dealer and select a new car. He advised me to telephone the dealer to expect you—and give you anything you wish. I shall do so at nine o'clock," she added efficiently, turning away to carry a file to her desk.

Marnie gazed at Dorothy's back and felt like an old shoe. "My goodness, Dorothy. You mean Patrick went without you?" she said. "I suppose this trip must not have been too important, then."

Dorothy lifted her gaze. "He took Mr. Turpin with him. There were more pressing things here I needed to attend to."

"Yes . . . like giving me a message." Dorothy opened her mouth to reply, but Marnie said quickly, "And I thank you, Dorothy. You are a wealth of information, a credit to your profession, and I shall bring the idea of a raise to Patrick's attention." It was quite gratifying to see Dorothy's pinched lips tighten almost to obscurity. "However, you don't need to telephone the Rodgers dealership on my behalf. I am perfectly capable of handling the matter."

"My orders come from Mr. Vinsand," Dorothy said with satisfaction.

"So they do." Marnie turned to leave.

"Oh, Miss Raines?"

Marnie looked back.

"How is your *secretary*?" Dorothy's face remained prim, but there was a superior twinkle in her eyes.

"She's not only efficient, she's lots of fun," Marnie quipped, and swept from the room.

But in the hallway, her straight shoulders seemed to melt. *Oh, Patrick....* No one to share breakfast with, and again no one to go to the fair with.

"I ordered you blueberry muffins to go with Mr. Patrick's cinnamon rolls, Miss Marnie," Tacita told her when she returned to the living room.

Marnie gazed at the linen-covered table sitting on the patio surrounded by pots of blooming flowers. The table was set for two, with the familiar large insulated chrome coffeepot and cloth-covered basket in the middle.

"Thank you, Tacita," she said faintly, then added more firmly, "I'm afraid Patrick won't be here for breakfast, and I think I'll just take the coffee into my suite. I'm sorry for all your trouble."

Tacita's face darkened with concern. "But you should eat, Miss Marnie. Let me bring you the muffins when they come, at least."

Marnie touched the small woman's hand. "Okay...muffins and coffee."

Back in her apartment, she looked around and wondered what to do with her day. She hadn't drawn the drapes the night before, and bright morning light filtered through the white sheers.

Blinking away irritating tears, she pouted. Her car was wrecked, Patrick was treating her like an afterthought and it appeared she'd been helping Ogden to romance Dorothy the warden! Oh, that was just too much! She might as well go back to bed and pull the covers over her head.

The self-scolding started immediately. Self-pity was just about the most useless thing on God's earth. Feeling sorry for yourself never put food in your stomach or a smile on your face.

*Just straighten up, Marnie Raines!* Patrick had his job to do, and she had *hers,* which was to see that Patrick had all he needed to do his job. She *did* have a job. She *did* count!

With a grand sigh, she went out to the rooftop and gazed at the city stretching out around her. Cars rushed by on the thoroughfare in front of the hotel, people were tiny, darting figures at the car wash next door, and construction workmen moved methodically on the new entry ramp to the highway. So many people with places to go, things to do. And her day stretched endlessly ahead of her. Nothing to do other than go down and purchase a new Cadillac, and that would take no more time than it took to sign her name.

Nothing to do, and no one to do it with. No one in the world who needed her. *Patrick could call the employment office and have her replaced in two minutes.* She was expendable.

She supposed she could go to the state fair by herself. Again. But seeing the fair alone was a lonely proposition. It was an event for people to see, to experience, together.

When she'd been a child, her father would take them to any fair or carnival they happened upon. They'd had so little money, but her father somehow always managed to come up with the small price of admission. At those fairs and carnivals they could forget their hard lives for a while and immerse themselves in a fantasy world of bright color and sound and miracles. Rarely had they been able to do more than look—at the bright colored lights, the rides going round and round and up and down, other people spending their money at the dart and ring throws, grand cows and horses and sheep displayed by rich people. Marnie used to dream of going to a fair and having all the money in the world to spend—to ride all the rides and see all the shows. Now that she could, she had no mother or father, no siblings living nearby and no friends to enjoy it with.

"Miss Marnie! Miss Marnie! Are you in here?" It was Tacita's voice calling with excitement.

Marnie hurried back inside and across the bedroom. "Yes, Tacita. What is it?"

"Look what has just come for you! Lonny just brought it up!" Eagerly, her face a bright sunbeam, Tacita came across the living room, holding a large vase of flowers.

With her heart lodged in her throat, Marnie slowly took the vase. The flowers wiggled and winked at her—bright white daisies and pink daisies and purple daisies and yellow mums.

"There is nothing like flowers from a man, eh?" Tacita said with a knowledgeable air.

"No... there isn't," Marnie replied softly, a smile wrapping around her heart as she recalled her advice to Ogden the evening before. Tacita quietly left, and Marnie set the vase on the coffee table, removed the card and opened it, fully expecting to see a message of apology from Patrick.

"Forgive me for running into your car—Jesse Breen."

Her breathing stopped, and her hand flew to her lips. She gazed at the gaily colored flowers. Not roses. She should have known. Patrick would have sent the most expensive roses, to impress. But these were flowers meant *to cajole*. And then, holding the card to her heart, she laughed.


Jesse had breakfast with Rory and was riding with him to the fairgrounds, when he told Rory to pull over to a convenience store.

"I need to make a telephone call," he said. "And I'll buy you a pop."

Sending Rory into the store for the soft drinks, he went over to the pay telephone, checking his watch again. It was nine-thirty. Marnie Raines should have received his flowers by now, and hopefully she hadn't gone out already. He fumbled with the coins, and his hand shook as he punched in the numbers from the card she'd given him. It had been months since he'd called a woman for a date—years and years since calling a woman for a date was something crucial to him. For too many years he'd simply telephoned Celeste to tell her he was coming over, or to get her Sunday dress on because he was taking her to dinner. He'd never had to *ask* her. He'd had to ask few women in his life—and the only one who'd meant anything had been Regina. She'd had him chasing her until she caught him, and that had been a hell of a long time ago.

And now here he was again—at fifty-two, feeling twenty-two. Didn't hardly seem fair.

He patted his foot while the ringing sounded across the line. Once, twice, three times. He let it go to five and was about to hang up, when she answered.

"Hello, Marnie... this is Jesse Breen."

There was a pause, and he imagined her surprise. "Hello." More silence.

"Hope I didn't get you out of bed or anythin'."

"I've been out of bed for a long time, Mr. Breen."

*Mr. Breen?* He frowned.

"I have also received your flowers," she said.

"That's good." He grew hopeful.

"They're beautiful."

And he grew more hopeful. "I'm pleased you think so. I...ah..." Sweat trickled. "I was wonderin' if you might join me for lunch."

## Chapter Four

The invitation came as a stunning surprise. In the back of her mind she'd assumed his call had something to do with the accident. Perhaps she had sensed his interest before, but . . . well, she hadn't been asked out in a long time. The few available men that she knew were Patrick's associates, and they knew she belonged to Patrick. Strangers she happened to run into about town, while often openly admiring, didn't go so far as to ask her out. And was Jesse Breen such a thickheaded bumpkin that he'd forgotten he was the one who'd demolished her car?

*You did smile at him across an entire restaurant last night.* So she had.

Finally she said, "I'm sorry, Mr. Breen, but I was just on my way out. There's a little matter of purchasing a new car that I have to take care of today."

"How about dinner, then?" he asked, apparently not at all fazed by her sarcasm.

She had to smile, though she wouldn't have revealed it to him. "I'm sorry, but I'm just not available. I'm . . . involved with someone."

"Patrick Vinsand?"

"That's right."

"Are you married to him?"

"No." Why in the world was she answering?

"Engaged?"

"Not that it's really any of your business, but Patrick and I have lived together for some time, so you see—"

"I've lived with a couple of dogs for some time," he said, breaking in. "I can still go to dinner with a woman if I want."

Marnie saw red. "I *choose* not to have dinner with you, Mr. Breen—and as I said, I was on my way out the door."

There was a moment's silence. "Thank you, Marnie. I'm sorry if I intruded."

She was absurdly sorry. "Oh, you didn't—"

But he hung up with a loud click.

She slowly replaced the receiver and wondered why she felt bad about hurting his feelings. He was the boldest, cockiest son of a gun. How could he dare to think she would possibly be interested in him? She'd left the country behind a long time ago— and country men, too.

Turning, she caught sight of herself in the mirror. Her cheeks were flushed. It was, she thought, most pleasant to be pursued.

*Oh, Marnie! He's a bumpkin-come-to-town.* A handsome bumpkin, yes, but certainly not someone she would be interested in. Dress him up, even with a nice watch and shiny boots, and he was still a country jake. She'd left his type behind years ago. Even if she were free to be interested in anyone.

Embarrassment washed over her as she recalled telling him she was *involved.* There simply wasn't a better word for her relationship with Patrick. They weren't married, nor engaged, and it seemed too juvenile to say she was Patrick's girl or they were going steady. Her heart sank.

The true description was mistress. She was Patrick's mistress, and that wasn't something she wanted to bluntly say to another person. She wasn't ashamed—but she wasn't proud, either.

* * *

Jesse, his hand still resting on the receiver, stood stewing. His gaze strayed, unseeing, to the store window, and he thought of the foolish things he'd said to Marnie. It made him mad. *He was too damn old for all this romantic foolishness! God had good reason to make people do that at a young age!*

Rory came out the door of the store and handed Jesse a cold can of cream soda, saying, "Finish your phone call already?"

Jesse nodded. "Guy wasn't there," he said and tilted his head to drink deeply.

If he'd succeeded in getting Marnie to have dinner with him, he might have told his son. He could have shared his success, but not his failure. A man didn't care to look like a fool in his son's eyes.

There was no need to let it bother him, he thought. He'd made a fool of himself a number of times through the years and probably would many more times before he died.

Rory shifted on his feet. "Well, Dad, can I drop you back over at the fairgrounds? I have a date this afternoon." He grinned. "Woman I met last night. Thought I'd go buy a new shirt, maybe boots, too."

"Yeah, let's go," Jesse said, feeling as sour as a rancid pickle. "But instead of the fairgrounds, you'd better drop me over at the car-rental agency."

What was it about that woman that unhinged him? he thought. Made him say the craziest things—like that crack about the dogs? Where had that come from? *It was the way she looked at him, the tone of her voice—as if he weren't worthy of her notice.*

But, by damn, she'd noticed him last night in the restaurant. He knew she had!

Well, he supposed, as the saying went, there was no fool like an old fool.

"Think I'll rent a Cadillac," he said.

The last thing Jesse expected to happen was to once again run into Marnie Raines. The odds against it had to be a million to one—or at least one in 438,000, which was close to the population of Oklahoma City. He would sooner have expected a lightning bolt to strike him. Then again, lightning struck a good many unsuspecting people all over the country everyday, and the southwest quarter of Oklahoma City wasn't all that big. And no one ever said fate had to make sense.

With Ham leaning against his leg, he stood next to Woody Greene in the spacious sheep barn. There was a bit of bleating, but more noise came from hair dryers and electric clippers, a portable radio here and there and the numerous fans stirring the early afternoon air in an effort to cool the stock.

"You're at least three thousand too high on the price," Woody said, and indicated Fancy. Woody was a breeder from down Lubbock way and as sharp a trader as they came.

Jesse tipped back his hat with his finger, gazed at Fancy and pretended to mull over the comment, because that was the way the dickering game was played and he was as good as Woody, if not a mite better. He and Woody had been at it for fifteen minutes, and Jesse had about decided Woody really and truly wanted to buy Fancy. The ewe lamb, oblivious to the attention she was generating, contentedly munched her hay in the same manner as a sheep worth a mere fifty dollars. It was nothing more than men's opinions that set the value on an animal. Jesse thought that said something for mankind, but he wasn't certain exactly what.

He shrugged and rocked back on his heels, saying, "I may not sell her. I only have one other ewe that shows as much promise."

Woody gave a smart smile. "You won't at the price you're askin'. Of course..."

Woody's words faded as Jesse suddenly caught a fleeting glimpse of a familiar head of deep sorrel color hair through the wide barn door. The woman disappeared behind the steel wall of the barn, and Jesse, his heartbeat doubling, shifted his gaze to the next doorway to catch another glimpse.

"...she may bring the four thousand on the top end, but I doubt it," Woody was saying.

"But I won't take less than five now," Jesse said and touched Woody's arm, starting away even while he spoke. "Excuse me, Woody. I think I see someone...."

"You won't ever get that!" Woody called after him.

Jesse kept his gaze glued on the opening where Marnie Raines should have appeared but didn't. He sensed Ham had followed him but didn't spare time to tell the dog to return. Bursting out into the bright sunlight, he blinked and cast around, looking for her. He *knew* it had been her. *He just knew it!*

He saw her then, along the opposite side of the narrow street that ran between the exhibit barns. Long auburn hair, pale blue shirt, white, tight-fitting pants that showed off a pair of long, slim legs. With a camera to her eye, she crouched, taking a picture of two boys in blue jeans and plaid shirts and cowboy hats big enough to fly with. They grinned and held corn dogs up like torches.

Jesse adjusted his hat and started off toward her with swift strides, watching her carefully and ready to slow down if she turned. He sure didn't want to appear as anxious as he felt. "No fool like an old fool," echoed in his thoughts. But he didn't want her to get away, because there was never a deeper regret than an opportunity allowed to pass.

She straightened and backed up. Camera to her eye again, she went for another picture as she kept stepping backward— not knowing that she was about to step in a big pile of horse apples.

Jesse reached her and put a hand to her back just as she was one tiny step away from the pile. "You don't want to back up any farther," he said.

She started, jerked the camera around and barely missed smacking him in the chin. "What . . . ?" She stared wide-eyed, then glared. "I need more room for a wider shot."

Jesse pointed to the ground, and she twisted to look.

"Thank you, Mr. Breen," she said dryly and sidestepped in her little gleaming-white sneakers.

"Okay, boys. . . ." She motioned to the youngsters, who looked curiously at Jesse. "Sit on that pipe fence there for me, will you?"

They did, happy as any boys out of school to do so. As if Jesse wasn't there at all, she took three more shots, making a great production out of it, too, and taking care where she stepped. Jesse crossed his arms and looked on, noting the way the silky blue fabric of her blouse draped over her breasts. The top buttons were undone, revealing pale, creamy skin. She was a full-breasted woman for her slim size, he thought. The kind of woman who exuded sex appeal as naturally as she breathed.

The kind of woman who could get a man to feeling alive, Jesse thought, as a bittersweet swelling began within him. And no matter how she pretended to ignore him, he would bet his ranch that she wasn't able to.

Pausing, she called to the boys to wait. She turned to Jesse, taking him a little by surprise by asking, "May I borrow your dog? For a couple of shots," she clarified, indicating the boys.

"I'm sure it'd be Ham's pleasure," Jesse replied, proud and happy to do so. "That's his name—Ham."

"That figures."

Jesse caught her murmur as he motioned for Ham to go with her. She placed a very pleased Ham between the boys for several shots, then had the boys play with the dog, and she caught a few more.

Finally she handed a dollar to each of the boys, and they bounded off. Slinging her camera strap over her shoulder, she wiped curly, damp bangs from her face and said, "Are you followin' me, Mr. Breen?"

"Why would you say that?"

"Here we are, runnin' into each other again." She cocked her head, and her silver earrings swayed. "Seems a little against the odds, doesn't it?"

Jesse gave her his most charming smile. "Odds have nothin' to do with it when angels get to arrangin'." He spoke with his best Western drawl, too. Women always seemed taken by that.

That smile she always wanted to hide played at the corners of her lips. "Angels?" She lifted a skeptical eyebrow. "You believe in angels—and that they arranged for us to meet? Just this time, or did they begin by having you smash into my car?"

"About our accident, I'm not certain. But, yes, I believe in angels and God and Santa Claus and winds of fate—all which is as practical as believin' in coincidence or karma or whatever."

He had a smile on her face now and strolled along beside her. Ham trotted along behind them—at Marnie's heels, not Jesse's.

Taking her elbow, Jesse directed her on a course through the horse barn, saying, "Why, just this mornin' I ran into my second cousin who's come up from Abilene. I haven't seen him in at least half a dozen years—didn't know he was comin'."

"You're makin' that up."

He made an X across his chest. "Cross my heart, it's the truth. I'll introduce you, if you'd like—he's showin' a horse around here somewhere...."

"I'll take your word for it," she said dryly, then added, "But I've met your type before, Jesse Breen. No one can tell tales like a farmer."

"I don't mean any disrespect to farmers, but just so you know—I'm a rancher, ma'am. I raise sheep."

Her expression told him she saw no difference, and perhaps, seeing it her way, there wasn't much.

"Yes, you do have sheep, don't you?" she said. "How are the obnoxious little critters?" Quite suddenly there was a teasing glint in her eyes.

"Safe and content, thank you."

"Heaven forbid they be anything else."

His smile widened, and so did hers, but just a fraction. He wanted to ask her to see his sheep, but caution told him that wasn't a good approach.

So he said, "I'll treat you to a corn dog."

But she shook her head. "I only have half an hour before my driver comes for me, and I want to get a few more shots."

"You can do a lot better picture-takin' with a fair corn dog in your stomach."

They had reached one of the main thoroughfares. Displays of stock trailers, portable buildings and farm implements filled the grassy median. Attention-getting flags fluttered in the wind. But it was still early on a weekday, and the crowd was sparse.

"If I take time for a corn dog, I won't have time to take pictures."

"Yes, but you'll have a full stomach, and I'll feel better having done somethin' to make up for smashing your car."

"A corn dog in exchange for a Cadillac?" she asked, raising that skeptical eyebrow again.

"It's a start—and the fair corn dogs are awfully special."

Marnie gazed at him, as if uncertain how to take him. "You are a most persistent man, Jesse Breen."

"My daughter-in-law tells me that's one of my best qualities."

Grinning, he found himself looking deep into her eyes. They were as blue as the western sky and remained locked on his. And it came as sudden and surprising as a whirlwind: a sizzling sexual attraction stirring deep in his vitals. Even more astounding, he saw quite plainly that Marnie felt it, too.

"I imagine she's right," she said in a low sultry tone. "I like my corn dog with mustard."

Jesse felt as though he'd won the lottery. Or as if he'd just shed twenty years. As they walked along beneath the bright sun toward a concession booth, he had the confused feeling of being at once supremely delighted and nervous as hell. And it seemed the sun had gotten about a hundred degrees hotter.

Jesse led her over to a display of outdoor furniture on the grassy median. With gold band bracelets tinkling on her wrists, Marnie held her mustard-smeared corn dog carefully away from her with one hand and her soft drink in the other. Jesse had the idea a corn dog on a stick and a soft drink in a paper cup were not normal fare for her.

Quickly he pulled two iron chairs from the display and arranged them together beneath a nearby tree, then stood waiting for Marnie to sit first.

She inclined her head politely and sat. "You are quite resourceful."

"Opportunities are always close at hand, if a man keeps his eyes open."

"You should have kept your eyes open the other day, when you ran into my car."

"I had my eyes open—I was simply concentrating on somethin' else."

She averted her eyes to Ham, and Jesse was surprised to see a pale blush steal across her cheeks. He watched her break off a tiny piece of her corn dog and feed it to Ham.

"So—what brings you to the fair today?" he asked. "Takin' pictures for some magazine or the newspaper?"

Her eyebrows rose; then she shook her head. "I came to the fair because I like it—and I take pictures for the same reason."

"I like the fair, too," Jesse said, pleased to have found a common interest with her. "Have ever since I was six and one of those traveling carnivals came around to our lonely neck of the woods. Used to be a lot of those operations that traveled from town to town. When I got to my teens, the only reason I raised calves was to be able to take them to the county fair and spend a day or two. I never got to go to the state fair until I was almost eighteen. I've gone to at least one state fair each year since."

She gave a grin in answer to his. "I'd never gone to a state fair until I came here to Oklahoma. But we used to go to those small fairs and circuses, too. One summer my brother got a job driving a truck for one—Mr. Bonaparte's Traveling Carnival. He got us all the rides, games and cotton candy we could handle."

"You're not from Oklahoma, then?" he asked.

She shook her head. "Arkansas."

"And you like to go to fairs and take pictures."

"Yes."

"My son is into photography, too. When he was twelve, he traded his twenty-two rifle for a 35mm camera. A couple of years ago he turned an extra closet into a darkroom."

"I tried developing my own pictures for a while," she said around a mouthful of hot dog, "but after spillin' my third bottle of developer, I decided it was a lot easier to take them to the lab. The one I use does excellent work and can do prints for me in an hour."

"It's a long way to a lab from out where I live," Jesse said.

"The thriving metropolis of Wings, New Mexico?"

"Yep." He watched her lick mustard from her lip with the pink end of her tongue.

"Where is that?"

"Northeast corner of the state, not far from the Colorado line. Nothing fancy, but a good ranch. Three sons, all grown, a daughter-in-law and a grandson." Somehow he felt the need to define himself to her. To reveal right up front that he was a seasoned man, mostly because he wished deep inside to act like he wasn't at all.

"A nice big family," she said softly.

"We like us."

She turned those blue eyes on him. "No wife?"

That raised his eyebrows. "No, ma'am," he said, shaking his head and feeling he should have made the point clear right from the first. "I've been a widower for seventeen years."

"Oh..." she said, but both her tone and expression remained suspicious. Jesse got the feeling Marnie Raines was skeptical of life in general. She definitely kept a high fence erected around herself.

They drank from their soft drinks. Ham lolled on Marnie's foot. A carny guy called loudly from the corner, offering to guess people's ages and weights, and a couple of riders on Appaloosas in fancy rigs clumped by. Jesse felt as aware of Marnie sitting inches away as he would have if she were in his arms. He wondered not only about her relationship with Vinsand but also about the urges twisting around inside him.

"I think they look so silly without tails," Marnie said. He lifted an eyebrow, and she pointed at the bobbing rear ends of the Appaloosas. "They look silly. Do they cut those tails like that?"

Jesse shook his head. "It's just a trait of the Appaloosa—they tend to have sparse tails and manes but real good feet. Hardly ever find an Appie with bad feet. So you live with Vinsand at the hotel?"

She blinked in surprise, then nodded and looked away as she took the last bite of her corn dog. He thought, a woman doesn't live with a man unless she had powerful feelings of some kind for him, Breen.

"Any kids?"

She shook her head. "No. Never got around to that."

"Well, you still have time yet."

"Not all women live and breathe only to have children," she said as she bent to pet Ham.

"I didn't mean that you should. Plenty of other things in this world," he said. "What do you do?"

It took her a second to answer. "I take care of Patrick." She didn't swing her gaze to his until after she spoke, and he saw the hint of a challenge in her eyes.

He spied a smear of mustard on her cheek and took his napkin to wipe it off. She jerked away.

"You have a bit of mustard…" he said, and took hold of her chin with two fingers, wet his napkin on the tip of his tongue, and dabbed again at the yellow smear.

She became very still, wary as an ewe sensing danger, and he felt her eyes sharp upon him. "You're wipin' spit on my face," she said.

He kept hold of her chin, and a warmth churned low in his groin at the velvet feel of her skin. "Well, I got the mustard off," he said with one last swipe before reluctantly releasing her. "So, just what does takin' care of Patrick entail?"

"Everything you think it does," she said, looking him in the eyes.

"Like what?" he persisted, though he knew just what.

"I do all the things for him that your wife did for you—I make certain his home stays in order, his clothes are cleaned, see to his meals, host his dinners and parties. I see to all his *comforts.*"

"All of that is a hell of a job."

"Yes," she said after a searching pause.

They gazed at each other; her expression was skeptical.

"Patrick Vinsand is a very lucky fella," he said.

She averted her gaze, and a pale blush once again slipped across her cheeks. The next instant she jumped up. "I have to go. My driver will be waiting. Since I no longer have a car," she said pointedly, "I have to make reservations for one."

"Thought you were buyin' one this mornin'."

"I did, but I have to wait for it to be serviced before picking it up." She hesitated. "Thank you very much for the corn dog."

"Sure you couldn't tell your driver to come back later? There's a whole afternoon left, and we could see the fair."

She shook her head. "No…I can't."

He wondered if Vinsand would be angry. Probably. In Vinsand's place, Jesse would be.

"I'll walk you out," he said.

"There's no need. Sidney will be coming to the front gate, and it's a long walk." She began walking quickly away.

He stepped fast to keep up with her. "I'd like to."

She glanced at him, and he saw the hint of distrust in her eyes, but she slowed down, and Jesse sensed she wasn't completely averse to him walking with her. Of course, he thought sarcastically, it could have been Ham she was becoming partial to. The dog remained at her heels.

Along the way to the front gate, he stopped to buy her a balloon. He had to grab her arm to get her to stop walking, but she laughed when he gave it to her.

He walked all the way through the gate and to the waiting black limousine, where a skinny, white-haired old man popped out to open a rear door. When they reached the car, the old man vanished back behind the dark glass of the front seat.

Jesse helped to settle both Marnie and the balloon into the car and was mildly gratified when Ham showed a preference for remaining with him. Marnie lowered the window, and Jesse propped his hands on the opening.

"Ham and I will be here tomorrow mornin' showing a couple of sheep down at the animal barn," he said, speaking very low, for Marnie's ears alone. "If you want to come and watch—around nine o'clock—you could take some pictures of my sheep."

Before she could give him an excuse for why she couldn't come, he tipped his hat to her and walked away. He refused to allow himself to turn back to see if she were looking at him.

Marnie was half turned in the seat before she stopped herself. She would not look after him!

But as Sidney drove away from the fairgrounds, she imagined how Jesse had looked walking away, his broad shoulders straight as a lodge-pole pine, his sauntering walk calm as a midsummer's day, the petite black-and-white collie dog padding beside him, both being swallowed up in the crowd.

Jesse Breen a was man out his time. A man made of the same stuff as all the guys in the white hats. And he deliberately assumed the role, she thought with a grin, as his image filled her mind.

"Did you have a good time at the fair, Miss Marnie?" Sidney's voice brought her back to the moment.

She met his smiling eyes in the mirror. "Yes. It's a good fair this year, Sidney. You'll have to make time to go."

He nodded. "My wife will drag me here before it's over. She likes to see the quilts and stuff, and we most generally come for the rodeo."

Only partially listening, Marnie tugged at the string of her shiny balloon and thought its colors, blue and silver, were very much like Jesse's eyes. Oh, those eyes were captivating! Full of himself, that was what.

"... I will be here tomorrow mornin' showing a couple of sheep ... if you want to come and watch ..." he'd said.

*He wanted to see her again.*

No! She wasn't going to, wasn't even going to entertain the slightest thought of it. There was no future in it.

But as she turned to gaze unseeingly out the window, she wondered exactly what sort of future lay before her. Just what would her future be like if she remained with Patrick?

At the Cadillac dealer's lot, she took the balloon with her. But as she was trying to trap it in the trunk of her new car it got loose and blew away from her. Both she and the salesman raced to catch the string, but it teased them on the tarmac, then lifted out of their reach. Up, up, up, the balloon rode the air currents, blue and silver winking in the bright sun as it headed for the heavens.

"I'm sorry, Miss Raines," the salesman said. "Thought I had it for a minute there."

"It doesn't matter—it wasn't important." She watched it rapidly growing smaller and quickly sent wishes with it, though she couldn't have put the wishes into words.

Early that evening, as Marnie was dressing in anticipation of Patrick's return, he telephoned to say he would be spending the night in Memphis. His trip had been necessitated by a guest's accident in the lobby and the staff's poor handling of the situation. He'd fired the head manager and was still involved with settling the claim and getting the staff straightened out.

"So, did Bud Rodgers have a Cadillac Allanté on the lot for you, or did you have to order one?" he asked.

"I got one from the lot," Marnie said. "Drove it home, in fact. A white one this time."

"You're sure a white one is what you want? You could have had a pink one—or whatever that color was—ordered from the factory."

"It was metallic mauve. And white is fine. Thank you for it, Patrick. I'll take very good care of it." Somehow she felt inordinately indebted to him.

"It's yours to take care of any way you want, baby," he replied with faint surprise. "You des—just a second."

The line hummed between them, while Marnie could hear Patrick speaking to someone there with him—room service, because she heard him instruct them where to put the table. She thought of telling him about meeting Jesse at the fair: "I ran into that Jesse Breen again today—at the fair. Imagine that. Isn't that some coincidence?" What would he say? Would he simply yawn? She didn't like the faint guilt that lay on her shoulders.

He came back on the line. "We're about to have a meeting here, so I have to go."

She gripped the receiver. "Why don't I catch a flight and join you?" she suggested out of the blue, surprising even herself.

"I appreciate the thought, baby," Patrick said after a second's pause. "But I have a dinner meeting, and then I don't want to do anything more than get a massage and hit the bed. I'd be poor company for you to go to all that trouble."

"It wouldn't be any trouble, Patrick. It's still early, and I can be at the airport in twenty minutes. I wouldn't really have to pack." The idea was impulsive, crazy, but she had an overwhelming need to be with him. An overwhelming need to kindle a fire in her heart.

"Marnie, what's this all about? What's going on?"

She rubbed her forehead, thinking of how to explain. Trying to get the courage to be honest, because maybe if she could tell him how she felt deep inside, there was a chance for them. "I would simply like to be with you, Patrick. To do somethin' fun and impulsive, like we used to. We haven't slept together in weeks, and we haven't had a good talk in months. About the only time I see you anymore is when I'm playin' hostess at your business dinners." *Oh, Lord, she sounded like a nagging wife—exactly what Patrick had made very clear to her that he didn't want.*

His irritation vibrated in the silence on the line, and she squeezed her eyes closed.

He said, "I'm sorry I've been neglecting you, but I do have a business to run. And I believe I give you enough to make up for it. Is there anything you want that you don't have?"

"Companionship, Patrick. Comfort." Her entire body was shaking.

"Marnie...look, now is certainly not the time to discuss this. We can't talk over the phone, and I have people waiting," he said impatiently. "Coming here would be a waste of time. I just won't have time for you. We can talk when I get home tomorrow afternoon."

"Yes. See you then. Good night." She replaced the receiver with a stiff arm, then knotted her hands, pressing her nails into her palms.

Whatever had gotten into her to make her say those things to him? Those stupid, stupid things! Oh, Lord, it never paid to reveal oneself so completely. It only opened one to heartache.

Then she stared at the telephone. Had he not wanted her to join him because he had a woman there? This thought seeped into her mind and filled it like a vapor. She wasn't jealous; she wasn't even too angry. What frightened her was that she merely felt accepting.

## Chapter Five

"Are you lookin' for somebody, Dad?"

Caught keeping an eye out for Marnie, Jesse shook his head and said, "No...just lookin'. There're a lot more breeders here than I'd expected. With prices down below bottom like they've been, I hadn't expected this many to show." He kept firm hold on Billy, who he was about to take into the show ring. The show was running behind time, as usual.

"Lower prices mean people have to hustle more," Rory observed. "Works in the sheep industry just like anything else."

Jesse nodded. He automatically watched Billy for signs of aggressive irritation—rams could get as riled as wild bulls on occasion—as he skimmed the crowd for a sorrel head of hair and dealt with the sharp disappointment at not seeing what he sought.

Marnie hadn't come.

*Did you really expect her to?*

Yes. He'd really thought she would show up. He had thought she liked him.

Well maybe she did, but there wasn't much reason for her to come to see him this morning. She belonged to another man.

He accepted this as truth, but a part of him that couldn't give up kept an eye out for her, though he tried not to let Rory catch him at it. Then the officials arrived and the show got under way, taking Jesse's attention. He studied his competition, and his heartbeat picked up tempo. The main reason he and the other ranchers, and some professional sheep showmen from as far away as Ohio, were there showing their sheep was to generate sales of their stock. Raising and selling sheep was their livelihood, as opposed to the Future Farmers of America and 4-H kids who would be coming a few days later.

But the secondary reason was the same for these grown ranchers as for the FFA and 4-H kids—to get that ribbon, by golly! And Jesse, a man, felt his heart beat like any kid's as he guided Billy into the show ring. Somehow the childish hope of getting that ribbon never went away. Jesse had it as bad now as he had at thirteen, the first time he'd shown one of his stock animals. Back when he used to show cattle, Regina and the boys had been with him. The first time he'd shown sheep, the boys had been with him, but in recent years, he'd usually been alone.

He wished mightily now that Marnie were there to see him and Billy.

If Billy didn't win first place, it was because of a judge's poor eyesight, in Jesse's opinion. He held Billy in place and watched the judges observe the rams, studying their form, coming in turn to dig down into Billy's wool, checking the density and seeking traces of black fiber, which Jesse knew they wouldn't find. The judges attempted to keep their faces perfectly blank, but he saw a gleam jump into their eyes when they looked at Billy. Woody Greene, who also had a ram in the class, shot Jesse a challenging grin. Jesse replied with a confident wink.

It seemed to take unnecessarily long for the deliberation, and then finally numbers were called. When Billy received the red ribbon of second place, Jesse was certain blindness had run rampant, especially when Woody's ram took first place. Losing first place to anyone was hard for Jesse. It was an especially bitter pill to lose to Woody Greene, as arrogant a fella as they came.

However, Jesse wasn't about to triple Woody's triumph by revealing the slightest disappointment. He was a big enough man to take things as they came, a sheep's worth being only a matter of opinion, after all. And Jesse wasn't ungrateful, either—second place was nothing to sneeze at. Billy's worth had just risen by about five hundred dollars.

"Congratulations, Dad," Rory said as he met Jesse bringing Billy from the ring.

Their eyes met, and they shared a silent camaraderie. "Leastways we won't go home empty-handed," Jesse said, and started Billy back for his pen. He had the fleeting wish that Rory was Marnie. A man's son was precious, but sometimes what a man needed was a woman's interest.

Kipp Stewart, wearing his wide cowboy hat, calico bandanna at his neck, approached at a quick, spur-jingling walk. "They're finished rakin' the arena, Rory, and about to start again."

"Okay," Rory said, then turned to Jesse. "It'll probably be half an hour or more before we get our go, Dad." Which was his way of indicating, without actually having to say so, that he wanted his dad to come watch the team penning competition.

"I'll be over," Jesse said and waved him on his way.

He took Billy to his pen. The big ram went instantly to chewing hay, oblivious to the honor of the red ribbon that Jesse pinned next to the Breen Ranch sign hanging from the top rail.

Jesse stood there a moment looking at the sign and the ribbon and feeling disconcerting flashes from the past—other shows, other ribbons. The first time his sheep had won ribbons was at the New Mexico State Fair, three years after Regina's death. He'd had a ram take best of show that year. Winning those ribbons had gone a long way to restoring his faith in the future. He wished they could do the same thing now.

Ham jumped up and hurried away, wagging his tail, and the hairs on the back of Jesse's neck stood up. *Marnie...* Slowly he turned, and there she was, crouched in the aisle between the pens, petting Ham.

A great wham-bang of emotion washed over him as he saw her rich, shining hair, then swept his gaze down over her body and back up again. *She had come!*

When she lifted her head, he saw long earrings dangling from her ears. Their eyes met. Slowly she rose, her blue eyes remaining on his, and his heart expanded like a billowing sail.

"I see you got a red ribbon," she said with a slow smile.

"You were over at the show ring?" he asked, a big smile blooming inside him.

"I came in at the last," she answered, her eyes skittering away from him.

"Billy got the red ribbon," he said, standing rooted to the spot and feeling a rush of pride. "But I get the twenty dollars that comes with it. I can treat us to the whole day at the fair."

She shot him a dry look. "Twenty dollars doesn't go as far as it once did."

"We can go Dutch, then."

Their gazes locked again for another long second. And then Marnie averted her eyes, running her fingers along the rail of the pens as she strolled forward. Ham, panting, followed at her heels.

"I'm glad you decided to come join me this mornin'," Jesse said, his attention caught by her subtly sexy movements. Her ruffly, soft blouse was cut in a low V and revealed skin as creamy as high-grade milk. A gold neck chain warmed against her skin.

"Oh, I had already planned to come to the fair this mornin'," she said.

"And you just happened to wander back here to the sheep barn?" he said, amused.

She lifted her chin and touched the camera hanging from her shoulder. "It's a good place to take pictures. Lots of little kids and animals, and they're my favorite subjects." She grinned. "Lots of big kids with their animals, too."

"I see," Jesse said, because he was a prudent man. But what he did see was that *she had come to see him.*

"Are these the same sheep that trampled my Cadillac?" she asked.

"Yes, ma'am. The very same, only in their Sunday best now."

She gazed at the sheep, as if determined not to look at him.

"Let me introduce you," Jesse pointed. "This is Billy, and in this pen we have Irma, Elsie and Sadie—Sadie's the one who had such a fondness for your car."

"A ewe with good taste," she said dryly.

"Very," he said and moved to the third pen. "These two little ones are Little Sue and Fancy."

"Billy had horns," Marnie said, her wondering gaze meeting his quickly before skittering away. "I didn't know sheep had horns."

"Not all breeds do, and many breeds that once did are now polled." He opened the gate to the lambs' pen as he spoke. "Come here, Little Sue. Say hello to the lady." He bent and caught the lamb in his arms.

Marnie came uncertainly into the pen, peered at Little Sue and reached out to pet her. She leaned close and sniffed. "She doesn't stink."

"Of course she doesn't."

"I always heard that sheep stink. Isn't that why cowboys never liked sheep? Hello, Little Sue." Marnie, her face going all soft, was almost nose-to-nose with the lamb now.

"That's just tales. Cowmen never liked sheep because they were determined not to like anything but cows. And a man who had to stay out with the flock for months maybe did smell—from lack of bathing. He wouldn't smell any worse than a cowboy doin' the same."

She dug her fingers into Little Sue's fluffy wool. She chuckled. "It feels so springy. Oh, look at those eyes! Don't sheep have the most wonderful eyes!"

Women always said that, and Jesse smiled, watching her set about petting both lambs, then leaning over to pet the yearling ewes, too, as if not wanting them to feel left out. After they came out of the pen, she tried to reach Billy, but he stubbornly refused to allow it.

Then they were standing there together. Not exactly alone, with so many people milling around the big barn, but those people were strangers, and no one was within hearing distance.

"So," she said in a friendly manner, "has your truck been fixed yet?"

"It should be fixed by tomorrow. The insurance company is still hemin' and hawin' about the trailer. How 'bout you? Do you like that new Cadillac you got yesterday?"

"Yes, very much," she said.

"Must be nice."

"It is," she said with satisfaction.

They stood there in silence, gazing at the animals. Jesse wondered if she felt as awkward as he did, while he cast around for something to say. He couldn't recall the last time he'd experienced bashfulness around a woman. Couldn't recall when he'd cared enough to worry about saying the wrong thing.

Marnie stepped back, startling him slightly, and slipped her camera from her shoulder. "You did invite me to take pictures of your sheep," she said.

"You might as well—since you were wanderin' around to take pictures and you just wandered back here," he replied.

She blushed and cast him a saucy look. Putting the camera to her eye, she focused on the sheep, clicking a number of times from different angles.

"And one of their owner," she said. "Move over there, so I can get your red ribbon in the shot."

He did as she said, using his finger to tilt his hat back from his brows. She grinned at him, and he grinned at her. He knew he'd always taken a good picture, but suddenly a sinking doubt washed over him. Perhaps his attractiveness in pictures was fading, like a lot of things in his life. He struggled to ignore the niggling self-consciousness and to be the forthright, distinguished man he'd always thought himself to be, while Marnie clicked away.

She finished with shots including Ham, then closed the camera lens. While Jesse put Ham into his pen next to the sheep, he thought frantically of a way to keep her from leaving. Striding to her, he reached for her elbow.

"The team penning show is going on in the horse-show barn down the road here," he said, smoothly guiding her outside.

"My son Rory and two of his friends are entered and will be competing in just a few minutes."

She hung back. "Oh, I should be getting on. I—"

Not releasing his hold on her, Jesse interrupted. "You don't really have anything you *have* to be doin', do you? Patrick Vinsand isn't even in town."

Her eyes widened. "How did you know that?"

"I overheard two desk clerks at the hotel this mornin'. And since he isn't here, he won't mind if you're with me."

She came to a firm halt and jerked her arm from his grasp. "You are *assuming* quite a bit. You don't know what Patrick would mind—nor what *I* might want."

Jesse gazed at her and decided to go with his instincts. "I may not know what Patrick would want, but then, I don't really care. I'm attracted to you," he said softly. "And you're attracted to me. And feelin's like this are gifts not to be wasted."

Her beautiful eyes took on a dark glint. "You do assume too much, if you believe I play around."

He gazed at her. "I never meant to imply that you do," he said. "I'm not tryin' to seduce you, Marnie. I'd just very much enjoy seeing the fair with you, and since you are technically a single woman, I didn't think I was steppin' on anyone's toes. If I've gone about telling you that in a clumsy manner, then I'm sorry."

Her expression turned suspicious. "I've never quite trusted a man who was both a blunt talker *and* a charmer."

"And how many of those types have you met?" he asked, coaxing a grudging grin from her.

"Not too many," she admitted. "They're usually one or the other. And I trust neither."

"I'm generally a forthright man," he said. "It saves time and a lot of unnecessary misunderstanding. Sometimes keeps a fella from gettin' shot. Come on. I'll bet you've never seen team penning before." And again took hold of her elbow, directing her toward a large blue building.

"Are you always this overbearing?"

"I think of it as masterful," he said with a grin. "Besides, you like it." He felt a growing virility, and it was great.

She shot him a sarcastic look. "That attitude is way behind the times," she quipped, while walking willingly beside him.

"And that's a shame, isn't it? I guess I'm about the last of the good guys."

He caught her gaze and held it, looking deep into her shimmering blue eyes. Sensual energy swirled around them like the dust from the street.

"Either that," she said with a deep drawl and that slow grin that Jesse was beginning to expect, "or a man who's a bit too big for his britches."

Jesse chuckled, delighted by the way she was making him feel. "I guess I can be that sometimes, too," he allowed.

Jesse held her hand, tugged her into the horse barn and across its dirt floor at a fast pace. His hand was large and work callused. And when he smiled at her, his thick auburn mustache slanted crookedly and his craggy features became quite surprisingly boyish. And his eyes sparkled right into her heart. He could charm coons from the trees, she thought. Oh, mercy! That was something her father used to say. A few minutes with this man and she was regressing!

But it had been a long time since she had held anyone's hand this way. Since she had felt that she was doing something that gave someone else a lot of pleasure.

She pushed aside all her nagging cautions. Seeing the fair with Jesse wouldn't take anything at all away from Patrick, and it would give her so much. It would give Jesse so much.

He led her over to introduce her to his son.

"Why do I feel like some prize ewe you've just bought?" she muttered good-naturedly.

And he winked. "Because you're a very special woman in the care of a very special man."

"A man whose hat's gonna bust at the seam any minute," she said, and he chuckled. The deep grooves from his nose to his mouth were laugh lines, she thought. He was a man to chuckle easily, to take little in his life seriously.

Jesse's son Rory leaned down from the saddle of his palomino to shake her hand. "Nice to meet you, Marnie." He grinned shyly with a heartbreak-handsome face, his features very much like his father's.

"Nice to meet you."

"She done favorin' that leg?" Jesse asked, indicating the horse and studying the animal carefully.

"Yep. Not a whisper of a problem today."

"Go out there and show 'em how it's done, son," Jesse said, and patted Rory's thigh. "We'll be watchin' from up there."

An old wound cracked inside of Marnie as she watched Jesse with his son. Showing how he felt was no problem for Jesse, Marnie thought, contrasting him to Patrick, and to Patrick's father. Her own father, with all his no-account ways, had been good at showing his feelings, too, when he'd been around.

"That's my middle son," Jesse said as they walked away, his hand warm on the small of her back.

"And you taught him all he knows."

"Matter of fact, I did."

He left Marnie sitting near the top of the dusty aluminum bleacher seats, while he went for soft drinks. She watched him clamber easily to the ground and she thought, he's such a bold man.

She suddenly felt very alone and out of place sitting there. The crowd was sparse, sitting in isolated groupings, family and friends of the contestants in the arena, most wearing the familiar Western-style clothes. She was wearing a designer-made silk blouse and linen slacks.

Bleak thoughts washed over her. Did Jesse find it a thrill to flirt with her because she was Patrick's mistress? Did he think her an easy woman, ready and willing for any man? There had been a few who'd thought that about her. Once, Herb Wallis had caught her alone in Patrick's kitchen and offered to double the allowance Patrick gave her if she would come with him. She'd managed to catch his roving hand in the silverware drawer hard enough to break his index finger.

But then Jesse returned, grinning at her as he came up to their seat, balancing two soft drinks and a box of popcorn. Very carefully, as if he were serving a princess, he put one cup in her hand and smiled warmly. "Here's somethin' to wet your whistle," he said and tilted a box of popcorn toward her.

"Want some popcorn? I didn't get butter on it 'cause I'm watchin' my cholesterol."

She had to grin. "Me, too," she said as she dipped her hand into the box.

He grinned back at her. Because of the dimness of the barn, for an instant she had the illusion of seeing only black and white, like an old film. She thought that, yes, Jesse Breen was bold and overbearing. Downright cocky, which had always been her stupid weakness when it came to men. Her father had been like that, she thought, and her mother had suffered from the same weakness as herself.

But Jesse Breen was also gallant and polite and warm-hearted. And, she thought grudgingly, she was very glad to be with him.

She *was* attracted to him.

That thought came sharp and unbidden. She looked at him, hesitantly but unable to stop herself. His head came around and he looked long at her, and the energy vibrated between them.

"Thanks for joinin' me," he said.

She simply shrugged, afraid to acknowledge the excitement swirling around inside her.


"This is very similar to work cowhands have to do out on the range," Jesse said, explaining the actions going on in the ring. "There're three on a team, and it's their job to sort three cows from the herd at that end and drive 'em into that pen there in the middle of the ring."

"That doesn't look so hard," she said.

He gave her a dry look. "There are numbers on the backs of those cows for a reason. Those boys can't choose any old cow. They are assigned a number and have to cut from the herd the three cows with that particular number on the back, without lettin' any others come across the line. And those boys have to push those three cows in the center pen in two minutes or less."

"They aren't all 'boys.' That rider is a girl." She repressed a grin and gazed into his mockingly pained expression.

"My mistake," he said. "And since you are being specific, let me admit that those aren't cows. They are yearling heifers. Sometimes yearling steers are used, but most generally they're all referred to as cows. No sexist slight intended. It's just easier."

Focused on the arena, his expression grew intense. "That rider's got too far behind the cow—he has to stay up beside it but not let his horse ride over it. Whoa...hold 'em back, now," he said, giving whispered instruction.

The event was action packed and hilarious, too, as the riders yelled at each other and worked furiously to get the swerving, darting, racing cows into the small pen without running over each other. In seconds, Marnie found herself as caught up in the act as Jesse. She'd never known that cows could run so fast!

Jesse gave Marnie a running narration on the ensuing rides. She listened closely, finding herself fascinated by the action. The only horses she'd ever seen as a child were an occasional plow horse. She had accompanied Patrick to a number of shows featuring horses that simply walked around and looked beautiful and were worth fortunes for doing so. Patrick had from time to time owned racehorses, and she'd gone with him to the track to watch them race. Once he had even taken her to the Kentucky Derby.

But she'd never seen horses like these, which were doing a task requiring them to do a little thinking on their own, requiring them to stop and turn in one motion and race off in another direction. "Cowy," was what Jesse called it, explaining that these horses were bred to work cattle, as opposed to those bred to run, or those bred for stamina or those bred for a certain smooth gait. These were Quarter horses, "the all-round horse," he said proudly.

And then it was Rory's team's turn. The two other team members were Kipp and Larry, Jess explained, as his son and two other riders entered the far end of the arena. Rory's horse was a beautiful palomino, but it wasn't the horse's looks that Jesse commented on. "That horse is real cowy," he said, leaning close and brushing against her arm. "Rory raised her from a foal and taught her the basics workin' cattle for real. If you can teach 'em well, the horse will do all the work." Fatherly pride echoed in his voice. "All those boys have raised their horses like that."

And then the race was on!

Quietly but quickly, Rory cut a cow from the herd, and his teammates drove it neatly into the center pen. Jesse cupped his mouth and called, "Whooeee!" causing Marnie to jump an inch and a number of other people to grin.

She looked from Jesse to the horses and riders in the arena and found it hard to believe she was sitting on a dusty bleacher seat in a warm barn, watching cowboys play. Actually urging them onward, clenching her fists, whispering oohs and ahhs, helping them with her energy to put those cows into that pen.

Her heart went to her throat when, in the heat of chasing a cow, Rory's horse jumped right over Larry, who quickly threw himself to the side of the saddle, out of the way, then popped right back up and went on chasing the cow. And then, well before the sounding of the buzzer, the three cows were in the pen, and Rory called for time.

Jesse again cupped his mouth and called, "Yeah! Whooeee!"

There were three more teams, and then it was over. Rory and his teammates had taken first place. Jesse held Marnie's hand tight as they came down the bleacher seats. They met Rory and his friends down near the arena, all in Stetson hats and boots and spurs. She sensed their veiled curiosity and admiration as she hung back, while Jesse hugged Rory and slapped the other two on the back, congratulating them profusely on their win.

Then he took her hand and pulled her forward, introducing her to the young men. Hardly giving her time to say hello, he tugged her away, saying, "I'll see you fellas tonight. Marnie and I are off to see the fair."

All three men focused sharp, curious eyes on her. Then Rory smiled. "See ya' later, Dad. Nice meetin' you, Marnie."

"Nice to meet you, Rory."

"Want to ride the merry-go-round first?" Jesse asked as he led her away.

She stared at him. She hadn't ridden a merry-go-round in years. She hadn't had a man paying her attention in years.

"I'd like that," she said finally.

Today was a special day, she thought. One of those days a person was simply handed as compensation for the much more numerous hard days that filled a person's life. And Marnie gave herself totally to the fun of it.

They rode the carousel three times, and Jesse's spirit soared as he watched Marnie's hair blow back from her face. As he watched her grin and as he felt more and more alive.

They went for corn dogs and ate them while strolling down the midway. Marnie stood back and snapped pictures of him at a coin-tossing game, where he won her a stuffed bear—using about ten dollars to do it. They went to the kiddie rides, and Jesse stood back, holding the bear, while Marnie took pictures of children. He remembered how she'd said she didn't want any; the piece didn't fit.

They sat in the shade of a small mimosa tree and listened to a fiddle player and watched clowns juggling. Coming upon one of the men who guessed ages and weights, Jesse stopped.

"Guess her age," he said, handing the young carny a dollar.

The man eyed Marnie, who hugged the brown-and-tan stuffed bear. "I can tell I'm in trouble. Twenty-nine?" he said hesitantly.

Jesse and the man regarded her expectantly, and she said, "A lady should never be asked to reveal her age."

"Now you all came to me," the young carny protested.

Marnie looked stubborn, and Jesse laughed.

"I didn't bring my driver's license with me," Marnie said, "so I can't prove you wrong." As they walked away, she told Jesse, "You deserved to lose your dollar. If you wanted to know how old I was, you could simply have asked, Mr. Forth-right."

Jesse was heartily embarrassed at being caught. So much for subtlety, he thought. "I'm fifty-two," he said and held his breath.

*Was she surprised? Was she put off?* He saw evidence of neither.

Marnie gazed at him and thought of how she hadn't thought about his age at all. She'd thought of him as a mature, attractive man. A virile man.

"I'm thirty-six," she said.

His eyebrows rose in surprise, and then he sighed. "I'm damn glad you're older than my eldest son. I'd feel even more foolish if you were terribly young."

His sheepish expression and the irony of him visualizing her as some young innocent made her both laugh and feel close to tears. "Oh, Jesse, I left 'terribly young' behind at the age of twelve!"

Something in the tone of her voice and the sad glimmer in her eyes caught him. His gaze slipped from her face to her arm clutching the bear, and he wondered what lay behind the remark.

Immediately her expression turned guarded, an expression he was beginning to recognize.

"Where to, next?" he asked. "How about the Ferris wheel?"

She shook her head. "Let's go see the pig races. If we hurry, we can just make the next show."

"Lead on, lady. I'm happy as a dog waggin' two tails just to be walkin' around with you."

"Oh, Jesse Breen, you are a dangerous charmer."

"No, ma'am . . . I'm just truthful."

But she cast him a thoughtful, skeptical gaze, and he wondered if there was something about him that she especially distrusted—or if she was naturally distrustful of everyone. Or maybe it was men in general. A woman as alluring as she was might have good reason to be distrustful of men, he thought. And he wondered what had happened to her to cause her to keep a careful distance and put into her eyes the sad dullness he occasionally saw there.

Jesse found himself becoming increasingly curious about her life.

They saw the pig races, toured the crafts-and-hobbies building, ate strudel, pitched pennies and rode the Tilt-A-Whirl and the carousel—Marnie's favorite—again. They laughed and teased and touched very hesitantly, always with propriety, but Jesse knew Marnie was as tempted as he was to touch a lot more intimately.

He succeeded when they joined in dancing to country music played by a band on one of the open-air stages. He slipped his arm around her and held her close while he guided her around the concrete dance floor. He leaned his head close to her hair and caught her alluring scent. Her thighs brushed his, her breasts his chest, faintly, but causing an immediate warming. *Lordy, what her laughing eyes did to him!*

"You're very good," she said, obviously surprised.

"And you're rusty."

"I haven't danced the two-step in ... well, in a very long time."

He wondered what she and Patrick did together. They didn't dance; that much was obvious. And apparently Patrick didn't take her to the fair. He did take her to company dinners. But he didn't romance her. Jesse had no doubt about that. Patrick Vinsand might sleep with her, but he didn't romance her.

After dancing, they got ice-cream cones and strolled around the Flag Plaza.

"You said you were from Arkansas?" Jesse prodded.

The familiar guarded expression swept her face. She licked her ice cream and nodded. "Eastern Arkansas, near the Mississippi. And you? Are you originally from New Mexico?"

He nodded. "Born and bred. Had two brothers, but they're both dead now. You?"

She hesitated. "There were five of us. I was the middle child. Two older brothers and two younger sisters. One of my sisters died as a baby. I lost touch with my brothers years ago, but my little sister's a CPA in Memphis. Should we go in here?" She indicated the Made In Oklahoma building.

Jesse remembered then. "Ah ... jeez!" He glanced at his watch. "I'm supposed to show a couple of my sheep this afternoon—starting in twenty minutes." He looked up to see stark disappointment cross her face, though the emotion was gone so quickly, he wondered if he'd imagined it.

"I need to be going anyway," she said quickly. "I need to pick up a few things at the market, and I haven't ordered dinner. I'm parked out front, so I'll just ..."

He grabbed her arm. "Wait. I don't have to show my sheep."

She gave him a puzzled frown. "But you're entered—and you came all the way here from New Mexico to show those sheep, didn't you?"

"That's *part* of the reason. The other reason was simply to go to the fair. I've shown those sheep before, and I'll show them again, God willin'. But right now I'd rather spend the rest of the day with you—and, hell, no one's gonna arrest me for not showin' those sheep."

She gazed at him for a long minute in which disbelief and suspicion flickered in her eyes. Then she said, "I'll go with you to show your sheep."

Jesse grabbed her hand. "Then let's get movin', gal. I'm hopin' for a couple of first places this time."

Marnie spent the rest of the afternoon with Jesse. She helped him quickly spruce up Sadie, and she even held the ewe while Jesse slipped away to the men's room to spruce himself up. She clapped the loudest when he and Sadie took a first place-ribbon and made a spectacle of herself taking pictures of the winning ewe and owner.

Back at the sheep pens she congratulated Jesse profusely and then scolded him for getting a swelled head, while both of them scurried to get fresh feed and water for the animals and to spruce up Fancy for her class.

"You've done this before," Jesse commented, his gaze intense and curious.

But Marnie only said, "How hard can it be to get a hose to put water in a bucket? Do you think I'm totally useless?"

"Oh, no, ma'am. I didn't say that at all," he teased with a sensual gleam in his eye.

"Jesse Breen! You are a total male chauvinist!" She teasingly shot a spray of water at him.

"No, ma'am—I'm a rancher," he said loudly, charging her and wrestling the hose from her hand, managing to spray them both in the process.

Marnie looked up and found her face only inches from his. His arms were around her. They were strong, and he was hot, and his pulse beat against her. The sexual urge flashed through her, hard and pounding, and she felt herself drawn to him and his lips.

He broke away, averting his eyes and clearing his throat. "I'd better get the water turned off."

Weak in the knees, Marnie took hold of the fence. She had wanted him to kiss her right then and there, and the realization shook her. Quickly she took up her camera and began taking pictures.

By the time Jesse had won a third-place ribbon for Fancy and once again had all his sheep settled in their pens, Marnie was hot and sweaty and dusty. Her white flats were scuffed and speckled with dirt, and her silk blouse and linen trousers were smudged and covered with dog hair and bits of fleece. She had smudges on her face, too, she learned, when Jesse dabbed his handkerchief to his tongue and caught her chin in his hands and went to wiping at her.

"Must you spit on my face?" she said.

"Just gettin' a smudge. Wouldn't want you to walk around that way. There."

They gazed at each other, and as it had before, as they both knew it was bound to do again, the attraction spread between them.

*Just once, very quickly,* Marnie yearned, looking at his lips beneath his thick mustache. She raised her gaze to his eyes and saw the wanting there.

The clanging sound of someone dropping a bucket broke the spell and brought them back to the reality of a public place.

"I really have to go now, Jesse," Marnie said quietly. Their eyes met again. "Patrick should be home soon."

Patrick's name brought the cool chill of reality.

"Ah, yes. Patrick," Jesse said and averted his eyes.

"Let me get one more picture," she said impulsively. "A close-up of you. Come on—give me that charmer grin."

Snapping pictures of him kept her from getting all mushy over this goodbye.

"Ham and I will walk you to your car," Jesse said as she slipped her camera strap over her shoulder.

"There's no need, Jesse."

"I want to, okay?"

"Thanks."

They walked slowly and didn't talk much. Ham padded silently at her heels, expertly avoiding being stepped on by the growing crowd of people. Marnie wished this time never had to end. Then she reminded herself of the old saw, "If wishes were horses, then beggars would ride." Her mother used to say that. Her mother who had taught her to live in the present and never cry over yesterday nor expect much from tomorrow, because to do either brought heartache.

About halfway to the front gate of the fairgrounds, Jesse took her hand. When they reached her car, he made a big deal of looking at it and complimenting it.

"I always wanted a white car—a car like that is a bit out of our league, though. Pretty nice machine."

She wondered if he was trying to prolong their special time, just as she wished to do. She wondered if he wanted her as she wanted him. She opened the car door, then bent and petted Ham, saying softly, "Goodbye, fella. It's been very nice to meet you."

"I'll be here one more full day," Jesse said. "Maybe I'll see you again."

She slowly stood and made herself look directly at him. "Maybe," she replied, though she knew it would be foolish on her part—on both their parts. A person couldn't hold on to good days.

Then he stood very still in front of her and put his finger beneath her chin and gazed into her eyes. She blinked and forced the tears back.

"Thank you for today, Marnie. I'm a man whose been thinkin' himself on the downhill slide. You helped to pick me up."

She smiled. "Oh, Jesse, nothin' about you is goin' downhill. And I thank you for making me feel like a lovely woman."

"You are, gal. You are. If Patrick Vinsand doesn't let you know that, he's a fool."

"Bye, Jesse," she said, forcing the words past the giant lump in her throat. She wanted to wish him luck with his sheep tomorrow but couldn't possibly get the words out.

"Bye, sweetheart."

She hoped for an instant that he would kiss her, but he quickly stepped backward and touched the brim of his hat, turned and started walking back to the gate. Ham gazed at her a moment, then whirled and followed his master.

Marnie started the car and drove away with happy-sad tears flowing down her cheeks and not understanding the why of them at all. She hadn't had such a good day in years. She hadn't been so unhappy in years.

Suddenly realizing she'd left the teddy bear—Jesse had won for her—back in a lawn chair beside Billy's pen, she began to cry harder.

## Chapter Six

Jesse gritted his teeth and told himself he could be proud of not kissing Marnie—an accomplishment of no small measure. It had been hell turning away from her soft face, which had been filled to overflowing with wanting. But that one kiss would have put him over the line.

Just what line he wasn't certain. Maybe it had to do with his age, and hers. Maybe it had something to do with thinking that if he kissed her it would have been a solid goodbye. He would never see her again. His mind couldn't accept that. He had no more turned his back on her in that white Cadillac than he'd begun thinking of ways to see her again. Foolish it might be, but he couldn't get the idea out of his mind. He wanted to spend another day with her, and maybe some of the night. Of course, there was the little matter of Patrick Vinsand.

Jesse studied that fact. He didn't think he needed to feel guilty in regard to invading Vinsand's territory, because a mistress didn't fall into the same category as a wife, or even an engaged woman. A mistress fell into the same category as a girlfriend, who was a woman a man adored and wanted but not enough of either to marry her—such as the way Jesse himself had felt about Celeste.

As far as Jesse was concerned, all was fair when it came to girlfriends. Unless the said girlfriend happened to belong to a close relative or personal friend of his, in which case honor forbade him doing any more than looking—and not much of that. However, Vinsand was nothing to Jesse; he didn't even particularly like the man. He especially didn't like Vinsand because he didn't think the guy could possibly be good for Marnie. If he had been, she wouldn't have that sad shadow in her eyes. If Vinsand had made her happy, she wouldn't have come to see Jesse today. So the matter was settled on that score.

But then his conscience set up all kinds of a ruckus. *What the hell was his intention here?*

The truth wouldn't be denied, and even at his worst, Jesse never hid from the truth. No matter how he tried to color it, what he was thinking of, what he was wanting so bad he could taste it, was an affair.

He had tonight, tomorrow and the following night left in town. That was it. And since he was telling truths, he might as well admit that it had been his intention, his hope, all along to meet a woman on this trip to the city and enjoy an exciting affair. He winced. What he was wanting was to be a young buck sowing wild oats again—and that sure as hell wasn't much to offer a lovely young woman like Marnie.

He felt guilty about that, but he guessed all the guilt in the world lying on his shoulders wouldn't have been able to make him quit wanting to be with her. He'd had a taste of her, and that had simply served to whet his appetite. He was like a thirsty ram who, having come finally to water after crossing a high, lonesome desert, wasn't going to be satisfied with two quick gulps. He wanted the whole damn river!

The hours left in which he could be with her taunted him unmercifully, as did fantasies of her all hot and pliable and liquid in his arms. He was both glad and ashamed of those erotic fantasies: glad because they indicated he was very much alive in that area—when he had feared himself dead—and ashamed because they seemed unworthy of Marnie. He felt protective of her, and if any other man had voiced what Jesse was thinking, he would have punched the man in the mouth.

He was settling Ham and the sheep for the evening, trying to cool the fire in his blood and erase from his mind images of Vinsand with Marnie, when Woody Greene and Clyde Barrow came by and asked him to join them in going to a party a couple of the professional sheep showers were giving over at their hotel. He readily agreed. Maybe he would meet a pretty woman who was of the same mind as he was about an affair. A woman nearer his age, that was for damn sure. Immediately a cautioning voice began whispering in his mind; he told the voice to shut up.

He was leaving the dimly lit barn when his gaze fell on the stuffed bear he'd won for Marnie. It sat in the corner of a green-and-white webbed lawn chair at the end of Billy's pen. Had she forgotten it? Or had she intended to leave it there?

Jesse picked it up and took it with him.

When he pulled his rented black Cadillac Eldorado into the hotel parking lot, when he walked through the lobby, all his senses kept on alert for Marnie, while he imagined all sorts of witty things he would say to her, always ending up with, "How about joining me for tonight?" Which would have been a lot more crass than clever.

He was heartily disappointed not to run into her, and found himself growing more irritable by the minute. He complained to the powers that be that had helped him and Marnie run into each other before. Where were they now? he thought as he entered his silent, lonely room.

He looked at the stuffed bear and thought about Marnie being only a few floors up from him. He turned his gaze to the telephone, then tossed the bear onto the bed. Cursing, he began jerking off his clothes as he headed for a cold shower. The day had been great—and had left him with one large knot of frustration.

On his way out Jesse stopped at the hotel desk. The clerk greeted him with a practiced smile.

"Could you direct me to Marnie Raines's apartment?" Jesse asked.

The clerk's smile was replaced by a cautious, curious one. "She lives on the private penthouse floor, sir." He reached for the telephone. "I'll need to announce you."

Jesse had expected as much. "No...that's okay. Please have this delivered to Miss Raines." He slid the stuffed bear, with an envelope bearing Marnie's name pinned to its chest, across the counter. He followed that with a five-dollar bill and said, "Don't forget."

"No, sir. It'll be delivered."

As he headed for the front doors, Jesse wondered what her reaction would be. He'd sent the bear to her on the chance that she might want it and thus would be thrilled to get it. And if she wasn't thrilled to get it, he still wanted her to have it. He wanted her to remember this day, for whatever crazy, insane reason. And if she had to explain the bear to Vinsand, so much the better. Since he was uncomfortable, Jesse certainly wouldn't mind if she and Vinsand were, too. Maybe it would make Vinsand quit pussyfooting around and make an honest woman of her.

And with that thought, he recalled her telling him that his attitudes were long out-of-date. Maybe they were, he thought, but they suited him just fine, so it didn't matter what *she* thought.

The sun was lazy in the evening sky, sending golden beams into Patrick's bedroom. While Patrick showered, Marnie emptied his suitcase. Freshly bathed, she wore a lavender silk robe, a bit of light makeup and had her hair twisted loosely atop her head.

Patrick, rubbing a towel over his hair, poked his head out of the bathroom. "Have you ordered dinner yet?"

"Yes—sirloin steak, okay? And I've set the table out on the patio, because the air's just perfect this evenin'." She'd set the table with fine china, silver and white tapered candles. She had champagne chilling, too.

"Great," came his muffled voice from the bathroom; then he poked his head back out the door. "Og's coming by for a few minutes after he stops to see his mother. But we only have a few things to clear up. He won't stay long."

Marnie's heart tightened. Og was returning, which meant their dinner would be cut short. She had so hoped they could talk tonight. Really talk. Communicate heart-to-heart. Though she wasn't at all certain of what she was going to say. Could she say she *needed* him? That she didn't want to go on living this way? Sure—and then he'd likely show her the door. Where would she go, and what would she do? How could she leave the only life she knew?

Moving nervously, she carried a pair of brown wing tips into the closet. She looked at the rows of shoes and thought of cowboy boots, which were all Jesse probably wore.

His face, his lazy smile, filled her mind.

Her heart squeezed, and memories of the day flashed in her memory: Jesse standing beside his blue and red ribbons, and the purple banner Sadie had won in the end as champion. His large, work-roughened hands holding the flimsy popcorn box, his expression as, completely uninhibited, he rode the carousel. His hand holding hers. She missed him terribly.

*But that was just nonsense!*

Suddenly Patrick's arm came around her waist, and he pulled her against his bare chest. "What's so interesting in the closet?" he asked in a low, amused tone and kissed her neck.

"Oh, nothin'...I was just thinking." She touched his hands, smooth, long-fingered, manicured hands, so very different from Jesse's. And Patrick's arm felt slight in comparison.

Guilt slid over her. She'd often hidden her feelings from Patrick, but she'd never had feelings of this sort to hide.

"I'm glad I could get back tonight," he whispered and pushed erotically against her, his breath hot on her neck. A feeling of panic swept her. *What if he wanted to make love tonight—which he obviously did?* Quite suddenly, for the first time ever, the idea was...was...impossible!

Shaken, she slipped from his embrace, saying, "Do you want me to have this coat cleaned?"

She felt his intense gaze, was inordinately aware of him standing there behind her in his bare feet and tan trousers unbuttoned at the top.

"Yes...go ahead," he said. "But don't bother putting the suitcase away. I'm leaving again tomorrow morning."

She whirled and stared at him. "Leaving?"

He nodded and moved to pull a shirt from the closet, averting his eyes. "That's why Og and I have to meet tonight. He'll be staying here to handle things on this end while I go to Atlanta to handle this deal for Williams's hotels. There are some problems that need ironing out, and the bank we're going to use is there."

"I see." Marnie went cold inside. Fear, which she had been trying to hold at bay, crept over her like evening darkness. She quickly gathered Patrick's dirty clothes, as if by moving, keeping busy, she could escape the dark.

"Look, baby," he said, slipping on his shirt, "I know I've been pretty preoccupied lately, but this deal is a big one. When it's finished, we'll take a trip down to the Caribbean. I had a call from Tom Worthington the other day—" He moved to look in the mirror and brush his hair. "He's decided it's time to sell the old Grand Bay Hotel and is finally coming to *me* now, which is a pretty good joke and goes to show how far we've come. He's invited us to come have a look. How does a few weeks stay down on St. Thomas sound? Hmmm . . . ?"

He stopped her and wrapped his arms around her, nuzzling her neck. A sense of suffocation engulfed her, and she fought the urge to push him away. *She did not want to hurt him, did not want a scene in which she would pour it all out. . . .* The doorbell rang, giving her an excuse to slip from his embrace.

"That's dinner," she said and practically fled the room. *Stop this nonsense! Stop it! You're going to blow your life right away!*

Before opening the door, she dashed the tears from her cheeks and fixed herself into a genteel Southern woman, just as Miss Phoebe had taught her to do. But that assumed calm was shot clean away when she found it wasn't someone with the dinner cart but Lonny, a young bellman, with the brown-and-tan bear that Jesse had won for her.

Trembling, she closed the door and walked into the living room, staring at the bear. Bittersweet joy flooded her heart as she squished its soft, plush body with her fingers. She unpinned from his chest the envelope bearing her name. *Marnie Raines.* Was that Jesse's bold and flowing handwriting?

She thought of Patrick in the bedroom.

Opening the envelope, she pulled out the small piece of hotel notepaper. "You forgot this guy. I won't forget this day—Jesse."

"I take it that wasn't dinner," Patrick said.

Marnie looked up to find him gazing at her. She shook her head and stuffed the note into the pocket of her robe.

"What is that?"

She gazed at the bear, held it out. "It's a teddy bear."

"I can see that, Marnie. Whose is it?"

She lifted her gaze to his. "Mine. Jesse Breen won it for me at the fair today. I forgot to bring it home, so he sent it."

"I see." Turning, he walked over to the bar. His back to her, he carefully poured bourbon into a glass as he said, "Just who is this Jesse Breen and have you known him long?"

"Almost three days. He's the man who wrecked my Cadillac. Remember—you met him the other evening up at the Top of the World."

"Ah, yes . . . the gentleman who came to the fair to show his sheep and who prefers feather pillows." He turned slowly to face her. She felt his tightly controlled fury, saw it in his bland expression and his curiously raised eyebrow. "And you spent the day at the fair with him?"

"Yes." What would he think about that?

His eyes darkened. "He must be a hell of a sheepman to be able to afford to offer you something I haven't already given you."

Anger flashed through her. "He could afford to offer me his *time,*" Marnie said through her teeth. "That's something money can't buy."

Patrick took a deep swallow of his drink, then gazed hard at her. "Oh, yes, it can. I buy people's time everyday. What do you think I pay my employees for? I pay them for their time and effort."

His words were cold and hard as frozen steel, and gazing into his eyes, Marnie felt that steel driven right through.

Trembling with fury, she said, "And that's what you pay me for—right?" She stepped toward him. "Well, let me tell you, if you think I've stayed with you for six years for nothing more than money, you don't simply underrate me—you underrate yourself. And you belittle Og and Dorothy, too. They, and most of your other employees, work for you for a damn good salary, yes, but all the money in the world couldn't buy you the loyalty they give you."

The tears came in an angry rush, and she turned so he couldn't see her face as she dashed them from her cheeks. An evening breeze stirred through the screen of the sliding glass door, soft and gentle, as if mocking the harshness of the moment.

"I'm sorry, Marnie. That was a low shot."

She looked round to see him standing there, his face and stance like a statue. Emotionless, not at all apologetic. But she knew him. Patrick wasn't given to hitting out in anger; he was too practical for that. And he simply wasn't good with giving an apology, nor receiving one.

"I know," she said. "I just want you to know it isn't only the money. It has never been *only* the money."

Silence was like thick fog.

"I know that, Marnie," Patrick said finally in his low, no-nonsense voice. He walked toward her and stopped. "What's going on with you? You've never resorted to trying to make me jealous before. You've never played games. What's going on?"

"I wasn't trying to make you jealous," she said sharply. "I had a day at the fair with Jesse. He was nice to me, and we enjoyed each other's company, plain and simple."

"All right," he said slowly, watching her closely. "What else? Something has been bothering you for weeks. What is it?"

And she thought: it has been bothering me for months.

She didn't know what to say. Gazing unseeingly at the teddy bear, she tried to find words to explain something she didn't fully understand. Something that could blow her entire life to pieces.

"It's just...I..." She regarded him helplessly while fear, anger and longing swirled inside her like a muddy whirlpool. "We've barely had time to see each other in months, Patrick. You've only slept with me a couple of times. I practically have to make an appointment to see you! Dorothy almost wouldn't let me into your office the other day."

He gazed at her. "Dorothy gets overprotective, but she's just doing her job as she sees it. And I've been busy running a business, Marnie. Vinsand Corporation can't run and grow all by itself. I guess I don't need to point out it's Vinsand Corporation paying the bills—buying all this—" he gestured with his drink, then gazed pointedly at her "—as well as the silk you have a penchant for... and look so good in," he added, pointedly raking her with a sensual gaze.

Marnie sighed. "I know that, Patrick. I live well, and I appreciate it. I'm grateful to you for everything. And I've always tried to show you that." She swallowed. "But... I am in the unique position of being your mistress and not having to hide that fact. Since you're not married, you don't care who knows. When people ask me what I am to you, I can't say I'm your fiancée or even your girlfriend, who could entertain hopes of someday being your wife. What I am is your mistress, and I don't like explaining that to people anymore. I don't like the way some people look at me." She tossed up her hand. "Half the time Dorothy doesn't only look down at me, she looks *through* me."

She couldn't meet his eyes and blinked rapidly, trying to clear her tears. The lump in her throat made breathing difficult, and she struggled not to break out sobbing. Silence fell like death over the room.

"Has Dorothy insulted you?"

She shook her head. "No...not really. She doesn't even mean to hurt me. She's just naturally head and shoulders above everyone."

"Has someone else insulted you? If they have, I'll—"

"No." She gave a dismissing wave and sniffed loudly. "Well, once Herb Wallis got pretty obnoxious, but I smashed his hand in a kitchen drawer."

Again the silence stretched, and Marnie knew Patrick wished he were already way down in the Caribbean, far, far away from this emotional confrontation.

"You have no reason to be ashamed of our relationship, Marnie," he said, standing stiff as a board. "Don't you realize what you do for me? I was right on target when I persuaded you to come with me. You handle my social life with ease, and you make a haven for me. You are my haven, baby. And I couldn't have built what I have in these last six years without you. I tell everyone that—and those looks you see are looks of envy. Half the men I know wish they had you beside them.''

She gazed at him, wishing to believe, wanting to see herself in the light he was painting. Maybe she even could, but it wasn't enough anymore.

"What do you want?" he demanded, a flash of anger in his movements as he raked a hand through his hair. "Marriage? Is that it? Is that what this is all about?''

"And if I said yes? If I said to you, 'Do you want to see if what we've built in these six years is a relationship worth going on with, worth deepening?' Would you be willing to try?''

Their eyes locked for long seconds.

"I know we have a relationship, and it's a damn good one!" he said, then gazed at her with a pained expression. "Marriage? You think that will make for a better relationship? I had two wives, and I never had with them what we've got, baby.''

Her heart sinking, Marnie turned away and hugged the bear to her chest.

"What more would a legal little piece of paper give you, Marnie, that I haven't? Just tell me that.''

She shook her head. He didn't understand—not at all. "It isn't the piece of paper I want, Patrick.'' She hesitated and then spun to face him, all the humiliating fear spilling out. "I'm thirty-six now, Patrick. Actually, I'm in my thirty-seventh year, because my birthday was last New Year's Day.''

His eyebrows rose. "But you said . . .''

"I know what I told you, but the fact is I lied about my age by four years. It's not a grand lie—half the women in the world do it. Miss Phoebe was not eighty-two, like everyone thought, she was ninety. But, Patrick, I'm not getting any younger, and I'm not going to be able to stay like I am now, being the *mistress* forever. And what will I have when this is gone? I can't do anything! I have no way to make a living beyond just scraping by. I have nothing, Patrick.''

He frowned. "Nothing? Haven't you been putting aside a portion of what I give you each month like I told you?''

"Yes, I've put somethin' away, just as you instructed. But it won't provide for a lifetime. And it's not simply *money* I'm talking about." Frustrated at not being able to explain what was actually in her heart, she searched desperately for words to make him understand.

"What I want is to believe in the years ahead. And, if possible, I want someone there beside me. Someone to remember my birthdays, someone who will watch reruns on television and take long walks with me. I even think I might like a child, Patrick. I think I might be a good mother. And I'd like someone to share that child with. Someone to share my life with and someone to share his life with me. Someone to grow old with. I want a *future*, Patrick."

Marnie found herself as shocked as he was. She hadn't known. None of it—until she'd been forced to try to explain.

The issue hung there in the air between them. Patrick studied her, and though he stood only three feet away, she felt he was far down the hall and getting farther all the time.

"A future?" he said with strong sarcasm. "What you want, Marnie, is a fantasy. The rainbow's end, the happily ever after, and it simply doesn't exist. Not for anyone."

It was equal to a good slap across her face. Marnie flinched, closed her eyes and looked away. She'd asked him, and he'd answered by not answering. She didn't think she could stand the pain of hopelessness.

"What will you have if you leave here?" he shot at her then. "What will either of us have that's better than what we have now? I can't do without you, Marnie. Is that what you want to hear? I need you here with me, doing what you do so well. I don't want to lose you."

She knew it had cost him dearly to reveal that much. Yet, still, he was offering no more than what they had. Not even a willingness to try, after all these years.

The lump and tears rose stronger than ever. She forced them back and looked at him. His eyes burned with bitterness.

"I'm sorry, Patrick. I...I need to be alone."

She whirled and strode to the door of her apartment, walking away from Patrick in anger for the first time ever. She slipped through the door, which was ajar as usual, and closed it behind her, softly but with a firm click.

Leaning against it, drawing in deep, sobbing breaths, she hugged the teddy bear to her chest as if holding to a lifeline.

Sometime after midnight, storms rolled in. Bright, jagged lightning split the sky, and great rolling thunder shook the walls. Marnie stood in the dimly lit bedroom and peered through the rivulets of rain sliding down the glass door. Country music sounded softly from her bedside radio, and once in a while a voice broke in with a status report on the storms. A tornado had been sighted on the ground out near El Reno.

Nights like this were perfect when a woman felt lonely and lost. As she stood there, hands in her pockets, forehead leaning against the cool glass, Marnie let the night sadness seep deep. Pictures from the past drifted across her mind. Every person was, she thought, a product of all they had experienced since birth. Perhaps, as some believed, a person was born with certain traits, good and bad, yet those traits were puffed up here, carved down there, by what went on in a person's life.

One of her strongest memories was of a time when she'd stood beside her mother in a small, dusty hick town, while her mother gazed through a store window at a bright, red-and-white polka-dot dress. The kind of dress worn by the beautiful women in the picture shows that Marnie had been to two or three times in her eight-year-old life.

"Maybe you can have a dress like that someday, Momma."

Her mother, her face as gray as the concrete beneath their feet, had looked at Marnie and shaken her head. "No, hon, I won't even think about that. Don't ever go expectin' much in this life, Marnie, 'cause you'll only end up with a broken heart. Expect the least, and you won't be disappointed."

And that was pretty much what Marnie had learned to do. She'd learned not to expect too much from life, or from people. That was how she'd endured the twenty-plus different schools she'd attended until she'd dropped out in the eighth grade, where children taunted her for being poor migrant-worker trash, stupid and slow. That was how she'd endured the third-hand clothes she'd had to wear and the hard work, heat, cold and sometimes hunger.

Not expecting otherwise was how she had endured a father who used to leave them sometimes on the farms where they were working, just up and leave for maybe weeks. He hadn't been a bad man, only weak, sometimes overwhelmed by life. Always he returned, all apologetic.

"I love you, my New Year's Day angel," he'd say, hugging Marnie fiercely and scraping his scruffy face against her soft one. He'd smelled of sweat and liquor.

"Why'd ya' go, Daddy, if you love us so much?"

"Aw, hon, that's a hard one. Let me study on it."

It was how she'd endured the heartbreak of Bo Bramwell. She'd been sixteen and still hopeful. He'd been eighteen, handsome enough to set a girl's teeth on edge and a landowner's son, too. He'd said he loved her, they'd talked marriage, and she'd had her first experience with sex with him in his daddy's truck. But Bo Bramwell's daddy had made it clear he wasn't having an ignorant field worker for a daughter-in-law, by damn! Bo had loved her, but he'd feared his daddy more. He'd turned from her without a word of defense and let his daddy ship him off to college.

It was a paradox of the human spirit, she thought, that a woman could look back on her life and understand why she was as she was and yet have so little power to change herself.

Those experiences, and shadows of others still hidden in her mind, had caused her to do just as her mother had said: never expect too much, because you're always sure to be disappointed. She'd learned, too, that even people who loved you would often let you down, a heartbreaking fact she'd never quite been able to come to terms with. Whenever she let someone down, she thought she would die, so she tried very hard never to commit herself to anyone.

She felt now that she'd let Patrick down by wanting more than he could give. She knew he felt betrayed, and she was heartily sorry.

Pictures of the years ahead with him formed easily—they stretched out empty and cold. And there would come a time when he wouldn't want her anymore; she would be alone.

She tried imagining her life if she left him and could picture leaving with a suitcase in each hand but nothing more. She couldn't figure out which picture terrified her more.

A future. Patrick had called it fantasy.

He hadn't understood that she wasn't looking for happily ever after. She was looking for love and commitment, and all the passion—good and bad—that came with it.

If she remained with Patrick it was certain she would never experience that. Perhaps she could learn a trade of some kind and make some friends, but she had absolutely no chance of finding a man to share love with, no chance of being a wife and mother.

It seemed to Marnie that she'd drifted with life, letting it be good to her when it would, trying to keep alive and as comfortable as possible when it was bad. But being alive and comfortable was no longer enough. She wanted, longed, yearned, to do more than simply survive. She wanted very much to have the courage to live. She wanted to have the courage to know love.

Slowly she turned, walked to her bed and sat near the bedside table. She gazed at the bouquet of flowers sitting beneath the lamp. The flowers Jesse had sent her. His face, with his cocky grin and luminous eyes, filled her mind. She reached out and plucked one of the daisies from the vase, brushed it against her cheek and recalled how Jesse had touched her.

The woman in Jesse's arms pushed her pelvis against him, and a reaction stirred within him while she whispered in his ear, "I *liii*ke tall men."

She was nearly as tall as he was, fully curved and all over him like stink on a skunk as they moved around the dance floor of the dimly lit bar. There were only two other couples dancing, so it didn't matter that Jesse had had too much to drink to worry about precise steps.

He pulled his face from the woman's billowy white-blond hair and tried to focus on her face. He had an impression of a pretty woman who'd been around the block a few times. Then he experienced an odd sensation of being able to see her features in a bright spotlight, right there in the dark.

He blinked and stared at the woman. She smiled at him with a ready look. "Do you have a room in the hotel next door?" she asked.

"Noooo...no, I don't." His gaze dropped to her deep cleavage. A man could suffocate there.

"Do your friends have a room?" She indicated Woody and Clyde and the others at the table.

"Yeah."

"Maybe we could borrow it? Or get one of our own." She kissed his ear and snaked her hands up underneath his coat and around to his back.

Jesse shivered and jumped back a space. He'd suddenly changed his mind.

"Well, now..." He gently extricated himself from her embrace, doing the exact opposite of what he'd planned a minute earlier. "I'm sorry, ma'am, but I find I'm not up to somethin' like that this evening. In fact, I really think I need to take my leave while I can still get myself where I belong."

"But...I thought we..." she protested as he politely saw her back to the table and made firm good-nights all around.

Seconds later he stood beneath the awning outside, feeling as if he'd just narrowly escaped falling off a cliff.

A heavy rain fell in already full puddles in the parking lot, and thunder rumbled in the distance. Pulling out the keys to his rental, he gazed at them a moment, then stuffed them back into his pocket. A man who was swaying as much as he was had no business driving.

Stepping from beneath the awning, he started off for the Vinsand Plaza Hotel, a walk of nearly half a mile. It was a punishment of sorts, doled out for his drinking more than he had in ten years, and a cure, too, for the fire in his veins.

There was a tall curb but no sidewalk along the thoroughfare. As he walked past another hotel, a gas station, two hamburger places, a swank restaurant and an office park, his boots squished on the soggy grass and splashed through puddled parking lots. Rain pounded on his hat, and water dribbled from its brim. He tilted his head once, and water ran like a river off his hat. Traffic was light at this time of night, but two cars did manage to splash him good. He walked slowly, letting the rain soak through his coat and into his soul.

His thoughts filled with memories of Regina, memories he hadn't had in twelve or thirteen years. It was as if he were back again in those god-awful months and years following her death, when he'd struggled so hard to find his life again without her. To find a future again.

The bleakness and splashing through as much water as possible and daring God to strike him dead with lightning sustained him until he reached the hotel. Beneath the portico, he removed his hat and drained the water from it. No doorman was in evidence; apparently they didn't bother at this time of night—or morning. The soles of his boots were slicker than snot on the marble floor as he dripped his way to the front desk. The young clerk winced as he looked at him.

"Would you have a pack of cigarettes back there?" Jesse asked.

"There's a machine down—"

"I don't want a whole pack. I just need two cigarettes." He wasn't about to take up the habit again after what it had cost him to quit.

"Umm..." The clerk drew back and began looking around. "Here we go. Is this brand okay?"

"At this point, brand has no bearin'." He shook out two and held them carefully away from his wetness. "Much obliged." He sloshed away to the elevator.

In his room, he stripped off his wet clothes and left them in the bathtub. Stretching out naked on the bed, he wadded two pillows, which he wished were feather pillows, behind his head and smoked in the room lit only by the reflection of outside lamplight. The storms had almost passed.

He thought of his mother. Sometimes he did that, trying to recapture the assuredness she'd always given him. He thought he'd been born with a natural appreciation of women, and that appreciation had been fortified by his mother. Every man should have had a mother like his—feminine yet strong as steel, and intensely loving, always grabbing her sons and hugging them, telling them she loved them, telling them they were the greatest people in the world. Telling them there wasn't anything they couldn't do.

The greatest hurt in his life, besides losing Regina, had been losing his mother when he'd been only thirteen. When his own sons had lost their mother early, he'd tried to make up the difference—unlike his father, who'd never tried. Maybe that was why his father had never tried, because he'd known only a woman could be a mother. Fact of nature. And, though Jesse wouldn't have revealed it to a soul, maybe losing his mother early had contributed to his lifelong thirst for a woman's touch.

The fantasies of Marnie lingering at the back of his mind pushed to the forefront, claiming him completely. A great longing for her swept over him. He longed to feel her lying naked against him. He longed to stroke her hip and feel her press against him. He longed to hear her throaty, sensual laugh and to see her eyes, those lake-blue eyes, so full of admiration for him.

He thirsted for her woman's touch, craved it, dreamed of it, while lying there, staring at the red glow of the cigarette in the dark.

He stabbed out the butt, and his gaze fell to the clock. It was going on two o'clock. He got up and got his wallet, pulling out the card he'd saved.

As he switched on the lamp, he thought it was crazy to call her. He switched off the lamp and lay there, thinking of how she'd come to see him and how it had been between them. Her telephone number echoed in his mind. He reached for the telephone and punched in the numbers.

When a thirst hit a man, it could overwhelm his good sense. And Jesse had learned that sometimes the greatest regrets in life were the chances, no matter how crazy, not taken. If the impulse was a good one, never let fear of failure hold you back.

His fingers tightened on the receiver as he listened to the line ring once, twice, three times. *She wasn't going to answer. She was probably with Vinsand. What if Vinsand answered?*

"Hello?" Her voice, low, curious yet cautious. Feminine.

"Hello... it's Jesse." Stunned silence hummed on the line. *Now what in the hell could he say to her? Would she under-*

*stand that he meant it as a high compliment if he told her he*
*was hot as hellfire for her?*

He said, "I know it's late, but I was thinkin' of you. I just want to talk to you. Just talk. It's a lonely night." He didn't apologize for waking her, because he didn't care if he had—but something told him she'd been awake. "Can you talk?" he thought to ask, then held his breath.

## Chapter Seven

"Yes..." she said in practically a whisper, and the hint of warmth in her voice sent a shiver through him. "It is a lonely night," she added, and he heard loneliness in her tone.

He imagined her in a big bed with flowery covers and lots of fluffy pillows, wearing a gown so thin her creamy skin shone through. Or, better yet, she was nude. Nude in the soft lamplight he added to the picture, letting his imagination go. He wondered where Vinsand was.

"What are you doin'?" he asked, heat rising.

"Havin' a party."

"What?" He didn't hear any noise.

"Now what did you think I was doin' at two o'clock in the mornin'?" she said with sultry sarcasm.

He defended, "You weren't sleepin'."

"No. I wasn't sleepin'." The sultry tone crept across the line to swell inside him.

*Oh, man, he had to be crazy to be doing this!*

He almost mentioned something else she could have been doing, but good sense made him ask instead, "Did you get the bear?"

"Oh, yes!" Her soft voice was as excited as a child's. "Thank you for sending him. I was so upset when I realized I'd forgotten him."

She *had* forgotten it! Jesse was glad and relieved. He wondered if Vinsand had seen the bear, but didn't ask that, either. Desire hardening his muscles, and needing to do something with his hands other than grip the phone, he lit the second cigarette.

"I'm surprised you called," she said, her voice almost a whisper again.

"I guess I am, too. I can blame it on liquid courage."

"Are you drunk?" There was disappointment in her voice.

"No. I was earlier, but I'm not now. The liquid courage I meant was the rain. Nights like this make people do things they might not do otherwise."

"Nights like this sometimes make people drink," she said. "Do you do that often, Jesse? Get drunk?"

"No. Used to go on wild hoots in my younger days on trips away from the ranch. Then I got to drinkin' some at the ranch and realized I was headed down a rocky road, so I turned around. Havin' a few beers is usually my limit."

"I'm glad. I don't care to be around people when they drink."

He'd had experience enough to know where the comment was coming from. "I know what you mean," he said. "My father used to drink."

"Mine, too," she said.

They both fell silent. Marnie thought of him on the other end of the line, lying in bed, in the dark. Naked, she pictured him, and smiled at her fancy. Naked and smoking a cigarette.

"Are you smokin'?" she asked.

"Yeah—how'd you know?"

"I don't know. I just pictured it all of a sudden. Maybe I could hear you. I didn't know you smoked."

"I quit about five years back." He chuckled. "You must be able to see me lyin' here buck naked." Pleasure laced his voice.

"I can't see you, but I have a good imagination," she said daringly.

"I do, too, gal. I do, too."

Marnie blushed and instinctively pulled up the sheet. "I'm not naked, Jesse," she said primly.

"You ruined it," he said, then added in his low sensual voice, "but not totally."

It was as if he'd reached across the phone line to stroke her. Heat flashed up from between her legs and trembled across her belly. She squirmed, pressing her legs tight. She wondered what she was doing, talking like this with a man on the phone. This strong attraction for a man was strange, wonderful, frightening. Was it to the man—or to the fantasy dream of a knight in shining armor? Whatever, it was too intriguing to resist.

"You certainly are *not* like any farmer I ever knew, Jesse Breen."

"I'm a rancher. How many farmers have you known?"

"Would it surprise you to know my father was a farmer?"

There was a second's pause. "Yes, I'd have to say it would."

"Well, I am a farmer's daughter, and I've spent my share of time with dirt beneath my fingernails and between my toes." It pleased her to surprise him.

"Did he farm out in Arkansas, where you said you're from?"

"Uh-huh. He and Momma had a small place for a while. He sharecropped for others, too." She stopped.

"A man has to be a good farmer to sharecrop for people," Jesse offered and waited for her to elaborate. He wanted to know all about her—something told him she'd endured great disappointments.

"Yes. Daddy was a good farmer, but like I said, he drank some. He lost his place and the sharecroppin' work, too." Her heart pounded; she hadn't spoken to anyone since Miss Phoebe about her family background.

"How'd you get so far from the farm?" he asked.

She played with the coiled telephone wire. "By a lot of hard work and plenty of luck."

"You never married?"

"No," she said softly.

"How long have you lived here in Oklahoma?"

"Five years."

"All that time with Vinsand?"

"Yes. We came from Memphis when he took over the corporation from his father."

"Long time. How come you and he haven't married?"

"How come you haven't remarried?" she countered. "Hasn't there been a woman in your life since your wife died?"

She heard him blow out smoke. Then he said, "There've been a couple."

"A couple of women over sixteen years—and none of them a serious interest?" She thought that he must have loved his wife very much.

"I saw a woman pretty regular for 'bout seven years. She decided to marry a hardware-store owner early this year."

"Oh. Why didn't you marry her?"

He sighed. "She and I enjoyed each other's company and filled lonely places for each other. That was all that ever came of it," he said quietly. "What does that Vinsand fella do for you? He doesn't fill your lonely place."

Anger flashed, and she thought to say it wasn't any of his business. But instead, the words poured out. "There are other considerations in life. I happen to like a nice place to live, credit cards without limits, silk nightgowns and Cadillac convertibles."

The line hummed for a long second, while her heart squeezed, awaiting his reaction. His censure.

Then he drawled, "Can't say as I blame you, gal. I happen to like all those things, too. All except the Cadillac. I like a good truck."

Marnie said in a thick whisper, "Patrick is good to me."

"He should be," he replied gruffly. "But he has to be several bricks short of a full load not to be there with you right now."

She breathed deeply and explained, feeling foolishly defensive of Patrick. "He gives me my own apartment separate from his penthouse."

"Oh?" The line tingled with his ripe speculation.

A hot tremor swept her body. "As rare a man as you are, Jesse, I'm not askin' you up." She gripped the receiver as the possibility flitted across her mind: of him holding her, speaking low, listening to her. She wouldn't be lonely then.

"That's probably wise, gal," he drawled at last.

Her mind filled with him, and desire tugged tauntingly.

"I think we should say good-night," she said, trembling.

"Wise gal, like I said."

"Good night, Jesse. I enjoyed talkin' to you." She was fleeing.

"Wait!"

Tentatively she held the receiver to her ear. "Yes?"

He said quickly, with force, "Before I leave town, I'd like to see you again—as much as possible. I'll be at the sheep barn in the morning until at least noon, and my room here is 508. I'll be registered through tomorrow night."

"I would like to see you, Jesse," she said softly, then paused. "But I can't promise."

"If you can. Sleep tight, darlin'."

The line clicked dead. Marnie stared at the receiver, then replaced it with a trembling hand. She lay back and gazed into the darkness. His low and sensual *darlin'* echoed in her mind.

It had been so long since she'd felt for a man what she felt for Jesse—this excitement, this longing. She thought she had felt it for Patrick long ago. And again she wondered if it were Jesse she felt this for, or if she was making fancies out of a great yearning for something that would forever be elusive.

Fantasy, Patrick had called it.

Fumbling around the bed, she found the stuffed bear. Hugging it to her chest, she snuggled down beneath the sheet. The bittersweet ache of unfulfilled desire stayed with her, and it was hard to sleep.

Marnie was up early the following morning, debating whether or not to go to see Patrick or wait for him to come to her. Perhaps he would leave without a word, thereby avoiding further confrontation.

She showered and donned a robe, demure with violet flower sprigs, that Patrick had once said he liked. She pinned up her hair, brushed on blush, then wondered why she was doing all this.

For courage, she thought. For Patrick might very well tell her to be gone by the time he returned. Such was her life. Though she'd never allowed herself to dwell on it, she'd always known it could happen.

The telephone rang, and she thought about not answering. She didn't want to face anything at all. Wanted to go back to bed and pull the covers over her head. She answered at last.

It was Dorothy to say, "Mr. Vinsand would like to see you in his office, if it is convenient."

"Yes, Dorothy, thank you."

And so she was *summoned*.

She shared a smile and a good morning with Tacita as she passed through the penthouse living room. In Dorothy's office, her gaze fell on the gay vase of flowers before she continued on to Patrick's office.

Dorothy's survey was brief but intense. Marnie met the woman's gaze calmly. She wouldn't allow anyone to see her fear. Dorothy bade a quiet goodbye and left Marnie and Patrick alone, closing the door behind her.

Patrick, tall and lean, every inch the CEO in a blinding white shirt and pin-striped vest and slacks, came toward her. He took her by the upper arms and kissed her forehead lightly. He searched her eyes, and she searched his, wondering. He didn't seem angry, as he had last night.

"You are beautiful, Marnie. And you will be beautiful ten years from now."

She didn't know what to say. It was a compliment, yet spoken more as a surface assessment only.

"I can understand your insecurity, though," he said, turning away and walking behind his desk. He stopped and gazed at her. "Do you recall when we first struck our bargain?"

She nodded. "Yes."

"It turned out very well for both of us, wouldn't you agree?"

"Yes, I would," she said softly. "And I have never regretted it, Patrick."

"Good. Because I'm going to make you a new offer." He lifted a piece of paper from his desk. "For these six years we both kept a bargain that fit well. Now that bargain doesn't fit you so well. Do we call it quits—or do we strike another bargain?'' He came around the desk toward her. ''Well, baby, I still don't want to get married—just as I told you from the beginning. But I still want you, just as I did then. You're still good for me, baby. So what I can do is give you a better bargain. A contract in writing.''

Perplexed, she looked from him to the paper he extended toward her. ''A contract?'' She took the paper, a piece of his letterhead with his handwriting on it.

''I drew this up last night, and I'll have Andrew make it all legal while I'm gone.'' He was brisk, businesslike. ''I'm offering to raise your monthly allowance, and I'll start an investment program for you in secure stocks and bonds. If we're still together at the end of the next six years, the money will belong totally to you. Each year that we are together after that, I will continue to add to it. If *I* decide to terminate our arrangement before the six years are up, I'll still be obligated to give you the investments. However, if *you* terminate the agreement, I won't owe you a thing.''

She listened to his words and scanned the handwriting on the paper, but absorbed little. She lifted her head, looked into his eyes.

''It's a pension plan, Marnie. Security for your future. Much more than a marriage certificate could ever give you.''

Great, heavy sadness washed over her. *He didn't understand. He would never understand.* Unable to look at him, she averted her eyes to the paper, blinking back the tears.

''Think this over, Marnie. With this, you won't ever want for anything, baby. You will be a woman of independent means in just six short years.''

He moved back to his desk, threw papers into his briefcase, snapped it closed. Marnie stared at the paper, forcing her mind to focus.

''This...is a lot of money.'' Starting at five thousand the first year, he would raise the amount by a thousand each following year for six years, until it equalled forty-five thousand dollars. Stunned, she raised her questioning gaze to his.

"When I want something, I'm willing to pay for it," he said. "I want to keep you in my life."

The telephone rang.

Patrick answered and said into the receiver, "Tell Sidney to go on down with my bags. I'll be there in a minute. Yes . . . I'll sign them on my way out." He hung up and looked at Marnie, saying as he slipped into his suit coat, "I'll be back on Sunday. I promise."

They gazed at each other for an intense moment.

"I'll be here," she told him.

He nodded and headed for the door.

"Patrick, wait!"

He turned. She went to him and rose on tiptoe to kiss him lightly on the lips. Gazing into his eyes, she caressed his smooth cheek. "You are a very generous man. You're very good to me."

Something, surprise maybe, flickered in his eyes. His smile was almost shy. "I'll call you," he said and left.

She watched him leave, thinking, he could spare all this money for her, but so little of his time. So little of himself. She had never been, never would be, as important to him as the business deals that absorbed him. Perhaps for another woman it would be different, or perhaps he would be this way with any woman. She didn't know, would never know. And as long as she remained with him, Patrick would never know, either.

Slowly she walked to the wide windows and looked from the golden morning light to the paper still in her hand. She read the paper again.

In exchange for her "attention" and care, he was willing to pay forty-five thousand dollars, which would be worth much more than that in investments, all of that on top of a generous monthly allowance.

She would never know want again, if she accepted.

Patrick was always determined when he wanted something. She supposed he couldn't stand the fact that she might walk away from him—it would definitely be different if he'd decided to break off first. Yet, she thought, this written offer of money spoke quite loudly the words he was unable to voice. She meant something to him. He did care for her, in his way.

But he wanted all of her, while giving only his money in return. And money couldn't fill her lonely "place," as Jesse had called it.

It came down to this: she could choose security or nothing more than a *chance* of fulfilling the longings tearing at her.

She squeezed her eyes closed, fear and uncertainty swirling inside her. Then, gently, she laid the paper on Patrick's desk and swept from the room. Dorothy looked up from her typewriter, peering over the top of her glasses.

Marnie pointed at the vase of flowers. "If I were you, I'd say yes when your admirer asks you out. Honest affection is too valuable to let it slip through your fingers."

Dorothy looked as surprised as if she'd just had a bucket of water dumped on her head. "I beg your pardon?"

Marnie stopped in the doorway. "You don't have to beg for it, Dorothy. I'll *give* it to you. Now take my advice and look up from that typewriter, from your career, which will never be able to warm your toes on a cold night, and appreciate a man who is crazy about you. A man like him may only come along once in a lifetime."

Then she swept from the room and on down the hall. She had promised Patrick to be there when he returned. Beyond that, she was on her own. On her own to spend a very special day with a very special man. A wonderful, warm, sexy, good guy, who made her feel as lovely and as lovable as a princess.

Jesse sat in the green-and-white lawn chair at the end of Billy's pen. Leaning forward, forearms on his thighs, he whittled on a small piece of tree limb he'd picked up that morning. Ham lay curled beside the chair.

As he cut and chipped with his knife, turning the piece of wood into a small, nondescript dog, he thought of Marnie. Would she come? Chances were she wouldn't. But it was just after nine o'clock and too early to give up hope. There was no reason why she should come, though. Except that she liked him.

Despite her relationship with Vinsand, Jesse knew Marnie was attracted to *him*. And he suspected her attachment to Vinsand was thinning, enough even to break, which would suit

## PLAY THE

**LUCKY**

# CARNIVAL WHEEL

## scratch-off game
## and get as many as

# SIX FREE GIFTS...

## HOW TO PLAY

**1.** With a coin, carefully scratch off the silver area at right. Then check your number against the chart below it to find out which gifts you're eligible to receive.

**2.** You'll receive brand-new Silhouette Special Edition® novels and possibly other gifts—ABSOLUTELY FREE! Send back this card and we'll promptly send you the free books and gift(s) you qualify for!

**3.** We're betting you'll want more of these heart-warming romances, so unless you tell us otherwise, every month we'll send you 6 more wonderful novels to read and enjoy. Always delivered right to your home months before they arrive in stores. And always at a discount off the cover price!

**4.** Your satisfaction is guaranteed! You may return any shipment of books and cancel at any time. The Free Books and Gift(s) remain yours to keep!

# NO COST! NO RISK!
# NO OBLIGATION TO BUY!

# More Good News For Subscribers-Only!

When you join the Silhouette Reader Service™, you'll receive 6 heart-warming romance novels each month delivered to your home. You'll also get additional free gifts from time to time as well as our subscribers-only newsletter. It's your privileged look at upcoming books and profiles of our most popular authors!

If offer card is missing, write to:
Silhouette Reader Service, 3010 Walden Avenue, P.O. Box 1867, Buffalo, NY 14269-1867

Jesse just fine. Vinsand didn't treat her right. Of course, Jesse had to admit he had no hard facts on which to base this opinion, and he was going on gut feeling here—but his gut feelings were generally right on target. Though why their relationship should have any bearing on himself, he didn't know. Marnie's relationship with Vinsand wasn't his business. He was only a brief visitor in the city. A brief visitor in her life, and wasn't that pretty selfish on his part, he thought, wincing inwardly. He was wanting to enjoy her while it was convenient, then to leave. That was all. Though he justified his actions by telling himself he intended to give to her as much as she gave to him.

Would she come? He hoped she would.

Ham lifted his head, hopped up and pranced away. A chill raced across Jesse's shoulders. He raised his eyes from the wood and saw her feet encased in blue sandals and the hem of a flowing blue skirt teasing the tops of her pale, sleek ankles. His gaze moved upward over the soft skirt to a leather belt at her waist, then to a creamy sweater that hung over the edges of her pale shoulders. Her hair was piled in loose curls atop her head, silver bell earrings hung from her ears, and she looked all soft and warm woman.

She straightened from petting Ham and smiled at Jesse, eyes dancing. "Hello. What'cha doin'?" she drawled.

He stood slowly. "Ah...whittlin'. And waitin'," he answered, following suit in drawing out her words, while his gaze drifted down to her breasts.

"For me?"

He looked up into her eyes and saw amused knowing there. "I was hopeful." He was amazed to find himself blushing, but his smile came from deep within him.

She bit her bottom lip, then looked him in the eye and said, "Patrick left this morning for business in Atlanta. He'll be gone until Sunday."

He held her gaze. Jumbled feelings swept across him—excitement, pleasure, humbleness, caution. He held out his hand, and she took it. He bent and softly put his lips to hers, very gently flicked his tongue across her warmth, then kissed her fully, taking the sweetness of the moment and trying to give it back again.

* * *

They spent the next hours at the remaining sheep classes. Little Sue didn't get a ribbon, though Jesse knew it was only because the judges couldn't see straight. But his flock all together ended up taking Best Exhibitor's Flock, which automatically raised the value of each one of the sheep. That was nice, but what pleased Jesse most was coming away with another blue ribbon.

Marnie snapped pictures all over the place—of Jesse, of the sheep, of Ham and Jesse and the sheep, of just about everybody and their sheep. Jesse delighted in watching her graceful, sensual movements and in that she was there to see him in his glory. That Vinsand wouldn't be back that night kept creeping into his thoughts. Not too proud of the ideas that gave him, he tried to focus on the moment at hand.

Rory came by, and Marnie took pictures of him, too, making him pose like an old-time cowboy. She got shots of Jesse and Rory together, then Jesse enlisted Rory to take a couple of shots of him and Marnie together. Being an intelligent son, Rory soon made an excuse about doing something with his horse and cut out.

It was near noon when Jesse and Marnie headed away from the sheep barns to again enjoy the fair. Jesse felt like a man in high-grade wool—a man living out his romantic dreams.

Then Woody Greene hailed him.

At first annoyed at the intrusion into his precious time, Jesse took one look at Woody's face and knew he'd come about the young ewe, Fancy. A mischievous possibility flashed into Jesse's mind as he made the introductions between Marnie and Woody.

The idea strengthened when Woody said, "Jesse, I'm still interested in that lamb of yours. I'll give you four thousand—which is about five hundred too high."

Drawing a deep breath, Jesse pushed back his hat and rocked back on his heels. "Well, Woody," he drawled and cut his eyes to Marnie. "Marnie here and I were just discussin' Fancy, and she's offerin' me forty-five hundred."

He held his breath, but Marnie didn't do any more than give a quick blink before coming back with, "I made you an offer and you accepted, Jesse. I'd call that a deal made."

Jesse swallowed his glee and pulled at his ear. "Well, I know we'd reached a tentative agreement." Out of the corner of his eye he saw Woody cast a speculative glance from him to Marnie. "But that deal called for waitin' until next month for you to pay and take delivery. And that means I have to haul Fancy back home and then on to your place next month." Assuming a blatantly pleased expression, he said, "Now, if you two want to fight it out between yourselves, I could do business with the highest bidder."

"Jesse!" Marnie indignantly stamped her foot. "I'm appalled that you would do this!"

"Business is business, gal."

Woody chewed on it for only two seconds. "I'll give you forty-five hundred right now," he said.

Marnie looked put out. "Daddy has authorized me to spend forty-seven. And I'll come get her."

Then Woody looked put out. "All right, Jesse. I'll give forty-eight. Right now."

Both of them stared at him. "Jesse! Daddy is gonna spit nails," Marnie said angrily.

"Your daddy'll get over it. He understands that business is business." It was all Jesse could do not to burst out laughing when he saw the glint in Marnie's eyes.

Marnie huffed, and Woody looked satisfied as he whipped out his checkbook.

After arranging to meet Woody that afternoon to load Fancy, Jesse took Marnie's arm, guiding her away. Loud enough for Woody to hear, she said, "And you think I'm still willin' to spend time with you after what you just did, Jesse Breen?"

They were barely out of sight of Woody when they both broke out in laughter.

"You are somethin', you know that?" Jesse said, when he could get words out.

Marnie looked pleased with herself. "I'm not just another pretty face."

He gazed into her deep blue, dancing eyes. "No, ma'am, you are not." He almost added, "It's no wonder Vinsand owns a string of hotels," but bit back the comment. He didn't want Vinsand intruding on their day in any way.

Then she said, "I deserve lunch for helping you make all that money."

He chuckled. "I'll take you to dinner tonight."

After a moment, she nodded. "It's a date."

It was hot between them for long seconds, before they both averted their gazes.

Jesse said, "I can't wait to see Woody's face when I tell him about this deal."

"You'll tell him?" she asked, surprised.

"Oh, yeah—eventually. We've been doing this to each other for twenty-five years. He'll soon recognize this as the same scam he pulled on me at a sale outside Lubbock about five years ago."

"You and Mr. Greene are very old friends, then?"

Jesse nodded, thinking back. "I've known Woody since we were both in our twenties. Other than being a show-off and know-it-all, he's okay."

She smiled. "You like him."

"Don't let him hear you."

"It must be nice to have a friend you've known so long," she said in the wistful, wondering tone of a person who had never known the experience.

His curiosity about her rose, as did his sense of wanting to take care of her, to give to her.


They wandered through the hobbies-and-crafts building again, looking at baked goods and jars of jellies, fruits and vegetables, along with every variety of sewn, spun, woven and glued thing, all in glass display cases. They ate messy pizza and drank soft drinks, saw an Old West-style play in a tent, the reenactment of a shoot-out, and Indian dancers. They attended the pig races and thoroughly investigated every horse and stock trailer on display—Jesse's insurance was sure to pay for a new one for him.

They rode the carousel twice, Marnie got cotton candy and fed bites to Jesse, and he wiped her cheeks, though he didn't tell her there wasn't anything there.

"Time for the Ferris wheel," Jesse said, feeling like the master of the world.

"You're joking," Marnie said.

"No. I've always loved the Ferris wheel. Why? Do you think I should have outgrown it?" He felt a twinge of foolishness.

She shook her head. "No. I think it's wonderful that you haven't."

A few minutes later Jesse realized he'd been too absorbed in his own desire to pay attention to Marnie's reluctance. He recalled then that he'd suggested several times in the past two days that they ride the big wheel, and always Marnie had drawn attention to something else. And it wasn't until the bar had fastened them into the seat that he'd noticed any uncertainty in her at all.

When the wheel slowly began to turn, lifting their seat, she closed her eyes and plastered herself to his side. "Hold me, Jesse."

He obliged with one arm around her shoulder and his hand holding hers. The wheel stopped to take on more people, and their seat swung softly.

"Oh... I shouldn't have gotten on this thing." Trembling, she kept her eyes squeezed tight and clenched his hand with both of hers.

"Why didn't you tell me you were scared of this ride?"

"Because you really like it. I thought I could... ohhh." The wheel lifted them higher.

"Jeez, I'm sorry, I didn't realize you were frightened of heights."

"It's not the heights," she said in a panicky voice. "It's Ferris wheels. I haven't been on one since I was twelve and the one I was on got stuck for four hours. It wasn't a very big one, but I was very small, and I was at the top. Alone." She shivered violently.

"That's the trouble. You were alone—and you should have gotten right back on again after your scare."

"I couldn't. I didn't have any money. The operator had given me a ride for fr—free." The wheel moved again, swaying them higher into the air. "Oh, Jesse!"

"You're okay, darlin'." He rubbed her upper arm, trying to soothe her. He saw her face go pasty, and he tightened his hold on her. "Marnie, open your eyes and look while we're stopped. It's not so high."

"It's not?" She opened one eye and immediately squeezed it tight again. "Yes, it is!" she said in a breathless, terrified whisper.

"Anyone who can work a deal with Woody Greene like you did can ride a Ferris wheel," Jesse said encouragingly, rubbing her shoulder. He glanced down, wondering if he could signal the operator to bring it around to let them off. That probability was slim, considering their angle.

The wheel moved again, and she drew a deep breath, shaking like a leaf in the wind. "Oh, Jesse, I think I'm going to throw up," she whispered hoarsely.

"If you do, you do. Won't bother me, because I'm up here. Of course, those below might be a mite perturbed."

She chuckled. "Oh, Jesse, you're somethin'. We're stopped again, aren't we?"

"Yes, darlin'. You should see it. We can see the whole fair. The colors are magnificent."

She peeked, then squeezed her eyes closed again.

"Marnie, you aren't alone this time. I'm with you, and I'm holding you tight. Look at me."

She turned her head, opened her eyes and stared at him. He kissed her softly. He felt her violent trembling ease.

"Now look out. Don't miss this chance while we're stopped."

She looked. Again her grip on him tightened; she closed her eyes, then immediately opened them. "Oh, Jesse. It's beautiful! Oh . . . oh!" She looked with one eye.

The wheel began to move again, over the top and down, stopped once, then went round and round.

"See, my eyes are open," she said with glee. "Oh, look! We can see the highway! Over there's where we had the wreck, Jesse! And look at the trees! The fairgrounds look a lot prettier from up here."

She was so weak-kneed and trembly when it came to their turn to get off that Jesse swept her up in his arms and carried her away from the ride. He guessed he didn't need to do that, but he wanted to. Laughing, she laid her head on his shoulder.

Finally he was chuckling so hard, he had to set her on her feet. She wrapped her arms around his neck and kissed him, a simple, appreciative kiss that nevertheless brought on his instant arousal.

Both of them growing tired now, they walked around, hand in hand, simply looking at the sights. Jesse felt like he was coasting on the edge of a high mesa. He knew he was racing toward the edge and would go over and straight down eventually, but right now the wind and sun were in his face, and he was having the time of his life.

They were on their way back to the sheep barns to meet Woody when a woman called to Marnie.

"Well, imagine running into you here," the woman said. She was attractive and stylish, with a painted-on face and wearing turquoise designer jeans and a white-and-turquoise shirt, along with diamond rings and an expensive watch. There was a feline quality about her as she looked, boldly inquisitive, from Marnie to Jesse.

"I'm surprised, too, Stella," Marnie said. "I didn't imagine the state fair was somewhere you might go."

"The Morgan horse show. My daughter is showing her yearling in the halter class today," the woman said airily. "You know we have the state champion mare—her father indulges her shamelessly. Are you here for the horse show, too?" The woman cast Marnie a doubtful glance, arched her perfectly formed left eyebrow and looked pointedly at Jesse.

"No," Marnie said coolly. "I've simply been enjoying the fair with Jesse." She politely made the introductions.

"How do you do," Stella said when Jesse shook her cool, limp hand. He was amazed to see a sultry, flirty look come into her eyes. "Are you an associate of Patrick's?" she asked.

"Not an associate...but we do have a mutual interest, ma'am," Jesse answered smoothly, and Marnie poked him with her elbow.

"*Ma'am?* Your accent must be West Texas."

Jesse shook his head. "New Mexico."

"I didn't know Patrick had any hotels there." She cast Marnie a questioning look.

"He's planning one," Marnie said. "If you'll excuse us, we need to see a man about a sheep." She slipped her arm through Jesse's and prodded him onward. "Nice running into you, Stella. Come up to see me sometime...you're always welcome."

The woman's mouth gaped slightly.

Out of sight, Marnie fell to giggling. "What a nosy-body! She couldn't wait to find out who I was with!" She gave a derisive snort. "Her husband is a lawyer at one of the firms Patrick uses. They've come to a dozen of Patrick's dinner parties, and I'll bet she hasn't said a full sentence to me in all of them put together."

"I don't think you should feel too slighted about that," Jesse commented. He noted how she'd referred to the parties as Patrick's alone.

"Oh? Didn't you appreciate her? She appreciated you, dear sir. Talk about mentally undressin' a person!"

"Yeah," he said, pleased. "She did." He lifted an eyebrow. "Jealous?"

"You are so full of yourself, Jesse Breen!" she said, giving him a shove.

He grinned warmly. "You like me."

She gazed at him with an amused smile. "Yes, I do." And her tone was very warm.

Jesse looked away as an uncomfortable sensation swept him—something very close to guilt. He inclined his head in the direction of the horse barn. "Does she mean trouble? Telling Patrick, I mean, 'cause she's gonna do that right away."

"She can't do it until Patrick returns from Atlanta, and when she does, knowing Patrick, he'll probably smile at her and make her feel terribly silly." Looking him in the eye, she said quietly, "I am not sneaking around behind Patrick's back, Jesse. I would never do anything underhanded to him."

Since there wasn't anything to be said to that, he simply nodded, hid the foolish jealousy that flashed through him and pushed it aside. He had no right to it.

Increasing curiosity about her relationship with Vinsand nagged at him—though it sure as hell wasn't any of his business, he reminded himself. He recalled that the relationship, which she'd given every indication was a physical one, had endured six years. Yet she had been sleeping alone last night, and had been then, as she was now, definitely highly attracted to Jesse. But her words just now indicated consideration, even a high regard, for Vinsand. It was all very puzzling. Even if it wasn't any of his concern.

## Chapter Eight

Jesse had his truck back now—"Never could tell it was wrecked," he said. But the three of them, including Ham, who squeezed in behind the two seats, took Marnie's Cadillac to the restaurant. Marnie tossed Jesse the keys.

"Are you sure you trust my drivin'?" he said, casting her a grin that was a mixture of boyish pleasure and manly seduction.

Delicious heat flashed through her, and she averted her eyes. "Just keep your attention on the road."

With the convertible top down, the early evening sun shone golden on them as they sped down the highway that circled the city. Ham propped his head on the side behind the driver's seat and squinted his black eyes, while one ear flopped in the wind.

Marnie kept casting Jesse quick glances, fascinated by him, but not wanting him to notice her interest. He'd tossed his hat onto the console between the seats, and wisps of his deep brown hair blew across his forehead. His face was very tanned, emphasizing eyes that were an iridescent ice blue. He smiled with

pure pleasure whenever he looked at her. He appeared to be
having a good time with her. She was so glad for that.

He was a quiet man but with an inordinate sense of power
about him. A controlled strength emanated from him and drew
her. He made her feel as if every nerve ending were alive and
humming and, oh, so completely, totally a woman.

He drove, following her directions, with an elbow propped
on the door and one hand hung easily over the top of the steering wheel, moving it with his wrist. His hands were rough and
strong. His shirt, long sleeves rolled up his forearms, was pale
yellow and looked magnificent against his tanned skin. He fa-
vored the color yellow; this was the third shirt of a similar color
she'd seen him wear. And it was a good choice for him.

She picked up her camera and leaned far back to get a shot
of him. He cut his eyes to her and looked sexy enough to make
her teeth ache.

"You are the ham," she told him, "not your dog."

He just laughed and took her hand. Just like that, he took
her hand. As if they were lovers, she thought. But, no, he was
simply a man who easily expressed himself with touch. That
was all.

He rubbed his callused thumb over hers, and sparks ignited
in her heart. Amorous images played at the edges of her mind,
teasing, as they had all day. She refused to let them grow. She
and Jesse had only this evening. He would be gone tomorrow.
Out of her life.

*Take this moment, enjoy it. But don't cry that there is no
more.*

It was a Chinese restaurant, small, in an older neighborhood and actually a bit garish. She'd chosen it because she
loved the food and friendly service and did not wish to be seen
by people who knew Patrick. She would not cause a lot of talk
to embarrass him.

Jesse switched off the ignition and cast her a curious glance.

"Don't make a hasty judgment," she said, patting her hair
into some semblance of order. "They have great food here."
Not waiting for Jesse, she got out and leaned over to pet Ham.
"We'll bring you some leftovers."

"I'm about to get jealous of my dog," Jesse said, again taking her hand. "You had a fit about the sheep gettin' in your car, but you let him get his dog hair all over."

"That was before I knew your sheep. We could have brought them along."

"That dog is enough competition." Jesse's blue eyes sparkled warmly, again stirring the heat inside her.

They knew her here. Mr. Charlie, the slightly bent, elderly Oriental gentleman who greeted them, called her by name and spoke with warm friendliness. Marnie introduced Jesse, and Mr. Charlie said, "So nice to see Miss Raines in the company of a gentleman friend. She always come alone," he said to Jesse, "but I know she cannot be a woman alone."

He showed them to a rear booth, one away from other patrons, near a large potted palm that was real, but surrounded by numerous plastic foliage. A mirror ran the length of the wall beside them, reflecting the brilliant red, green and gold decor.

After Mr. Charlie had left them, Jesse slid the bud vase of artificial flowers from the middle of the table to the edge next to the wall, saying, "I'm allergic to these things." He gazed at her thoughtfully. "You come here alone?"

She nodded, averting her eyes. "This place isn't exactly Patrick's style." She leaned her arms on the table. "It may be gaudy, but I find it relaxing here. The people are wonderful, and the food really is delicious."

Suzie, Mr. Charlie's granddaughter, appeared with menus, water and hot tea. Smiling broadly, she told Marnie about starting college, and shared news about her brothers and sisters.

"You're right," Jesse said after she left. "This is a nice place."

And Marnie was foolishly pleased. His gaze darkened with intensity and held hers. The heat rose again. She crossed her legs tightly and opened the large menu, scanning it but not reading a thing.

*What was she doing with him?* She wanted him, and he wanted her, and they were both flirting with it, when they were both old enough to know better. Or perhaps they did it because they were both old enough to appreciate the experience.

*She was with him because this was as close to love as she might ever come for the rest of her life.* She blinked rapidly, telling her tears to be gone.

Mr. Charlie brought them, on the house, a cold bottle of beer for Jesse and a glass of white wine for Marnie. After several sips of the wine, Marnie felt herself relaxing. They settled into easy, casual conversation, talking about the excellent repair job on Jesse's truck, saying that his beer was good, her wine fine—she rarely could tell expensive wine from cheap.

Over dinner, as they became more relaxed and trusting of each other, the talk gradually became more personal. Beginning by pointing out that his opportunities for Chinese food were limited because the only place to eat in Wings, New Mexico, was the lunch counter at Cobb's Drugstore, where the specialty was fried-onion burgers, Jesse began to describe his life.

He told her of Wings, "a tiny freckle on the giant stomach of the world." Situated on either side of a blacktopped county road, the town had three real businesses and a church, where services were held every other Sunday, if things went just right, and six houses, half of them usually empty, and all at least sixty years old.

Marnie had seen many, many towns like Wings in her life, and Jesse had the ability to make her see this one clearly, because he loved it and the people who lived there. He had lived there for most of his life, except for a few years in Albuquerque, when his father had experimented with city living.

She learned of Jada Cobb, who ran Cobb's Drugstore and was known in three counties for her melon-sized breasts and the warm heart beneath them. There was fiery Kelly, who ran the Tavern and Lemonade Parlor—selling lemonade on Sundays just so he could claim the title—and who spent a good deal of his time romancing Jada. Miss Loretta was an ex-school teacher with wild white hair who ran the post office like a five-star general, and Joe Shatto was a plain old boring fellow who operated the garage. The Breen ranch was far enough from town that they didn't get mail delivery. Portions of the Sante Fe Trail cut across it, and half of the ranch extended up into Colorado. The core of the present ranch house was made of logs, many of them hauled from miles and miles away, because the area was some of the best grassland in the world. Jesse was obviously proud of his home.

Enjoying his vivid stories, Marnie asked about his family. Digging out his wallet, he showed her pictures.

"Matthew is my eldest son. He's thirty-four, solid, dependable and romantic, but if you want to stay on his good side, you don't mention the romantic part." Chuckling, he lifted his sweating bottle of beer to his lips.

There was Matthew's wife, Annie, a pretty yet somber woman, at least in the picture. Marnie could tell by his tone of voice that Jesse was very fond of his daughter-in-law, and she felt a prick of envy of Annie for getting to live with him. For being the recipient of his affection.

There was little Jess, his grandson, and his pride and joy. And Rory, of course, whom she'd met. Jesse said Rory had a hair-trigger temper he was learning to control, finally, at the age of thirty-two. Oren was the youngest at twenty-eight, devilishly handsome and beloved by women. Matt ran the ranch, except for Jesse's sheep operation. Rory and Oren both worked the ranch, too, but Rory had his interest in horses and rodeo, and Oren had his interest in photography and women.

"It seems your sons are most definitely reflections of their father," Marnie commented.

Jesse nodded. "Good and bad, we're a lot alike. But they're also very much like Regina—their mother." He said the name *Regina* with a certain warmth. "She was passionate about the land, like Matt, and about horses, like Rory, and was something of an artist, like Oren."

"You two were married young."

"Yeah. I stole her away from her family the second day after she'd finished high school. Her folks were madder than hell, 'cause I was just another rodeo cowboy in those days, and a pretty good rebel at that, while they could trace their family back to the first New Mexicans of Spanish nobility. It was one of those spur-of-the-moment things two young people in heat do, but it worked out well."

"Do you have a picture of her?"

He gazed at her a moment, then said, "Yeah." The picture was the last one in his wallet, where nothing would rub against it.

"She was beautiful," Marnie said, gazing at a woman with laughing eyes, delicate features and light hair waving to her shoulders. Other than that, though, the picture could tell her nothing of the real woman. The way Jesse looked at the photograph before he put it away told her the most.

She regarded him thoughtfully. "Most men who have enjoyed a good marriage marry again. Why haven't you?"

He shrugged, gazed at his bottle of beer and wiped the sweat off it with his thumb. "I was pretty lost after she died. And then I was busy with the ranch and the boys and havin' a good, single time. I met some good women—like Celeste, who I guess you could say I 'courted' for seven years." An expression so sad that Marnie's heart felt the pain crossed his face. He sighed and said, "Time has a way of passin' before it's noticed. A man thinks, 'I'll get to that tomorrow.' One day I looked up and tomorrow had come and gone. It was the summer of my life, and the time for marryin' had just passed me clean by."

"Why should you think that? For heaven's sake, Jesse, marrying someone has no age requirements."

"No…but any women I might be tempted to marry are a hell of a lot more scarce."

Marnie swallowed, looked away at the table, feeling odd. When she looked again at Jesse, he was speaking from deep thought.

"Marriage requires a person to do a lot of bendin' and rearrangin' of themselves and their life," he said. "When we're young we do it naturally, mostly because we don't realize it has to be done or that we're doin' it. But when a man gets older, he knows everything has its price, and he tends to think, 'What will I have to give up to share my life?' I'm not willin', nor able, to give up what I've become, or to change my life around. I've been on my own too long. I just don't have it in me to give what it takes to be married anymore." He tipped his moist beer bottle for emphasis, then drank deeply.

She nodded. "I see." She understood only too well; she felt very much the same. And her heart cracked a little, though she told herself it was a silly fancy. It didn't matter to her what Jesse's attitude to marriage was. It didn't affect her at all.

"Is it you or Vinsand who doesn't want to get married?" he asked her then.

She took a deep breath. "Both of us, I guess. The time never seemed to come around," she said with a sad smile. When she looked back up from her glass, he was regarding her intently.

His brows furrowed. "I know what you said about the monetary considerations, but it seems to me you're gettin' the short end of the stick. A woman such as yourself could do a lot better than Vinsand."

"Patrick is a fine man," she said firmly.

"Maybe, but he leaves you lonely."

"I'm not going to discuss my relationship with Patrick."

"Why not?" He leaned forward and took a deep swallow of his beer, while keeping deceptively lazy eyes on her. "We're close enough for you to talk about him. Why were you sleepin' alone last night when I called?"

"I wanted to."

"That's not the impression I got on the phone."

"Aren't you leavin' town tomorrow?" she said with a cool-ness Miss Phoebe had taught her. "We've had a couple of days of fun and flirting. I don't see that that gives you license to ad-vise me about my life."

"Maybe not, but I think someone needs to do it. You've got a lot of life ahead of you, and you're wastin' it with a man who doesn't appreciate you. Seems to me you could find a man who'd not only enjoy giving you credit cards and luxury cars but wouldn't take you for granted." He paused, then added, "A man who would fill up your lonely place."

She gazed at him, feeling anger and bitterness rise on her tongue. "Rich or poor, Jesse, there are few people who fill up the lonely places inside of others."

"You don't love him."

"I'm not required to love him. But make no mistake—I ad-mire Patrick. He's been very good to me."

"You feel gratitude."

"There's nothing wrong with that. It's an honest emotion, much more honest and reliable than love. Love, as songs are sung about, comes and goes like the wind."

He inclined his head. "Sometimes," he said, speculation in his eyes.

They both fell silent, eating.

"What are you thinkin'?" Jesse asked, and she realized she was staring at him.

"Oh, just wondering if you'd be willin' to give me a bite of your shrimp," she said, desperately wanting the warm easiness to return between them.

She was rewarded when he grinned that sensual grin of his. Speared a shrimp and extended it toward her. Her eyes on his, Marnie ate from his fork. She ran her tongue over her lips and, mesmerized, watched the heat dance in his eyes. She looked quickly back down to her own plate.

Jesse turned the conversation to his youth, speaking of a mother he had adored and a father he still hadn't been able to fully forgive for his drinking and meanness, of brothers, and things he'd seen and done. Gradually Marnie realized that with what he said he was drawing her out about herself until, in a few brief bits and pieces, she told him, for the first time since she'd revealed all to Miss Phoebe, about her early life as a child in a migrant-worker family.

"It was before Lyndon Johnson's great War on Poverty program," she explained. "And even when that began to get off the ground, most people like my parents had no idea help even existed, much less how to go about gettin' it."

Discovering that he had an understanding of what it had been like because his family had been poor in his early years and he had friends back in his rodeo days who'd come from similar backgrounds made the telling easier. Or maybe it was simply easier because Jesse was from a rural background, the first she'd come in close contact with since she'd escaped the country. Or maybe it was that he truly listened to her.

Jesse ordered another beer and sat back, absorbed in listening and watching her eyes fill with emotion. He had to read between the brief things she told him. Her father had left them on occasion to drink; she didn't say, but he could tell, they'd been left in abject poverty without the head of the family. She said they had once lived in an old '49 Buick, and he could imagine the places she'd lived, how she'd lived and knew it had been a hard life; it certainly explained a lot of things to him. It gave him a peek into her childhood wounds, enough to understand the innate distrust of people that she carried with her.

As if unable to speak of herself, she spoke mostly of a Miss Phoebe, who took on an image for him as a "grand Southern dame." This Miss Phoebe had saved Marnie from the unwanted attentions of her boss at a hosiery mill, when the guy had cornered Marnie in the parking lot.

"Miss Phoebe poked her head out of the back seat of her car—she rode around in this long pink Cadillac with fins. Remember them? Well, she yelled for Rudy to *unhand* me." Marnie smiled with amused memory. "Scared Rudy to death, because everyone knew Miss Phoebe was related to the mill owners. He took off as if she'd set fire to his pants. Then she called me over, gave me this inspection, even told me to turn around so she could see the back of me. Then she asked if I'd like to take the job as her companion, and I said yes. I was so sick of that hosiery mill, I was nearly ready to go back to the cotton fields," she said and gazed thoughtfully at her plate. "Miss Phoebe taught me about photography—it was her hobby, too. And she taught me about manners and decorating and arranging dinners and parties."

Jesse figured Miss Phoebe had taught her a lot more than all of that. And he also doubted that Marnie had ever revealed any of this to Patrick and felt humbled that she would talk to him, even as briefly as she was, about her past.

"She sounds like quite a lady," Jesse said. "A lot like Regina's sister, Ina."

He lit into a couple of good ones about his sister-in-law, who was in her sixties, had just married husband number three and was off on an extended honeymoon at some nudist colony. They traded tales of the two eccentric women and enjoyed some good chuckles. It was good to see Marnie laugh. But then, out of the blue, she started crying. Jesse sat helpless. It wasn't the tears that upset him; it was not knowing their cause. He wanted to comfort her and wasn't certain how.

She dug into her big purse, saying, "I'm sorry. Sometimes I just...feel things. I'm sorry," she repeated, red-faced. "I'll be fine in a minute. I really will. In just a minute. If I can just find a tissue." She brought a hand to shield her face and appeared to shrivel right there in the seat, as if she would disappear if she could.

"It's okay, darlin'," he assured her, and leaned across the table to take her hand from her face. "Tears are nothin' to be ashamed of. It's good to be able to feel and to express it." She gazed at him with that suspicious look of hers and blinked rapidly. "The time to worry is when you can't feel enough to cry, gal," he said, speaking from hard, bitter experience.

"Oh, Jesse..." She stared into his eyes, and a trembling smile tilted her lips.

"Here..." He dabbed a napkin at her eyes, then moved to the edge of her lips. "And you have a little sauce right there."

"I do not." She rubbed at the spot.

"Yes, just a bit."

"Don't spit on that napkin and expect to put it on my face again," she told him.

But she stilled, and he took his thumb and caressed her silky cheek and gazed into her deep blue eyes while thoughts of making love to her filled his mind.

The restaurant was closing when they finally got around to breaking open their fortune cookies.

"Mine says, 'Joy comes in the morning.'" She smiled softly. "I'm havin' it now, I think. What's yours?"

"'You will soon come into riches.'"

"Oh, you're makin' that up. Let me see."

"I am not." He handed the slip of paper to her, and she read it.

"Hmm. What will you buy?"

He winked as he rose. "It may not be money. There's all sorts of riches, darlin'."

After thanking Mr. Charlie profusely for a delicious meal, they walked out into the starry night.

"Oh, Jesse, what if Ham ran away?" Marnie asked, concerned.

"He wouldn't...see?"

"I brought you dinner, boy," she said, crouching to set the foam plate of rice, bits of rib meat and chicken on the ground. Ham jumped out of the car and immediately went to eating.

Marnie stood and bumped up against Jesse, who'd come to stand right behind her. She froze. Her back brushed his chest; his breath was warm on her hair. His warm male scent whispered around her, and she thought she could feel his heart beating.

"Ham forgives us for leavin' him so long," he said softly.

"Yes."

His hand closed around her upper arm, and he gently turned her. She gazed into his face, lit by the silvery parking lot lamps. Desire swelled and seeped through her body. Her gaze drifted to his nose, to his mustache, and focused on his lips. She couldn't move, and her heart beat like a wild thing in her chest.

He reached into his pocket and pulled out the keys, handing them to her. "I think you'd better drive. I've had three beers, and you only had one glass of wine."

Without a word she took the keys and walked around to the driver's side, then slipped behind the wheel. They sat there in silence for several minutes, while Ham went over to a grassy area to do his business, and then Marnie started the car and headed back to the fairgrounds. Jesse, for some peculiar reason, slouched in the passenger seat, head reclining on the headrest, and placed his hat over his face.

"Are you going to sleep?" she asked, amazed.

"Nope. Just relaxin'," he answered and thought he was doing a masterful job at it.

Consciously he told his muscles to loosen, trying to ease the hard knot of desire. He reflected that his years were a double-edged sword. Impressed into his memory were all the feelings that came with each sexual experience over the years. Those memories rose and nourished new desires, which in turn fed on the memories, causing passion to grow hotter and hotter. When he'd been twenty-one, he might have had the healthy desire of youth, but he hadn't had the memories of age to stimulate it onward to a blazing inferno. Yet the experience of years had also taught him the dangers of being irresponsible. And none of it seemed fair.

Marnie kept her eyes on the road, but her thoughts remained with the man draped in the seat two feet away. A part of her touched him, whispered sweet things in his ear, felt him against her. Longed for him so badly that she squirmed in her seat. She blinked back tears, wishing to hold back time, to let this night go on and on. To just keep on driving down this highway with him lying beside her. She thought of tomorrow with dread. Somehow, in less than four days, he'd come to fill her life. It would be empty without him.

Nearing the fairgrounds, she said in a hoarse voice, "You did say you were parked on the south side, didn't you?"

"Yeah," he said, and gestured with his hat. "The second entry up there."

She turned into the black-topped road. Vehicles stretched out into the darkness, row upon row. In the near distance the fair lights glowed brightly, lighting the dark sky. Laughter and music floated easily in the night air. The green-and-orange neon lights of the Ferris wheel towered above it all.

Following Jesse's directions, she drove until she came to his truck. Distant light reflected off the deep red hood. She pulled up behind it and turned off the engine.

They each sat there in awkward silence.

Marnie wondered if he would kiss her. What would she say if he suggested they go to a motel? They couldn't go to his room at the hotel, for people would be bound to see her. *How could she be thinking this?* Because she was human, and she adored this man.

Jesse considered smooth ways to get her into his arms and to suggest they go to his room. Probably wasn't such a good idea to go to his room, though. They'd need to go to another hotel. *How could he suggest that? He'd really be in deep then.*

They turned to each other at the same time. And the next instant they came together in a hot embrace, kissing each other as if there was no tomorrow. Which there wasn't for them.

His kiss gentled with sweet seduction, and Marnie, losing all comprehension of anything but him, felt herself melting into him. He smelled of manly cologne and pleasant male sweat, and tasted of beer and soy sauce. His hair was silky to her fingertips, his muscles enticingly full and hard. He was wonderfully hot, pulsing with life. She moaned for him when his mouth broke from hers and moved to her neck. His hand cupped her breast, and emotions exploded inside her.

"No . . . no!"

It took Jesse several seconds to realize Marnie was struggling—*against him*. He released her as her flailing fists hit his arms and chest.

Stunned, he tried to catch her hands. "What's the matter?"

"No!" she cried in a hoarse, breathless whisper as her fist got him again. "You think . . . you think I'm easy. That I'm loose and available and you'll just have a little quickie fling in the city and be gone back home in the morning."

She pulled far back on her side. The glow from the distant lights shone on her angry features and hair falling all down around her face as she glared at him.

"I thought no such thing!" Jesse replied, while his conscience pricked. "What in the hell gave you that idea?"

"Then what were you thinkin'? What was this?" she demanded.

She had him there. He *had* intended this to be a quickie affair in the city and then return happily home. But it hadn't sounded so sordid in his mind.

He raked his hand through his hair, thinking. Ham whined from the back seat, then jumped out of the car. Jesse had the urge to do the same—yet the reluctance to leave her kept him where he was. He did owe her an explanation.

"I want you. I can't deny that, and I don't think I need to. I'm certainly not ashamed of feelin's put into me by God himself—or of anythin' I've done. And *you* are as hot for me as I am for you, so don't go gettin' on your high horse. And don't belittle what's between us by makin' it out to be dirty. Yes, I was sort of hopin' for an exciting affair when I came here," he admitted. "But I . . ."

A pickup truck came up from behind, spotlighting them in its headlights. Jesse broke off and glared at it. Curiously, the pickup didn't move on.

"Damn!" Jesse whispered through clenched teeth.

"Jesse!" a voice called from the truck, and a dark shadow of a head showed itself from the driver's door. "Is that you, Jesse?"

"Yeah!" Immediately alert, Jesse got out of the Caddie and began walking to the truck, his mind assessing everything, knowing instantly this had to do with Rory.

Rory's buddy Larry Young came out of the darkness. "I've been lookin' for you everywhere—drivin' by your truck every so often, hopin' to catch you. Rory and Kipp are down in jail. They got in a fight at a club down the road and busted it up real good. Between us, we don't have the cash to bail them out."

Jesse sighed deeply. "You boys sure do have rotten timing. Okay. Wait here a minute."

He walked back to Marnie. She'd gotten out of the car and stood, the door open behind her, staring at him. Her face in the bright light of the headlights was white and drawn with concern.

"What is it?" she asked quickly.

"Rory. He got in a fight and landed in jail. I have to go bail him out."

"Do you need a lawyer? I know a good one I can get right away."

He shook his head and bent to retrieve his hat from the Cadillac. He screwed it in place, drew a deep breath and rested his hand on his belt. "Look, I want you to know I had one of the greatest times of my life with you. I never meant you any disrespect."

"Oh, Jesse . . . I'm sorry about before." She reached out, rested her fingers on his shirtfront. "I was . . . oh, I was just crazy." Her lips trembled. "I truly didn't mean what I said."

He understood. He was caught between a rock and a hard place himself.

He reached for her, and she came readily into his arms. He sensed her gulping back tears as he hugged her, rubbed his face into her silky hair, trying to take a part of her with him. *He could ask her to wait for him to come back from bailing out the guys.* But he didn't know how long any of this would take. He had to let her go. *It was for the best anyway.* Anything else would only bring great complications.

Gently pulling away, she held out her hand. He slipped his into hers for a soft handshake.

"Thank you, Jesse, for one of the greatest times of *my* life. If you get back this way, you look me up."

"If you get up my way, *you* look *me* up."

"Yes," she said breathlessly, blinking furiously but smiling. He brought her hand to his lips, kissed it. "I have to go."

She nodded. "If there's anything I can do to help you about Rory, call me."

"It'll be okay. I've done it before."

"Goodbye." Her voice was choked. She rose on tiptoe to quickly kiss his lips, then turned to get into the car.

He closed the door for her. "You drive carefully."

She nodded and started the engine. He turned away, whistled for Ham and strode to Larry's truck, inwardly cursing wayward sons. He slammed the door and sat there watching Marnie drive away into the darkness. Ending his dream.

"For two cents I'd leave him there," he said, and Larry had the good sense to keep his mouth shut.

## Chapter Nine

Marnie rolled onto her back and lay very still, listening for her heartbeat. It beat steadily on, as if mocking her. And the sun was shining, birds flying, morning traffic moving below, she saw when she stepped out on the rooftop patio. All the world keeps on turning, she thought with disgust, wondering how it could, when her life seemed to be at such a dead end. It made her feel small and insignificant.

She moved listlessly back inside and went to pluck a white daisy from the bouquet Jesse had sent her. Twirling it in her fingers, she looked at the telephone and thought of him, imagined the telephone ringing, him calling to ask her to come with him for another day. But of course he was gone by now, on his way back to Wings, New Mexico. Back to the bosom of his warm and loving family. While she was left here, waiting for phone calls that never came. Patrick hadn't even called her last night as he'd said he would; there had been no message on her machine when she'd come in. There were rarely messages on her machine, but Patrick had insisted she have it.

With a sigh, she took the vase of flowers into the bathroom to add water. As she bent over the tub, which was the only place the vase would fit beneath the faucet, her tears plunked on the colorful petals.

As she showered, she told herself that longing for what could never be—like simply lying down and dying—never did a person any good. She had to deal with what was. And of all the people in the world, she had no reason to complain; she lived well and had been offered the grand opportunity to become a wealthy woman.

What was she going to tell Patrick? Could she really turn down his offer? She patted her skin with a thick, electrically warmed towel and glanced about the gleaming bathroom, looking at the marble, the brass fixtures, the costly bottles of perfumed skin lotions. Could she turn her back on all this? And go where? she asked herself as she sprayed herself with expensive perfume.

There were several important things she would have to tell Patrick, she thought bleakly. As for any further deliberation, her mind refused. It obstinately drifted with fragmented thoughts and fuzzy imaginings, totally out of focus. The day stretched before her, cold and empty, without purpose.

She wondered how Jesse felt, imagined him driving down the highway, with his wrist cocked over the top of his steering wheel. She saw again his slow and sexy smile, his sparkling eyes. And she cried some more.

After doing nothing more to her hair than shake it out, she slipped into a blue satin robe and slippers and went through to the penthouse to tell Tacita she wouldn't require breakfast.

Concern filled Tacita's eyes. "Oh, you should eat. Breakfast is the most important meal of the day, and I have set the table on the patio for you. Won't you even have a couple of blueberry muffins?"

Marnie smiled, grateful for the concern. "Yes, blueberry muffins would be nice."

"And a little milk?" Tacita coaxed.

"Yes, a little milk."

"Good!" And she went off happily to the kitchen to phone in the order and get coffee.

Marnie looked around the room, thinking that there really was nothing she needed to do in the penthouse. She wasn't needed here.

Someone clearing their throat caused her to turn. Dorothy stood there. "Good morning, Miss Raines. Mr. Vinsand just telephoned. He left you a message." She nervously cleared her throat again, and Marnie noticed there was something different about the woman, but she couldn't put her finger on it. "He said to tell you he apologized for not calling you last night. He was hung up for the evening in a business meeting. If you need anything, please call me. I have his number here for you."

"Thank you, Dorothy."

Marnie stepped forward and took the paper, wishing Patrick would quit using his secretary as a go-between. Then she noticed it—Dorothy looked different. She had done something with her hair. She'd curled and fluffed her bangs, fluffed her hair all over. And she'd put on blush and lipstick! And Marnie could guess why.

She said, "You look very lovely this morning." She looked as if she might actually be an attractive woman—younger, more feminine.

Surprise jumped in Dorothy's eyes behind her large, dark-rimmed glasses, and her hand flew to her hair. "Thank you. I..." She met Marnie's gaze and blushed furiously. Marnie had never seen Dorothy blush, or be anything less than a perfect iceberg. For that surprising second the woman seemed a very natural match for Ogden. But then Dorothy lifted her chin and said in an acerbic tone, "I'd love to stand here and exchange pleasantries with you, Miss Raines, but there are those of us who must work." Prim and proper, she turned away.

"Yes, and there are those of us who get to do nothin'," Marnie called sarcastically after her. Watching the woman's stiff back go down the hall, Marnie thought that help was needed here or Og could work forever and never thaw Dorothy Hines. "Dorothy!" she called and hurried to catch up.

"Yes?" Dorothy raised not only her chin but that irritating eyebrow.

"Would you join me for breakfast this morning—I mean, since Patrick's gone, and we're both on our own?"

Surprise appeared again in Dorothy's eyes; then suspicion replaced it, and she shook her head, saying, "Og... Mr. Turpin will be here in a few minutes. And I am expected to be in the office should Mr. Vinsand telephone."

"You can arrange for the telephone to ring out in the living room, can't you?" But Dorothy's expression wasn't relenting. "Oh, forget it," Marnie said. "Forgive me for tryin' to be nice and thinkin' it's past time we buried the hatchet." And she turned with a huff, while the back of her neck prickled with hope.

"Miss Raines..."

Marnie stopped and slowly turned, using her best innocent look.

"I'm sorry," Dorothy said stiffly. "I suppose I could go with a cup of coffee."

"I'd like to dress," Marnie said. "Could you join me in...say, fifteen minutes?" She hoped that was enough time.

"Yes...that would be lovely."

Thinking that the word *lovely* seemed a little foreign on Dorothy's tongue, Marnie flew away to the kitchen to find Tacita and change the breakfast order. Tacita cast her a curious look, but Marnie urged her to make the call and raced away to pluck several flowers from the huge vase on the entry-hall table. Leaving the penthouse door open in order to hear Ogden's arrival, she quickly grabbed a small vase from a display cabinet and put the flowers on the patio breakfast table. As she checked the place settings, she thought that if she could not experience love, she could nevertheless occupy her time helping two others to do so. A bit of romance was exactly what old stiff-backed Dorothy needed.

Tacita appeared with a small pitcher of orange juice and two glasses. "I thought perhaps, with all that food, someone would be joining you, Miss Marnie?"

Marnie shook her head. "This is not for me. This breakfast is for Mr. Turpin and Miss Hines," she explained with a sly smile.

"Oh..." Tacita's eyes widened with disbelief. "You mean Mr. Turpin and Miss Hines are..."

Marnie nodded with amusement.

"It will surely help Miss Hines," Tacita said matter-of-factly. "That woman needs some good loving."

"We all do," Marnie commented wistfully.

"Yes...yes, it is so," Tacita said so gleefully that Marnie had to chuckle.

There came the whir of the elevator arriving in the outer hallway. Marnie touched Tacita's arm. "You tell Mr. Ogden I expect him for breakfast. Miss Hines should be here in a few minutes, and it's up to them after that."

And she raced away to her own apartment, leaving a grinning Tacita hurrying to catch Ogden.


Following the studious young Ogden Turpin from the elevator, Jesse stepped into a curved hallway with a double door standing open directly opposite and another single door off by itself about twenty feet down the wall.

"She's probably in the penthouse," Ogden said, walking through the double doors, calling, "Marnie?"

Jesse stopped at the other man's elbow, swept his hat from his head and observed an enormous room with cool white couches and chairs and glass and black lacquer pieces. It was definitely the modern, wealthy look. Coming across the pale carpet was a small, dark-haired woman in a maid's uniform with an eager grin on her face. "Miss Marnie said you are expected to have breakfast on the patio, Mr. Turpin." Her gaze fell on Jesse then, and her eagerness turned to uncertainty. "You have a guest?" Jesse would have said the woman was disappointed.

"A guest?" Ogden said and glanced at Jesse. "Oh...yes. This is *my* friend, Mr. Breen." The young man's dark eyes skimmed over Jesse and back to the maid. "We need to speak to Marnie. Where is she?"

"She's...ah, Miss Marnie is in her apartment," the woman said hesitantly, her eyes revealing curiosity and confusion as she gestured behind her. Jesse followed the gesture to see a door on the far wall.

"Thank you, Tacita," Ogden said, backing up. "We'll go this way," he said to Jesse, and with swift strides, he went down the hall to the single door and rapped.

While waiting, the young man regarded Jesse with thoughtful speculation. Jesse smiled. "I appreciate this."

Ogden blinked and nodded.

The door was jerked open, and Marnie stood there, shimmering in a blue robe, her sorrel hair curling damply, her pale face devoid of makeup. "Ogden! What are you doing...?"

Her voice trailed off as her gaze met Jesse's. Her eyes widened with astonished disbelief. Then pure, vibrating joy flooded them, as her hand pressed between her breasts, and her lips trembled into a beautiful smile.

*It was Jesse!* Brown hair with stray wisps across his forehead, tan sport coat over his broad shoulders, yellow shirt, sharply creased denims, shining boots. Jesse Breen standing right there in her doorway, with his hat in his hand. Yes, it was, she thought as she gazed into his shining blue eyes. Feeling faint, she took hold of the doorknob with one hand and touched her damp hair with the other. Oh, mercy, she had no makeup on; she looked a fright!

"I ran into this gentleman downstairs at the elevator, Marnie," Og was saying. "He had a message for you, and I thought he might just as well bring it up himself. I hope that was all right."

She shifted her gaze to see Og watching her carefully with uncertain eyes behind his thick glasses.

"Oh! Yes...yes, th—thank you, Og," she stammered. "Oh, both of you, please come in. Uh, Og, this is—" she began, but Jesse interrupted.

"Ogden here and I have exchanged handles," he said.

"Oh." Her gaze fastened on Jesse's, and her heart beat ninety miles an hour.

"If you'll excuse me," Og said, already backing out into the hall again. "It was nice to meet you, Mr. Breen."

"And you, too, Mr. Turpin. A million thanks."

Marnie watched Ogden disappear before she recalled the tête-à-tête she and Tacita had arranged. "Ogden!" Clutching the folds of her robe together, she quickly stepped out the door after him. "Breakfast is set on the patio. Dorothy should be there any minute."

He gave a puzzled frown. "Breakfast?"

The elevator doors opened, and a waiter stepped forward with a food cart. Marnie pointed at the cart and said plainly, "Dorothy has agreed to have coffee with *me*—but I ordered *you and her* this breakfast. The table is set on the patio. Once Dorothy gets there, keeping her there is your problem."

Understanding dawned. Gratitude and excitement glimmering in his eyes, he bobbed his head and headed through the penthouse double doors. Marnie stepped back into her apartment, closed the door and leaned against it. Jesse stood in the middle of her apartment, looking around.

She was alone with him. In her apartment. It was almost too much to take in. *He hadn't left her!* She ached to throw herself into his arms but stood, holding onto the doorknob as if it were an anchor.

"Nice young man," Jesse said, with a wave of his hat in the direction Og had taken. "And he likes you."

"We're friends. You were hanging around the elevator?" she asked in an intense whisper.

"I was leanin' next to it. I was certain someone would come up—or I'd figure out the combination. Couldn't be all that hard with only six buttons." His eyes roamed the room as he spoke with breezy assurance, as if this were the most natural thing in the world.

"Why didn't you simply call? What if Patrick had been here?"

"I did call. Got your silly machine, so I hung up. And you said Patrick was gone until Sunday."

"He could have returned unexpectedly." She watched him begin ambling around the room. "I . . . I must have been in the shower when you called. What are you doing here? I thought you were going home today."

"I decided to stay a couple more days."

Their gazes collided and smoldered.

"I wanted to see where you live," he said.

"Where I live?" It seemed odd, too close for comfort.

He nodded and grinned that slow grin. "It's a natural inclination to be interested in what a person's home is like. You know—haven't you ever wondered what the president's real living room is like? Or Burt Reynolds and Lonnie Anderson's place?'' He stepped around to peer into her kitchen. "You won't cook a Thanksgivin' dinner in here.''

She moved beside him. "I could if it were for two people— and if I could cook.''

He slowly turned his head to look at her. "You can't cook?'' He was close enough for her to catch the warmth of his breath.

She shook her head and gazed, lost, into his eyes. "I haven't cooked a full meal in years,'' she said softly. "I do make pretty good coffee, though.'' Her gaze moved downward to his lips.

Jesse didn't dare let himself reach for her. He moved quickly away, looked at anything and everything but her. It was unbelievably cozy, this place, like a tiny cottage right here on the fifteenth floor. And he thought that by seeing this, he could believe in her country roots. The place fit her perfectly—and how different it was from the penthouse. Hell, she didn't go at all with Vinsand.

"You have a nice place,'' he said.

"Thank you,'' she said. Out of the corner of his eye he saw her watching him.

"Did you take all these pictures?'' The walls were covered with photographs. A few prints here and there, but mostly photos in old-fashioned frames—and mostly of people caught doing some activity.

"A lot of them. A few were Miss Phoebe's. A few I've bought.''

"Did you take this one? I like it,'' he said of a man walking along with a hound dog at his heels.

She said, "You would,'' and drew his gaze. "Yes, I took it.'' They smiled at each other. Like lovers, Jesse thought, catching fire and cursing himself for being here, for knowing he should crush his feelings right now but denying that knowledge. It felt too damn good to give up.

"What about your sheep?'' Marnie asked. "Don't they have to be removed from the fair barn?''

"I had Rory take them home early this mornin'. He was more than ready to go back,'' he added with a low chuckle and moved toward her bedroom.

"Aren't you worried about being nosy?'' she asked, following as he stepped into the room.

"No," he said. "I'll show you my place—even my closet— if you come out."

"You're quite safe there, aren't you?" she said with amusement in her voice.

It was thoroughly a woman's room, as totally feminine as she was. Flowery wallpaper, pastel colors, lace and ruffles, womanly fragrance, with no sign of a man anywhere. Not a cast aside tie or socks, nor a robe. Not one iota of a man, and Jesse would bet his bottom dollar that Vinsand had never slept here with her.

Marnie moved in rapid steps to the bed and sat to hide the stuffed bear whose ear was peeking out around a pillow. She didn't want Jesse to see it there, in her bed, where she'd obviously slept with it. He shouldn't know she did that.

As it was, he saw the flowers he'd sent her sitting on her dressing table. "Are those the ones I sent you?" He shot her a raised eyebrow.

She nodded. There was no way he would know she'd set them there because she'd wanted to see them last thing at night and first thing in the morning.

And again they gazed at each other, each having sensual thoughts.

"Can you come with me today?" he asked.

She smiled softly. "Yes!"

They were playing with fire dangerously now. But how could she have said no? Her heart would surely have stopped.

He nodded and started for the door. "Hurry up and get dressed in something casual. We're drivin' down to the Wichita Mountains for a picnic."

"You really are bein' overbearin', Jesse Breen."

"I'm bein' masterful. You'll love a picnic." He looked around, obviously intent on waiting for her.

"You can't wait. We can't leave together," she said softly. "It would cause talk."

His eyes darkened, yet he nodded with understanding and strode to the front door, saying, "I'll meet you at the 7-Eleven—the first one south on MacArthur Boulevard." He settled his hat on his head and cast her that winning grin. "Don't be too long. The day's far gone already."

"I won't," she promised.

The door closed behind him, and she flew into motion. *Oh! Oh! The joy was enough to take her breath!* And she teared up as she raced to the bedroom, pulling off her robe as she went.

Dear, dear Og, she thought. How had he known? He'd seen her looking at Jesse that night in the restaurant. But that had been such a small thing. Perhaps he'd brought Jesse up because of his own romantic inclinations at the moment.

Speaking of which, how had it gone with Dorothy? she wondered. Buttoning her blouse, she padded barefoot across the carpet and carefully slid open the door to the rooftop patio, stepped out and peeked around the corner. They sat there at the small table. Dorothy's back was to her, Ogden's face clearly visible. He was smiling.

Pleased as punch with herself and certain that life was worth living, Marnie quickly moved back inside. There was no worrying about tomorrow. Jesse was waiting today.

It was as she went down in the elevator that she recalled her fortune cookie—"Joy comes in the morning."


Jesse glanced at his watch for the second time in three minutes. *Where was she?* It had been forty minutes since he'd left her. On the seat across from him sat a food basket and on the floor a cooler of drinks—all the ingredients he considered necessary for a top-notch picnic. He hoped she liked fried chicken and wine coolers.

How long did it take a woman to get dressed? Maybe something had happened to waylay her. *Maybe Vinsand had returned.*

And then he saw her white Cadillac coming down the street. He was out and waiting when she pulled up beside his truck. His eyes shaded by the wide brim of his hat, he watched the sun glint on the gleaming finish of her car and her shimmering hair. She slowly got out, and they gazed at each other. She was beautiful, eyes like costly opals, a smile as warm as the sun, and wearing a simple deep blue sleeveless blouse and skirt that looked sexy as hell on her.

"Thank you for coming," he said. Standing in the open in a public lot was a lot less intimate than standing beside her in her apartment, and it was cooler between them.

"I'm glad you stayed," she said.

"I can take a couple of days if you can."

And she put him in his place, saying, "Let's take it a day at a time." She glanced around him. "You didn't bring Ham?"

"I sent him back home. I'm tired of him cuttin' in on my time."

She raised a saucy eyebrow. "If I'd known that, I wouldn't have come."

"I've got somethin' Ham doesn't have," he said suggestively. "I have the food."

"Oh...you have a lot that Ham doesn't have," she told him with her practiced sultry expression and tone.

He smacked her on the behind. "Day's a wastin', darlin'. Let's get goin'."

"In the Cadillac," she said.

"Hey, my truck has all the luxuries—radio, CD player, air, reclining seats."

She cut her eyes to him. "Yes, but it isn't an Italian-designed convertible roadster. And if you think I'm leaving a fifty-six-thousand-dollar car here in this public lot, you need to think again."

"You have a point."

Stepping lively, he transferred the large picnic basket of food and small cooler of drinks to her trunk. He also grabbed several of his compact discs.

She looked at the discs. "Mantovani and Don Williams?"

"I have eclectic tastes."

"Okay...but we get to listen to Stevie Nicks, too."

He wondered who that was and had a twinge of feeling old, which he pushed aside.

While he'd thought of the food, she'd thought of comfort, bringing a quilted blanket, two small pillows, bug spray and sunscreen lotion, a package of towelettes and a straw hat with a brim large enough to shade her shoulders.

"I do not tan," she said, plopping the hat on her head and tying it beneath her chin. She gazed pointedly at him. "I don't tan, I don't care to sweat nor to walk through grass and I despise bugs."

"You're going to be fun on a picnic," he said, watching her carefully check her camera.

She quipped, "Your idea, not mine."

They were both grinning and having the time of their lives.

"Do I get to drive?" he asked.

She handed him the keys.

Impulsively, he bent his head beneath the brim of the mammoth hat to kiss her. He'd meant it to be a fleeting thing, but, caught by the surprising fire that flashed through him and the sweetness of her velvet lips, he lingered. Slowly straightening, he gazed down at her flushed face. There was heat in her eyes. And a wanting that made him feel both prince and pauper.

He opened the passenger door for her. She slipped gracefully into the seat, and he closed the door. Rounding the car, he tossed the keys in his hand and he knew that the reason he was so hot, was that he was playing with fire.

As he sent the roadster squealing out of the parking lot, he felt a rush of exhilaration at controlling 200 horses under the gleaming hood. And he thought how the desires boiling inside him were equal in power—and in their destructive capability, too.


They drove along the turnpike to Lawton, Don Williams singing from the CD player, a warm and humid wind blowing around them, the sun shining brightly between cotton-puff clouds. Marnie again snapped shots of Jesse driving and thought her state of being had to be what was referred to as seventh heaven. She couldn't clearly see Jesse's eyes behind his sunglasses, just as he couldn't see hers. But she could see his smile and returned it. He took her hand and rubbed her thumb with his callused one. Desire played at the edges of her mind, as she knew it did at his. Teasing and taunting. She tried to ignore it, yet it was too sweetly seductive to be ignored. She pretended it didn't exist, just as she knew he pretended. What would she say should he suggest they stop at a motel? No, of course. That would be the responsible, proper thing. But what consolation were "responsible " and "proper" on cold, lonely nights?

She was very thankful for this day, she decided at last, and would live it moment by wonderful moment. Even doing something as basic as stopping for gas and iced tea was to be savored.

When she saw a sign for the Museum of the Great Plains, she shyly asked Jesse if they could stop. "I've wanted to see it for a long time." She didn't explain that the reason she'd never gone and rarely saw anything was that she didn't care to do it alone.

"Then that's where we'll go," he said easily.

She was thrilled. "Oh, Jesse, I love museums!" And this was one she wouldn't have to see alone.

But even before they went inside, Marnie found delight in the prairie-dog village right out front. The little critters sat up on their hind legs and twitched their noses, diving for their holes the instant Marnie tried to move in for a close-up.

She hadn't brought a zoom lens, so she contented herself with the shots she could get. Jesse helped by getting an apple from the picnic basket, slicing it with his pocket knife and tossing the pieces near the holes. Marnie watched avidly as the prairie dogs skittered out of their holes and snatched up the treats.

At last Jesse dragged her inside. "I want to see this place and still have time to eat."

He proved to be a knowledgeable tour guide, taking up with more detailed explanations where the small museum plaques left off. Walking with him hand in hand, Marnie saw the displays, diagrams, and old iron and wooden artifacts in a new light. He helped her with any words she didn't know the meaning of, and she plied him with questions, delighted to be seeing and learning so much. He *knew* so much and clearly enjoyed being the teacher, without ever acting superior.

"I was weaned on all this stuff, darlin'," he explained, the glow of warm memory in his eyes. "My mother set great store by history, and I guess I do, too. And I am quite a bit older than you," he added, a trace of regret in his eyes. "When I was a kid, I could go to my grandparents' home and see half of this stuff still in use.''

He was brooding over his age again, she saw. "Jesse, you may be a *mite* older than me in years," she said, "but certainly in no other way."

He regarded her thoughtfully, as if turning a question over in his mind.

They continued on, and he told her how certain rock formations came about and how the Indians and early pioneers had used the oil that seeped from the ground not only for burning on torches and greasing things but for healing potions of all sorts. He explained the workings of certain tools and guns and peppered all his teaching with anecdotes of real people who had lived and breathed and struggled on the grassy western plains.

"You are a born storyteller," Marnie told him.

"That's what Woody Greene tells me all the time," he teased.

When they returned to the car, Jesse presented her with a pair of dangling silver earrings that he'd bought in the gift shop while she'd been looking at books.

"Oh, Jesse, they're beautiful," she said, immediately taking off the ones she wore and putting on the new ones. She admired them in the mirror and in front of him, too. Then she handed him the gift she had bought for him, a book detailing early sheepherding on the high plains of early New Mexico.

He slipped it from the bag and gazed at it. "Thank you," he said with emotion.

She leaned over to kiss him softly. They drew apart and searched each other's eyes, each seeking answers to questions they could neither understand nor voice.

From Lawton they drove to the mountains, which, compared to the Rockies or Appalachians, were only rocky hills, covered with grass and craggy shrubs. Their magnificence lay in the way they jutted to the sky from the surrounding flat land, as if pushed there by an enormous machine. Following the winding road, they drove to the top of the highest peak, Mt. Scott. There they got out of the car and gazed out at a good deal of the state. Marnie had the sensation of being able to reach up and touch heaven, or at least one of the puffy clouds.

She drew Jesse's attention to darker clouds to the west, and he said, "Far away, yet. We've got hours more." He reached out and took her hand, a simple gesture that swelled her heart.

Once more driving in the car along the two-lane rural highway that cut through grassland and wooded areas, they searched for a picnic place. That Marnie was exceedingly particular about how tall the grass was and how much shade a tree provided made finding a good spot a little tricky, but at last a place was chosen at a graveled pull-off area complete with picnic table and trash barrel and several nice trees. Refusing the picnic table, which was covered with peeling paint, grit and unidentifiable substances, Marnie went to the tree farthest from the road and spread the blanket beneath it, while Jesse followed with the food basket and cooler.

The foods Jesse had chosen were simple and what every picnic should be made of: fried chicken, potato salad, baked beans and crisp fresh apples, with a fancy jug of cold tea and two strawberry wine coolers.

They ate, Jesse stretched out and propped up on one elbow, and Marnie with her legs curled to the side. Neither of them said much, but they looked at each other a lot. Jesse's looks made her conscious of everything about her that was female. She grew agitated both with being so very alone with him and being in so visible a place. True, they were in the country, with no farmhouse or anything in sight, and only one car passed on the road for the entire time they ate. Still, they were out in the open, in plain view for any passerby. Which was probably best, she told herself. Their situation was a good substitute for weakening willpower.

After they'd finished eating and replaced everything in the food basket, Jesse opened the wine coolers and offered a toast. "To us."

"Yes, to us," she said as he clinked his moist bottle to hers. "Mmm . . . this is good." She looked surprised.

"You never had a wine cooler before?"

She shook her head.

"Ah, darlin', there're some things equal to or better than five-hundred-dollar bottles of wine."

And she teased, "Not much." Taking up the can of bug spray, she sprayed the tree trunk.

"What are you doing?" Jesse asked.

"It's okay—this won't hurt the tree. I want to lean up against the trunk, but I don't like creepy-crawly things."

He shook his head, chuckling. "You wouldn't exactly have made the best pioneer woman."

"I never claimed to be the outdoorsy, country-girl type," she said, propping a pillow and then her back up against the tree. "I had my fill of country livin' as a kid. Give me good old clean concrete and glass any day."

"I'm sorry I dragged you on a picnic."

"Oh, I didn't mean that. Really. I'm having a very good time, Jesse."

"Me, too. . . . Mind if I lay my head in your lap?"

She patted her thigh and smiled a welcome. Grabbing up an apple, he propped his head against her and took his pocket knife, cutting the apple into thin slices. He held one up to her. She bent her head and took it with her teeth. She ate that piece, and he ate several, then offered her another, feeding it to her slowly, all the while watching her with heat in his luminous eyes.

Once more looking at the apple he sliced, he said, "I was wonderin'."

"What?"

"If we should indulge in a little neckin'."

Her breath caught in her throat. She swallowed as desire swirled deep in her abdomen.

He said, "And I imagine you've been thinkin' about it, too."

"I was wonderin' why you hadn't made a pass."

His eyes flicked up to hers. "You could have made the pass," he said with a slow grin.

"I considered it and came to the decision to leave it up to you."

"Why heap it all on me? You were the one who accused me of being a male chauvinist."

"You were the one who told me you were an up-front kind of man."

"True...and I am." He nodded thoughtfully, tossed the apple core away and stabbed his knife in the ground to clean it before folding it away. He muttered, "That's why this has all gotten so complicated. I'll have to think about this." He closed his eyes.

Hesitant at first, she gently stroked wisps of hair from his forehead. His skin was warm and damp, as was the air around them. Again and again she caressed his forehead and down his temples, savoring the sight of him.

*She was falling in love with him.* Her heart constricted with the thought.

"There's nothin' like a woman's touch," he said, eyes remaining closed as he turned his head against her fingertips.

Pushing aside thoughts of love, she gazed down at him, noting the lines from his eyes, the hard, rugged look of him, so in contrast with the inner man she knew. His warmth seeped through the thin cotton of her skirt to the juncture of her thighs. Her gaze moved to his lips.

As if he'd heard her thoughts, his eyes flew open. They were bright, hypnotic. "It's a hard job," he murmured, "but since you won't do it, I will." Pushing upward, he slipped a hand to the back of her neck. His eyes glazed and his lids lowered heavily as his lips parted beneath his mustache.

He kissed her deeply, strongly and with purpose. Her heart leapt to her throat, and she responded, opening for him, savoring him. In a swift, rough movement, he sat up and pulled her across his lap. His eyes ate her up.

"So," he said huskily, "what do you think? Should we do a little neckin'?"

"I..."

"Think about it while I kiss you again."

And kiss her he did, as she'd never before been kissed. Desire flashed like heat lightning through her. They kissed again, frantic and fierce, her hands in his hair, his rubbing her back.

"I take that as a yes," he murmured, pulling away and holding her to him, rubbing his rough cheek against hers.

"Yes," she said breathlessly.

The first burst of fire seemed to take the edge off the hot, gnawing hunger. Marnie melted against him, and his hold relaxed. Drawing away, he gazed at her. Holding her with his eyes, he placed a hand lightly on her breast, then drew circles over the nipple with his thumb. She pressed her legs together and bit her bottom lip, enduring the bittersweetness of it. Closing her eyes to his hypnotic gaze, she kissed him, softly parting his lips, feeling the tickling sensation of his mustache.

Their movements became seductive now, sultry as the afternoon air. As frustrating as the restriction of being in full view of the world was, it also gave them security. There were no choices to be made over what they should and should not do. They couldn't possibly have sex, and that gave them wonderful freedom to think of it, to gaze longingly into each other's eyes, to touch, to *feel* the heavenly sweetness that was both ecstasy and misery.

Jesse buried his face in her neck, and she did likewise into his, inhaling the maleness of him. It mattered not at all that layers of fabric separated them. Their touches had the same effect as if they were naked. And there were ways around and under clothes. His hand came up under her loosened blouse and very tenderly kneaded her breasts through her thin lace bra. Her nerve endings screamed.

"Oh, Jesse..." she moaned, stretching her legs, trying to ease the ache between them. The richness of his passion astonished her, as did the rock hardness of his muscles. She couldn't get enough of the way his muscles felt, nor of the way he smelled, like sunshine and heat and lightning. Their kisses became hot and wet, and they pressed tighter and tighter, the tension building into painful frustration, bringing Marnie to tears.

Then, suddenly, Jesse lifted his mouth from hers and hugged her to him. She trembled as she listened to his heartbeat pounding in her ear. Body aching unbearably, she wrapped her arms around him and held on for dear life. They clung to each other, as if fearful of being swept away by their overwhelming desire.

Jesse felt caught in a tornado. His feelings were taking him to places he'd had no intention of going. *Lord, he couldn't recall ever feeling this for a woman!*

Lust for her was one thing, but he'd suddenly realized that what he felt for Marnie was far beyond any simple lusting. He *cared* for her, and that scared the hell out of him. His conscience and fears did battle with his desire as he raised a hand to softly stroke her silky, fragrant hair. And he held on to her, kept her face pressed into his shoulder, for fear of looking into her eyes. Of having her look into his and know the confusion inside him.

Then he felt her suck in a trembling breath. She was crying. He pulled away to look at her, and she averted her face and blinked rapidly.

"I'd forgotten the price paid for heavy petting," she said, a note of strain in her voice while she flashed him a smile. A tear trickled down her cheek.

"Yeah. Me, too." He fumbled around to find one of the cloth napkins and grabbed to turn her face to him.

"Don't you dare spit on that."

"I'm not. Here..." He dried her eyes and wiped at the mascara smudges beneath them. He looked again into her eyes, and it was all he could do not to kiss her again. "You are a beautiful woman."

Her expression dropped and a great sadness seeped into her eyes. "Is that all this is? That I'm beautiful?"

He shook his head. "No. It's not. I want you, Marnie. All of you, and I have a feelin' you could have a crooked nose and warts and I still would." Her expression lifted. "But I'm not in a position to offer you any more than this day and tomorrow."

She searched his eyes. "I didn't ask you to," she said softly.

She was offering herself with no strings attached. And that told him a lot, because Marnie wasn't a woman to do that without caring a lot. He gazed into her sky-blue eyes and thought of taking her to a motel, of laying her down in a bed and loving her until neither of them could move. She sat there waiting for him to ask.

A gust of cool wind tugged at his hair, and he said, "We'd better be gettin' back to the city. Looks like it could rain."

Turning from him, she nodded.

As Jesse packed their things back into the car, he cursed himself for a damn fool. The most foolish thing was getting himself in this predicament in the first place. He couldn't say why he couldn't ask Marnie to go to a motel. He just couldn't, for a thousand and one reasons that probably wouldn't amount to a hill of cow chips a year or ten years from now. But they did matter very much this day.

It wasn't until after they'd started north down the road that either of them realized they hadn't put the top up.

"It'll probably just blow over," Marnie said of the approaching clouds. "We can always stop and put up the top if it starts to sprinkle." She hadn't put her hat back on, and her hair blew in the wind, beautifully, sexily.

Jesse looked ahead and watched the black road disappear beneath the car. He was speeding, trying to rid himself of his frustration. His mind, as if addicted, again took up the idea of making love with Marnie. He stared ahead and mulled it over. There were a lot of miles and a number of places to find a motel between here and Oklahoma City.

Marnie gazed at the surrounding pristine grassland and plowed fields, miles and miles of nothing, rarely even a farmhouse. The emptiness held a certain raw beauty. She glanced surreptitiously at Jesse; he gazed straight ahead. His jawline was tight, as if he were angry. She sensed he'd withdrawn from her, and that caused the ache inside her to double. Was he angry at the circumstances, or at her? He'd wanted her, she knew. Why hadn't he asked her to go to a motel? *You could ask him, if you're so brazen.* No, she wouldn't do that, because this was for the best. Whether he were being gallant and wise, or simply irritated with her, he was correct in refraining from giving in to foolish desire, she told herself and tried to be content. And she thought how every minute brought them closer to Oklahoma City.

*Look at the moment. Just look at the moment, and don't ask for more.*

Two big raindrops splattered on the windshield. Jesse glanced at her. Two more hit. Splatters covered the windshield as Jesse quickly slowed the car. Then, before the car came to a full stop, rain fell in the biggest torrent since the Great Flood; lightning was flashing and thunder rumbling.

"Stay here and push that button when I tell you," Marnie cried as she jumped out.

In a blur of swift motion, ducking her head against the driving rain, she jerked off a side plastic panel and ran around to the driver's side to take off another. Lightning flashed very close, and she screamed as she flipped open the compartment where the soft top was stored. Praying not to be struck by lightning, she grabbed the top and pulled it easily to cover the car. The procedure took only seconds.

"Push the button," she called to Jesse and ran back around to flop into the wet, slippery seat, slamming the door and pressing the button for the door window.

She looked up to see the top open, buffeting in the wind.

"Push the button!" she yelled at Jesse.

"I'm pushin' the damn button!" he yelled back. "Nothin's happening."

"Oh, for heaven's sake!" Frantically Marnie leaned over him and pressed the button.

Still nothing happened. The top sat there as if dead, while rain sprayed through the small opening, soaking her Italian leather and electronic everything.

"It's supposed to close and lock!" Marnie cried, looking helplessly at Jesse.

"We can't go anywhere with it like this," he said, raising his voice over the rain.

"My other one never did this!" she wailed.

The rain eased, and she gazed out, hopeful for a miracle. But lightning crashed again, and then there came a pinging sound. There, before her eyes, white balls bounced on the windshield and the shiny, water-beaded hood.

"Jesse! It's *hailing!*"

He opened his door to get out.

Panicking, she grabbed his arm. "You can't get out. You'll get killed!"

He shook her off. "We've got to put the top back down!"

And in amazement she watched him jump out and push the top back into its compartment, letting hail pound down upon her and her beautiful car.

He jumped back behind the wheel, started the engine, and took off as if driving the Indianapolis 500, with marble-size ice balls pelting them with a vengeance.

## Chapter Ten

Ducking his hat against the stinging hail, Jesse spun the wheel, barely letting up on the gas as he made the turn into a road leading off into a pasture. The car handled unbelievably, effortlessly, totally in control, never losing traction, not even squealing the tires. It was, after all, fifty-six-thousand-dollars' worth of the best in vehicle engineering—which was being beaten relentlessly by hailstones and rain from above and a rutted farm road from below. It ran over that bumpy dirt road as easily as it had the smooth paved one, and in less than a minute and a half—a very *long* minute and a half—he pulled it to a stop in the shelter of a weathered tin hay barn. He gave hearty thanks that there was room in the middle of the tall stacks of hay bales.

Relaxing his grip on the steering wheel, Jesse took a deep breath and turned off the engine. Hail pattered on the tin roof far above, but the sound was buffered considerably by the hundreds of bales of hay. He looked at Marnie. Slowly lowering her hands from covering her head, she looked back at him. Her eyes were like stormy blue splotches of paint on a white plate. Her hair dribbled down around her face and onto her blouse, which clung to her skin. One lone drop of water ran down her nose. The term *drowned rat* was apt.

They both broke out in laughter.

"Oh, Jesse!"

"Ooo-weee! I do like this car, darlin'. Did you see how it handled on that wet road? And it was no slouch on that dirt one, either."

"Was that a road? I thought it was a cow path."

"That, too."

She twisted, gazed out the barn opening and gasped. "Oh, my, Jesse, look at it."

He looked around to see the hail coming down about like a blizzard.

"I've never seen it fall like that," she said with wonder.

"I saw it fall three inches thick once," Jesse said. "Back at the ranch. We had to shovel it away from the porch and the barns. Clean knocked out one of Rory's horses."

They watched another minute, until the hail gave way to rain, changing from the chiming to a dull roar on the tin roof and falling so thick that it was hard to see the fence posts or the road. Jesse glanced around the barn—weathered and nothing fancy, but it was sturdy enough. Hay bales that still smelled of summertime, stacked twelve feet high and eight feet deep on either side, would hold the barn up even if it tried to fall down.

He looked back at Marnie to see her peering into the mirror on the visor. "Oh, my heaven...." Looking downward, she brushed away hailstones and lifted her skirt with two fingers. "Ewwwuuuu." Then she looked around at the car, and her shoulders slumped.

"This car's a lot tougher than a little rain and hail, darlin'. It'll get dried out and be good as new."

"My camera!" They found it safely tucked back into the pass-through to the trunk.

They got out of the car. Jesse took off his hat, and hailstones fell off the brim. He shook his jeans free from clinging to his thighs, with a modicum of success. On the opposite side of the car, Marnie was doing the same to her skirt and blouse. His gaze lingered on her. Every curve was now perfectly visible, calling attention to what he already knew—that she wore a little nothing bra and scrap of panty and that was all beneath her skirt and blouse. Clamping his jaw, he thought that the Fates were conspiring against his good intentions. Here he was again, alone with her and his desires and willpower that was growing about as weak as a cheap battery left on for eight straight hours.

He walked to the wide opening and gazed out. Marnie came to stand beside him. The rain had lessened but showed no sign of stopping completely and fell upon a blanket of white hailstones that covered the ground to more than an inch thick.

"It's like snow," Marnie said with amazement.

And Jesse said, "But a hell of a lot harder." He crouched and reached out, scooped up a handful of the ice crystals, one as large as a golf ball. They were melting quickly with the rain, which was a good thing, because he and Marnie were going to have to drive back out as they'd driven in. Provided they could get that top latched.

Marnie pivoted and walked back to the Cadillac. She began brushing and scooping pockets of melting hailstones from the dash, the seats and the floorboard. He helped her, then got a couple of cloth napkins from the basket in the trunk to wipe away the dribbles and puddles. There were places where the leather was soaked and would take a day or more to dry completely. However, they found no damage to the car's finish other than a few very small scratches and one tiny dent.

"You were lucky, darlin'," Jesse said. "I've seen hailstones of that size break windshields and cause fist-size dents."

"I was lucky because you thought to drive in here. Thanks, Jesse."

"I'm not just another pretty face," he said, as she once had said to him.

"No... you're not at all," she agreed.

They grinned at each other, and the fire that burned ever below the surface flickered to life. The rain drummed a rhythm on the tall tin roof, and the cool breeze teased wet curls around Marnie's pale face. Drawn of its own accord, his gaze drifted downward to where the nipples of her breasts showed through her wet clothes.

Turning away to the open trunk, he pulled out his sport coat and thrust it at her. "Here. You'd better put this on before you catch pneumonia," he said, not looking at her. "And I'd better take a look at that top before it gets much darker. If this rain keeps up, night's gonna come early—and I imagine I'm correct in assumin' you don't have a flashlight?"

He glanced at her. She clutched the coat to the front of her and shook her head.

"And no tools, either?"

"Why would I need tools when I have a brand-new car?"

"Because things happen. Even a brand-new Rolls-Royce can break down," he said, frowning as he studied the latch at the top of the windshield.

"What do you think is wrong?" she asked, crowding in beside him and peering over his shoulder, making his skin tingle.

He looked over his shoulder at her. "It doesn't work."

"Oh, my, aren't you the comic," she said and stepped back.

"You haven't put this top up since you bought the car, have you?" he accused as he slipped into the driver's seat.

"Why would I have to put the top up?" she said airily, walking away. "The only time it's rained, the car has been parked in my private garage at the hotel. Don't look."

"What?" He looked up to see she'd moved into the shadows beyond the car.

"I said don't look. I want to take this wet blouse off. If I don't, I'll just get your coat all wet. Oooo—there are some big leaks in this roof."

"Hmm." He focused on the floor and felt up beneath the dash, muttering, "Don't bother to put up the top for such a simple reason as to make certain it works." He imagined her full, ripe breasts and again clenched his jaw.

"I heard that. And everything was checked out at the dealer's. There was no reason for me to do it."

"Don't ever trust others to do what you should do yourself."

"You have that right. The only time I get into trouble is when I trust other people."

He heard the point aimed at him and struck back sharply. "It wasn't trustin' other people that got us into this fix. It was not allowin' that cars and the parts that go into makin' 'em are put together by fallible human beings. Even the best new vehicles can have little problems. Just things that get overlooked. Anybody with common sense knows to test everything everyday or so at first in order to prevent times just like the one we're havin'."

"Well, it's plain to see that I don't have any common sense, or I wouldn't have come out on this rural excursion in the first place," she said with drippy sarcasm as she came back along the opposite side of the car. "It's all my stupid fault. Does that make you happy?"

Jesse spared her a glance, enough to see her spread her wet blouse and scrap of bra over the side of the door and that his coat dwarfed her and would have showed everything had she not held it wrapped around her. "I wasn't placin' blame, darlin'," he said, with patent patience, moving out of the car again and thinking it was just like a woman to tie a man's words in knots. "I was just talkin' sense. And if you hadn't wanted to come, all you had to do was say no." And he knew she'd wanted to come, so she might as well not complain. Of course, women tended to overlook such logical things.

Getting on his knees outside the door, he twisted and wriggled into a position where he could look up into the wires and connections underneath the dashboard.

Stretching over the door to jerk her purse from the pass-through area, Marnie dug her brush from the bag. She again turned her back to Jesse so she could let go of the front of the coat and use both hands. She bent forward, shook out her hair and brushed. Jesse's scent wafted up from his coat, and she paused, feeling something odd flow over her. Angry at the feeling and at Jesse, she brushed with a vengeance. It was just like a man to make a big deal about knowing the perfect way to do everything. Must be a part of their genes. She never would have thought it of Jesse, but he was, after all, a man. *A hell of a man.*

Straightening, she tossed back her damp hair and threw her brush into the car. Then she remembered to pull the coat closed. She hoped Jesse hadn't noticed and tried buttoning it, which would suffice if she didn't make any hasty moves.

She breathed deeply of the scent of fresh, fragrant hay and damp rain and thought, for an instant, that being there wasn't so bad. It was quite romantic, or it could be. It was silly—their arguing.

Determined to smooth things over, she went around to the driver's side, where Jesse still had his head buried underneath the dashboard. Curious, she crouched beside his extended legs.

"What are you lookin' at?" she asked.

He jumped and banged his head. "Damn it!" He tucked his chin and glared at her.

"I'm sorry. I didn't sneak." His glare rankled, and she added, "Who did you think I was, anyway—a burglar joinin' us in this barn?"

He glared at her again. "I need a flashlight," he stated, his voice full of accusation; then he looked dreary. "I don't suppose you have matches?"

"I don't smoke," she said. "And why don't you have any of these things you keep askin' me for?"

"Because it's not my vehicle," he said acidly. "If we'd brought my truck, I'd have it all—plus a solid roof."

She straightened as if smacked. "Well, fine! Hindsight is always twenty-twenty!" She gestured wildly. "If we'd brought your truck, we wouldn't be stuck here in this stupid barn—but I wouldn't be here at all if I hadn't made the stupid mistake of goin' off with *you!*"

"Turn on the interior lights," he snapped.

She stood there and stared at his chest. "Why?" Why should she do anything for him? "What are you doin' under there? This isn't just any ol' car, you know. Maybe we should wait and get a certified mechanic."

He rose up and smacked his head a second time, then tucked his chin again and gave her a look that would have withered artificial flowers. "Just where do you suppose we'll get a *certified* mechanic?"

He had a point, and she cursed the fact she hadn't gotten a telephone in the car yet.

"I've been fixin' cars since you were in diapers. Now, turn on the lights."

She bent forward the switch and hesitated. "What are you doin'?"

"Checkin' fuses. I need some light to see these labels."

"Maybe you need glasses."

"That, too, but they're back at my truck, just like everything else. Just turn on the damn lights."

"Is it safe? You are all wet, you know, and aren't fuses electrical things?"

"Yes, ma'am. I know I'm wet—and I do happen to know what I'm doin'," he said impatiently. "Turn the lights on, *please*. I'd like to get out of here sometime tonight."

"Okay." With a nagging worry, she turned on the interior lights and saw that a little glow did indeed shine underneath.

Silence for two seconds, and then he murmured, "There it is." The next instant came, "Yeooww!" He jumped, cursing and bumping his head.

"Jesse! Are you all right?"

He wiggled out and sat up in the seat, shaking his fingers and blowing on them.

"Oh, I just knew somethin' would happen. Let me see."

"It's nothin'. I just got a little shock." He refused to show his fingers.

She said, "You have a scrape on your forehead."

He found himself staring down at her two full and swinging breasts, clearly visible with her bending and the coat gaping a mile. He couldn't stop looking, while what happened inside him was a repeat of the electrical shock. She jerked upward and clutched the coat together. Then he was gazing into her eyes. They were as dark as the storm clouds.

She jutted her chin. "You told me to turn on the lights."

"I know that." Guilt swept over him, and he stood, moving back to the compartment holding the top. "I'm sorry for snappin' at you." He fairly growled the words and didn't face her.

"Why in the world *are* we fightin', Jesse?" she asked after a moment. "I'm sorry the top didn't work, but it really wasn't my fault—and I thought we'd had fun today."

He sighed deeply, turned slowly. "It doesn't have a single thing to do with this car." He paused and looked her in the eye.

"It has to do with bein' all alone in this barn with you, and you bein' naked underneath my coat, and me bein' sixteen years older than you and goin' back home in another day."

Understanding dawned in her eyes and she looked away. Silence hung there between them, and he realized that the roar of the rain on the roof had ceased. A glance out the door and he saw a fine mist falling.

"Let's give this thing a try now," he said, flipping open the compartment. "I traded fuses. Won't be able to use the air conditioner, but we should be able to lock this top in place."

Without a word she passed him and disappeared behind the open trunk lid. Jesse ground his teeth and stood there. Then he pulled up the top and stretched it out. He slipped into the driver's seat and pressed the button. With a whispering whir, the top moved and locked into place. The car was now ready to head out on the road, back to Oklahoma City and the Vinsand Plaza Hotel.

He sat there for long seconds. He heard movement, the whispering of footsteps in hay, and wondered what she was doing. Maybe she had gone between the bales for some necessary privacy. He hoped she didn't come upon a snake. He thought of how she looked in his coat and of how they were alone, here and now. If she ran into a snake, it would give him a good reason to take her into his arms.

When total silence had lasted for a curious while, he rose and went around to the trunk. She wasn't there. His gaze traveled quickly to where she sat, five feet away, on the quilt that was spread over remnants of dry hay left behind when bales had been removed. Warmth bloomed in his gut and shimmied up his chest.

"There's quite a bit of food left," she said. "We could have a snack before we leave."

Their gazes held, and then hers skittered away. Bright splotches appeared on her cheeks.

"Yes . . . we could," Jesse said. He breathed deeply, raked a hand through his hair and turned his back to her. He thought how he was years older than her—but not *that* many years— and of how she had a life with Vinsand and he had one back on a New Mexico ranch.

Then he turned slowly and walked across to stop at the edge of the blanket. She stared at his boots, while he stared at her silky hair.

Pulling at his damp denim jeans to ease them, he sat and scooted his back up against a hay bale. They sat there, neither of them opening the food basket. Jesse plucked a stem of hay and played with it while he regarded her. Her hair was drying and curled femininely. His coat hung from her shoulders, nearly covering her hands, baring her chest to a deep V between the swells of her breasts. She looked up at him, her eyes questioning. Desire thrummed through him like a steady breeze across tall grass.

He said, "Do you use the Pill? I have . . ."

She nodded, and a faint knowing smile lit her lips. He knew she'd guessed he'd been about to admit to having a condom. "I'm on the Pill," she said. Again her gaze flickered shyly downward, then back up to his. "Patrick is the only one I've slept with in fifteen years."

Her words took his breath. She was reassuring him. *She'd only been with Vinsand for six years . . . and before that—no one for all those years?*

He reached for her hand, rubbed his callused thumb across her satiny skin. "I slept with the same woman for the past five years. And since we parted company last New Year's Day, I haven't slept with any woman."

Her eyes were deep and haunting and set him on fire.

He tugged gently, and she came to him. Holding her gaze with his own, he gently laid her down on the quilt and stretched out above her, just barely brushing her body with his. Hay rustled beneath the quilt; its summer-air scent came to him mingled with her womanly perfume.

"You made us a soft bed," he said, a smile surging from deep within.

"Yes. . . ." she replied in a bare, breathless whisper.

She gazed at him, waiting. He slowly slipped a trembling hand beneath her hair to the creamy satin skin of her neck. He drew circles with his thumb, watched the desire fill her eyes and felt it in the tensing of her body. Savored the sweet throbbing in his groin.

And the fear rose, too. The one he'd refused to acknowledge within himself, the one he certainly couldn't voice, and was, after all his practical, high ideals, the true reason he'd hesitated: that he was over fifty and hadn't been with a woman in almost nine months. *What if he'd lost it? What if he couldn't fulfill her?*

He cared very much about fulfilling this woman. He wanted to please her. He wanted to be her hero.

"Oh, Jesse." She breathed his name like a whisper in the wind and pressed against him. *"Please hold me."*

He heard the need in her voice, saw the shadows of self-conscious embarrassment in her eyes, and his heart reached for her. Wrapping his arms around her, he pulled her hard against him, buried his face in her fragrant hair. "Oh, darlin', I could live and breathe to hold you."

As she melted against him, her need went to the core of him, a need that was far greater than the physical. Tenderly he curved his hand to her delicate skull and stroked her hair. He ran his other hand up and down her back, massaging, savoring the feel and scent of her. The *essence* of her. His fear evaporated in the heat of rising desire and a sense that not only did he need her, she needed him. And he knew he had it in him to give her what a younger man would not, could not.

He pulled back enough to find her lips with his, kissing her and fumbling to find the buttons of his coat. She moaned into his mouth and sent excitement pounding through him. He sought to temper it, because he intended to take her with him to the moon and the stars. The coat fell open. Slowly he pressed his palm against her bare skin and watched her reaction. She froze, and he caught a glimpse of her eyes, glazed with passion, as he bent his head and put his mouth to the swell of her breast. He wet her breasts with his kisses. She trembled and twisted, pressed against him and pulled at his shirt to free it from his pants. He was so intent upon her, he didn't realize she'd gotten his shirt unbuttoned until her hand touched his chest. He swelled painfully.

Sitting up, he pulled her with him and slipped his coat from her shoulders. He gazed at her and swallowed, tightening all over. He'd never seen skin so milky white. He rubbed the backs of his knuckles just above one nipple and watched her chest move with rapid pants. Her skin was warm as fresh milk and her lips moist, her eyes wanting.

She reached out and pushed his shirt from his shoulders, and he helped remove it when, damp, it stuck to his skin.

"Oh, Jesse..." Her voice trailed off as she regarded him with wide-eyed appreciation.

Feeling a giant of a man, Jesse grinned and whispered, "You, too, darlin'," as he unbuckled and unzipped his jeans.

Foolishly embarrassed, Marnie turned her back and fumbled with the buttons on her wet skirt. Her fingers didn't seem to want to work, and she wasn't truly seeing the buttons but his powerfully built body. It had been a long time since she had been intimately close with a man who did hard, physical work. She heard the faint swoosh of his jeans as he removed them, and then the rustling of the hay as he hopped, lost balance and whispered a curse.

As she unfastened the final button of her skirt, Jesse's lips came to her back. She gasped and stretched, indescribable sensations washing over her. A hand to her shoulder, he turned her to him. Her gaze fell on his magnificent chest, then swept across and downward, over his muscular body. Amazement mingled with hot desire. Upon reaching the line where his tan stopped just below his belly button, she immediately flicked her gaze back up to his face. The tender edge to his rugged features brought emotion welling up and spilling all over her like a great flood.

"Jesse, I..."

With fire in his eyes, he reached out and stopped her words with a hard, demanding kiss that went on and on, wonderfully, druggingly. And then she was pressed flush against him, against those hard, swelling and sweating muscles. Her flesh against his, her breasts fitting against his, her belly to his, her legs entangled with his. Caressing and rubbing and stroking, with sighs and moans and gasps. Now there were no thoughts of stopping, of what should or shouldn't be. There were only two people loving each other with their hearts and their bodies.

Consumed by passion, they moved together quicker than either had planned. At the last second, getting a feeble grip on himself, Jesse gentled as he slipped inside her. He peppered her face with kisses and listened to her body's response, testing, growing, heating. Then they moved in rhythm, until, in a burst as bright and hot as the lightning and liquid as the rain, they melded and pooled into each other.

For heart-stopping seconds the white glow of passion lingered as they held to each other. The cool, damp breeze wafted over their hot, damp bodies. Jesse held her, kissed her temple and tasted salty tears.

"Shush, darlin'...."

He kissed her eyelids, the corners of her mouth and her temple again, and savored her fingertips stroking his back.

She heard and felt the pounding of his heart against hers. *I love you, Jesse.* She spoke silently, moving her mouth against his shoulder as she drifted back from the ethereal glow. She could not tell him. He wouldn't want to hear. But she would not deny her heart the satisfaction of saying it as it wished.

With a soft, sensual grunt, Jesse moved and rolled to his side, taking her with him. He held her tightly with one arm, pulled back and brushed the hair from her face. "Oh, darlin', my darlin'," he said in a husky whisper, "you just took me to heaven."

"Did I?" she whispered and dared to gaze up into his shining eyes.

"Oh, yes." He grinned, and a wondrously satisfied glimmer lit his eyes.

She smiled. "I think you gave me wings."

"Well, I tried to give you somethin'." With a throaty chuckle, he wrapped his arms around her and hugged her with such happiness that grateful tears sprang into her eyes. *He was happy with her.* She pressed her cheek to his sleek, hard chest and inhaled the scent of him, hoping to etch it into her memory. He continued to hold her, she to lie in the warm comfort of the strongest arms she'd ever felt, for a long time, while rain again began drumming on the roof and gray light slipped into night black.

* * *

Jesse seemed to have no trouble finding his clothes and putting them on in the dark. Marnie didn't find it as easy. Slipping away to the car, Jesse turned on the headlights, and the glow reflected through the barn enough for her to find her things and put them on straight. Just as she was slipping into his sport coat, her blouse and bra came flying through the air at her.

"Thank you," she called to him in a loud whisper, amused and touched that he gallantly kept his back turned to her.

"You're welcome. Why are we whisperin'?"

"So we won't wake the mice."

Quickly, like two mischievous children trying to cover their tracks, they stowed the blanket and food basket in the trunk. They kept grinning at each other. He took her hand, and helped her into the car and bent to kiss her before closing the door.

He drove down the road, away from the barn, more carefully than when he'd come in. The car slipped and slid, and there came the thudding of flying mud. Marnie held her breath for fear of getting stuck.

Jesse's confident grin flashed in the silvery glow of the dash lights. "You're gonna have to scrape mud from this fancy car, but it sure as hell is no slouch on any road."

"Maybe you should trade your truck in on one."

"Can't quite see this ol' sheep rancher drivin' one of these out in my neck of the woods—nor payin' for one, either."

And she thought how far away his neck of the woods was, and that soon he would be gone from her.

They came to the paved county road, and he turned north, pressing the accelerator and sending them racing away. They fishtailed on lingering hail, and he flashed her another grin, took her hand and held it on his thigh, then focused straight ahead.

Marnie listened to the faint swooshing of the windshield wipers and looked through her reflection in the side glass to the black all around her. Her heart constricted. She wished she could hold on to the night, wished they could go back to the barn and suspend time. The memories started already—the feel of his callused hand upon her breast...his kiss...his scent...his magnificent muscles. The way he made her feel as no man ever had....

Jesse spoke and tore her away from her thoughts.

"What?" she asked.

"I said I could use a shower. What about you?"

She sighed. "Yes . . . and a shampoo and dry everything."

"Want to spend the night in Chickasha?" He glanced at her. His expression remained noncommittal, but his hand tightened around hers.

"Yes. Very much."

They smiled at each other. He winked. "I'll buy you a steak dinner."

"Let's just bring hamburgers in," she said.

They got a room at a nice reliable motel that was part of a huge national chain. The car had to stay out in the open, but Marnie wasn't worried. "It could hail, but there shouldn't be any theft problem here in Chickasha, America."

Their room was clean and done in blond oak veneer, with brown-and-gold plaid fabric everywhere and generic prints above both double beds. Marnie called first dibs on the shower, and Jesse went to get their hamburgers.

She was delighted to find a tray of toiletries—facial soap, body lotion, shampoo, rinse, toothbrushes and toothpaste— sitting on the bathroom vanity. When Jesse returned, she was wonderfully clean and lotioned, scented with White Shoulders from a bottle in her purse, and wrapped in a giant bath towel and sitting on one bed, watching an old John Wayne movie on cable TV.

"Don't you look comfortable?" he said and tossed the bags he carried onto the table by the window.

Inhaling the aroma of hamburgers and French fries, Marnie hopped up and dived for the bags. "I'm starvin'!"

"So am I." Jesse grabbed her, pulled her against him, nuzzled her neck and tried to remove her towel. "And don't you smell good!"

She playfully slapped him. "Oh, no, you don't. A shower is greatly required." And she shoved him toward the bathroom. After he'd disappeared, she dug out the French fries and hurriedly ate several, then went to pick up the shirt that he'd thrown onto the floor outside the bathroom and hung it beside her own in the closet. She shook her head at the sorry wrinkled state of their clothes. A couple more French fries, and she turned down the covers, took two pillows from the second bed and fluffed all four on the turned-down bed.

When Jesse, wearing his jeans with the waist button undone, stepped out of the bathroom, he looked at the floor. "Where'd my shirt go?"

"I hung it up. I'm sorry—did you want it?"

Walking forward across the room, rubbing a towel on his hair, he shook his head. "I was gonna hang it." He paused when he noticed the bed. "That's nice." He took a second look, then smiled at her. "That's *very* nice."

Marnie blushed with pleasure.

He sat in the chair across the tiny, wobbly table from her and they dug into their hamburgers. Marnie thanked him for getting her a vanilla shake, too, and he commented on how she'd set their food out nicely.

He said thoughtfully, "When men live for so long without a woman's touch, like my sons and I did, we sure do appreciate when we have it."

The offhand comment that he needed a good wife came to the tip of her tongue, but she held it in the nick of time. She didn't want him to misconstrue, didn't want him to think she was hinting about herself. But the foolish fantasy of being his wife lodged in her mind, though she scolded herself severely.

They snuggled together in the dark room beneath the cool, crisp sheets, Jesse with his head on two fluffy pillows, Marnie with her head in the curve of his shoulder. Their bodies were cleanly smooth and fragrant, and to move against each other without sticking was heavenly. His pulse beat in her ear. She felt the powerful movement of the muscles of his arm beneath her neck and down her back as his hand caressed her, moving in a rhythmic pattern, sensitizing her nerve endings. With her fingertips she drew the same pattern on his hard chest. Slowly, sweetly, desire, like the misty rain outside, grew and swirled around them and through them.

When both of them were trembling, they turned, and hands sought flesh; lips sought lips; body sought body. Two lonely hearts and souls seeking intimate alliance. This time they made love leisurely, exploring each other's bodies, discovering with hands and lips every delicate sensitive area. Discovering the texture of each other. They entwined, caressed and rubbed. Chuckled and sighed and moaned, wet each other with kisses and dried with each other's skin. When, at last, they climaxed, it was a fine and glorious thing.

And when Marnie, languid as a cat lying on a hearth, lay with Jesse curled around her, she knew she had never been so loved in all her life.

A long time later she gazed into the dark. Jesse slept, his warm breath brushing her back, the fronts of his thighs heating the backs of hers. Only then, when she knew he was deeply asleep, did she dare whisper, "I love you, Jesse." Content to have said it, she, too, drifted off to sleep. And Jesse held her all night long.

"What shall we do with the rest of today?" Jesse asked, gazing at Marnie across the table in the motel coffee shop, where they were having a late breakfast.

She was beautiful, with a happy, satisfied light in her deep blue eyes. It made him feel shamefully proud to know he'd been the one to put that light there.

Holding up her coffee cup with both hands, she gave him that potent sultry look. "Oh . . . I can think of a few things."

"We can *try* to do that again, certainly," he replied in a low voice. "I'm always willin'."

They had awoken early and made love again—much slower and with less fire, but there had certainly been nothing poor in it, Jesse thought. He felt a rich, satisfied, grateful man. He felt reborn and credited Marnie with bringing about the miracle. They gazed long and warmly at each other across the table.

"You know what I'd really like to do?" she said shyly.

"What?"

"I'd like to go back to the fair again. I'd like to ride the Ferris wheel once more. With you."

"You got it, darlin'," he said, pleased to give her anything she desired.

Out in the lobby, Marnie paused. "I should check in with Dorothy at the hotel."

"Sure. I'll bring the car around front."

Using the pay phone in a corner, she called her apartment number first, wondering if Patrick had telephoned while she'd been gone. She punched in the numbers to play back her answering machine. After a beep, Patrick's voice came across the line.

"Sorry I missed you, baby. It's about eight. We're leaving for a late dinner, so I'll be out of touch. You can call me in the morning at that number I gave Dorothy. Things are on schedule, and I'll be home Sunday morning. See you then."

There came another beep and then quiet whirring. Patrick's was the only message.

She pressed the disconnect button, and her finger lingered there while she thought that Patrick hadn't appeared the least bit perturbed that she hadn't been home. She wondered if he'd noticed it was the first time he'd telephoned at night that she hadn't been there.

Coming to life, she dialed Dorothy, then quickly pressed the switch hook, cutting off the call. It was Saturday; Dorothy wouldn't be at work. Besides, neither Dorothy nor Og would even have known she was out all night. And Tacita didn't work weekends.

No one in the world would miss or worry about her.

Jesse was leaning against the car, with the passenger door open, when she came out. "Your chariot awaits," he said merrily.

He took her hand to assist her into the seat, then bent to kiss her before slamming the door. She thought how she was getting used to this.

When he got behind the wheel, she said adamantly, "The first thing we have to do is buy fresh, clean clothes."

## Chapter Eleven

Jesse pulled into a parking space on Chickasha Avenue, and they parted company—Marnie going into a women's shop, while Jesse headed across the street to a Western-wear store.

Forty-five minutes later, wearing stiff new jeans and a crisp shirt in an Indian print of yellow, turquoise and brown, his boots shined and hat cleaned, Jesse was leaning up against the Cadillac when Marnie came sashaying down the sidewalk, swinging a shopping bag. She had fastened her curls back from her face, and she wore a fluid peach-colored, long-sleeved blouse, belted at her waist by colorful cords woven together, over a soft flowing, brown skirt. The shape of her legs showed with each step.

"Ooo-weee." He swept his hat from his head. "May I offer the most beautiful woman in the world a ride?"

She came to a stop an inch from his chest, tilted her head upward and smiled sexily. "Oh, I don't know. What are you offerin'?"

"A trip to the fair." He gazed into her eyes and, unbelievably, felt rising desire again.

"Then I'm comin'—and with the handsomest man in the state." Laughing, she threw her arms around his neck, hugging him. "You look wonderful in that shirt."

He ran his hands up and down her back. "Where in the world did you manage to find silk in this town?"

She chuckled and went around to get into the car. "This woman can smell silk a mile away."

"And you look damn good in it, too," he said huskily.

They drove away, the top down, the sun shining on them, the wind in their hair. Jesse holding Marnie's hand atop his thigh. Neither allowed themselves to think of the time slipping rapidly away.

They went again to the fair. They saw paint horses perform, watched draft horses pull, enjoyed the pig races again. They ate pizza, cotton candy and corn dogs—and Jesse wiped Marnie's cheek, though she'd figured out by now that she didn't have mustard there; he just liked touching her, and she him. She wanted to impress upon her fingers the memory of him.

They watched square dancers and country-and-western singers, and they danced some, too. They road the carousel three times and the Ferris wheel twice. Marnie held tightly to Jesse the entire time on the Ferris wheel. She would never ride another, because she couldn't imagine doing so without him. And Jesse knew he could never ride another one again without thinking of her.

They played darts, the ring toss and the target game. Jesse won Marnie another stuffed bear, and she won him a monkey on a string. They tried their hand at spinning rabbit hair into yarn, watched a glassblower and perused the photography exhibit.

"You should have entered some of your photographs," Jesse told her.

Marnie shrugged and laughed.

"I'm serious," he said. "You had some as good as these on the walls of your apartment. You're very good at it."

Pleasure so deep she could hardly bear it, washed over her. Few people had seen her photographs, no one had ever given her such high praise and she knew Jesse wouldn't have said it if he hadn't meant it. "Maybe I will enter next year," she said, looking at the photographs.

"You'd better," he said and winked. "And you'll get a blue ribbon."

Curiosity whether he would come to the fair next year flashed through her mind and made it to the tip of her tongue before she pushed it aside. Both were careful not to mention anything about tomorrow. Theirs was today, and only today.

That evening they returned to the Chinese restaurant, and Mr. Charlie greeted them with excited pleasure, beer for Jesse and wine for Marnie. When their fortune cookies came at the end of their meal, Marnie let hers lie. Jesse gazed at her for a long minute and didn't touch his, either.

After dinner they drove to a motel on the far west edge of the city to spend one last night together. They each grasped all they could from the precious time as it slipped faster and faster away.

Marnie awoke and lay in the dark in Jesse's arms. It was such a pleasurable experience, that she refused to go back to sleep and savored the feeling—his strong arms holding her, his hard chest rising and falling gently against her, his warmth, his scent. She would never forget his scent.

At last, very gently, she slipped from him, rose and went to peek out between the heavy draperies. Her Cadillac and his big red truck sat side by side in front of the room, gleaming in the yellow porch lights. It was the deep dark just before dawn. Marnie thought of Atlanta, where Patrick was. It was dawn in Atlanta, and Patrick would be getting ready to return.

It was time for her to go.

The thought fell indelibly into her mind. It was time. She couldn't put it off, try to deny it or hide from it. It was best to get it over with.

Dropping the drape, she turned and gazed at Jesse's dark form in the bed, blinking as her eyes once more adjusted to the dimness. Crossing her arms across her bare breasts, she hugged herself against the pain. Her heart felt as if a sharp, huge wedge was being driven into it. Slowly, certainly, it split, soon to crack wide open.

She'd faced heartache before, she thought. She could face it again. *She just couldn't let Jesse know. She couldn't bear for him to feel guilty or pity her.* Quickly, silently, she swallowed her tears and went to the closet for her clothes.

Jesse awoke, becoming aware of his empty arms first and then hearing the rustling of movement. Light fell into the dark room through the opened bathroom door. Marnie was sitting on the end of the opposite bed.

"Marnie?"

She turned her head to him. He pushed himself up and switched on the lamp. She was dressed, holding her purse, digging into it.

"Where are you goin' so early?" But he knew.

"I have to go back to the hotel. It's Sunday."

"I know what day it is," he said and stared at her. "Were you goin' to leave without sayin' anything?"

She shook her head. "No, Jesse," she said with gentle patience that irritated the hell out of him. "I wouldn't do that. I just didn't see any need to wake you any earlier than I had to."

"Yeah," he muttered suspiciously, though he really did believe her. But he didn't want to believe her. Being angry at her made things easier.

He slung back the covers, grabbed his pants and strode to the bathroom, closing the door hard and fast. After an unsettling glance in the mirror, he bent to splash water on his face, then vigorously rubbed with a towel. He gazed into the mirror. A haggard, drawn face gazed back. It was almost a surprise, because yesterday he'd thought he'd looked pretty damn good. His eyes moved down to his body; it looked the same, hard and strong, belying his sudden weak, helpless feeling.

He didn't want to let go of this time. He didn't want to let go of *her.*

Well, the time had arrived to come down off that mesa, he thought with rank bitterness, threw down the towel and jerked on his pants. And it was going to be a hard, crashing ride. He'd known it all along, all the while he'd been being a damn fool and ignoring it.

Had he gone and fallen in love with her? He stared at the man in the mirror for an answer.

*Yes.*

He squeezed his eyes tightly, wincing in every cell. Oh, Lord, this was a hell of a mess. Sixteen years and two entirely different life-styles separated them. Things that could be overlooked for five magical days plucked from reality but not for the mundane everyday of forever. ·

He was an old buckaroo who didn't want to be attached to anyone. No, sir, he didn't want to be married! That just took more than he had to give anymore. He didn't want to have to worry about someone else's feelings, didn't want a woman depending on him, or to begin depending on her. He didn't want to have to consider how another person liked her coffee or her meat, or to have to make room for a woman's things in his bathroom. He wanted to come and go as he wished and answer to no one. He didn't have the energy for anything more.

And any thought of marriage was stupid, anyway, because she belonged to Vinsand and the city and credit cards and Cadillacs and silks and a different generation. Not only did she dislike the country, she *hated* it, and as far as Jesse could see, she wasn't very fond of marriage, either.

With a deep breath, he went out to get it over with. She was standing beside the outside door. Beyond her, he saw the eastern sky turning pink.

They gazed at each other, each trying for a smile.

"No time for breakfast?" Jesse asked, forcing a lightness into his voice as he sat to put on his socks and boots. It seemed a silly thing to do at that moment, but he couldn't go through all this without being fully dressed.

She shook her head. "I'd like to get in without anyone seeing me. And I have things to do before ... Patrick arrives."

He nodded as he slipped into his shirt but didn't button it up. "Got everything?" Automatically he glanced around the room, at just what, he wasn't certain.

"Yes. I just had that bag of clothes and my purse—and the teddy. I've put it all in the car."

He walked over, propped a hand on the edge of the opened door, and again he was gazing down at her. She'd put on just a bit of makeup; she looked fresh, beautiful, he thought as he cupped her chin and ran his thumb over her cheek. *And, oh, so damn young.*

The next instant she threw herself at him, wrapping her arms around his neck. He brought his arms around her, cupped her silky head and thought he was going to shatter if he had to let her go.

"Thank you for these days, darlin'," he said, his voice squeezing past the lump in his throat. He couldn't believe, after all his years of living, that he'd been so foolish as to ignore the price that would have to be paid for his days of enjoyment.

"Thank *you*, Jesse," she replied in a husky whisper.

He sought her lips, but she pulled away and pressed her fingertips to his mouth and shook her head.

"If you start your kissin' on me, I won't be doin' anything but closing this door and jumpin' into that bed with you," she said with her practiced drawl. Her voice was ragged. Tears shimmered in her eyes, and a smile trembled on her lips.

He overrode the objection and kissed her anyway. He had to—it was the way he saw it ending. And he wanted this to be the memory he carried away with him, her all soft and warm and womanly in his arms.

Then he took her elbow and walked her the few feet out to her car. "Want to put the top down?"

"No."

They stood there, gazing at each other in the first glow of morning.

Jesse propped his hand on his belt. "Do you still have that card I gave you with my address?"

"Yes . . . back at my apartment somewhere."

He looked her in the eyes. "If you ever need anything—anything at all—you call me."

She smiled softly and touched his cheek. "And the same goes for you." Quickly she looked away, opened the door and got inside the car.

He shut the door, placed his hands on the opened window and crouched to her level. "Put your seat belt on."

She did, then sat there with her hands on the wheel.

"You drive careful," he said.

"You, too. You're goin' home to New Mexico today?"

He nodded, averted his eyes.

"Goodbye, Jesse. It's been grand."

He looked up to see her smiling wonderfully at him. It seemed like they were always saying goodbye.

"Ah, darlin', if I were just a few years younger...."

She chuckled. "'If wishes were horses, Jesse, then beggars would ride.' Take care...*darlin'*."

She started the car and shifted into gear. Jesse stepped aside, and she backed away. She waved; he did, too. Then he stood there beside the white wrought-iron post, a fresh breeze teasing the edges of his shirt against his chest, and watched the white Cadillac drive off down the road into the golden rising sun. And he felt as if all his passion, his light, went with it. With Marnie.

Slowly, with a deep, nagging ache in his bones, he went back inside and began gathering his things to head home. Seeing her again nagged at his mind, just as it had the times before when he'd told himself he was leaving her. He pushed the thoughts aside.

Crying so hard she could barely see, Marnie drove east along the interstate highway. *Oh, Lord, thank you, thank you, that I didn't cry in front of him.*

She didn't dare pull off the highway until she could stop crying, because she might never stop. She just wanted to get home to the security of her apartment. Fumbling around, she found her sunglasses, put them on against the awful glare. The sun had become a full red ball on the horizon, and she had to drive directly into it. Thankfully, it was only a fifteen-minute drive, even as slow as she was going, to the Vinsand Plaza Hotel. Upon arriving there, meeting no one, she hurried from the private garage, through the back door and up the elevator.

The quiet of the entry hall closed around her. She entered her apartment, slammed the door behind her, stood there breathing deeply while the tears streamed down her face. Impatiently she brushed them away and refused the sobs that wanted to burst from her chest. She was a big girl. She'd known all along what was going to happen in the end. Regrets, recriminations, wishes, weren't going to change a thing. And the only thing oceans of tears were going to get her were wrinkles and bags. By heaven, it was time she gave up this foolish, emotional propensity for crying!

The blinking light on her answering machine indicated that there were two calls. She pushed the button to listen and grabbed a tissue to dab at the tears that stubbornly continued to flow from her eyes.

Beep . . . "Marnie?" It was Patrick's voice, clipped and a little curious as he waited. "It's 7:20 in the evening, and I'm leaving in a few minutes for dinner. I should be back here in the suite by eleven at the latest. I'm still scheduled to return Sunday morning. Sorry to miss you, baby."

She sniffed and thought of him in his dinner jacket and of how, when he'd made this call last evening, she'd been laughing with Jesse at the gaudy Chinese restaurant. The beep for the second call sounded.

"Marnie, this is Patrick." His voice was traced with impatience. "Marnie?" he said again, then, "It's 11:20. If you've called and left messages, I haven't gotten them. The number here is 404-555-4022. In case you don't return this call, I'll be arriving at the OKC airport at nine-thirty tomorrow morning. I trust you'll be waiting at the penthouse."

So he'd finally noticed that she'd been out and hadn't returned his calls, she thought. It was about time. She looked around the room, her vision blurred. He would be here in a matter of hours. With a deep sigh, she headed to the bathroom for a shower.

She had two open suitcases on her bed and was having a difficult time choosing what to put into them when Ogden called.

"Marnie? Boy, am I glad you answered," he said with great relief. "Did you check your answering machine? Patrick called here earlier, wanted me to check on you. He said he's called and you haven't been there and haven't returned his calls. Dorothy said she hasn't seen you since Friday morning, when I saw you, too, and we were kind of worried." He spoke with frantic swiftness.

"I'm fine, Og," she answered, her heart swelling. *Dear, sweet Og.* "You are very sweet to be concerned."

"Well, of course I was concerned, and so was Patrick. We thought maybe you were sick or something. I was coming over there if you didn't answer."

The emotion in his voice surprised her. "I'm sorry to have worried you both. I just got in this morning and listened to the messages, but it was too late to try to reach Patrick. I never thought about you being worried. I am sorry, Og."

"Uh...that's okay, Marnie," Ogden said after a minute, no doubt taking in what she'd said about just getting in. "Just so you're okay."

"I am, and I'll be here when Patrick arrives."

"Okay. You can tell him I'll be over later this afternoon. I have to take Mom to church, and then—" his voice dropped with shyness "—I'm taking Dorothy to lunch."

"You are?" Marnie smiled while tears filled her eyes. "That is very good to hear."

"Yeah . . . we went to a show Saturday night. She likes comedies. One of the reasons she doesn't go out much is that she has to take care of her mother a lot." This was the first Marnie had ever heard of Dorothy having a mother; it was hard to process. Og continued, "She's taking her mother to church this morning, too, and my mom offered to have her mother over so Dorothy and I can go out today and Dorothy won't have to worry about her. I think my mom has plans of getting her mother involved with her poker and gardening buddies."

As he spoke, she envisioned the mothers and Dorothy and Og, hearts in love, and Marnie's tears and smile increased.

"Thanks for what you did Friday morning," Og said, shy again. "I doubt Dorothy would have joined me, except it was all set up there in front of her, and that made it a lot harder to resist."

"I'm happy to have helped. And I thank you, too, Og."

Og took that quietly. Then they said goodbye, and she replaced the receiver, standing there thinking a moment about Dorothy and Og and how alike they were and that she'd never seen it. Then she recalled what Og had said about Patrick being worried. It was a little amazing to think of it. Had he been concerned about her, she wondered, or had it simply been that he felt inconvenienced because she wasn't where he'd expected her to be?

Then her heart glowed. Ogden's concern had been real, and that touched her deeply. She had at least one friend in him. She wasn't totally alone, she thought as she returned to her packing, and somehow that knowledge gave her strength.

Time ticked faster than she'd imagined. She had such trouble keeping her thoughts focused, and seeing nine o'clock upon her, she left her packing to dress. She chose an oversize ivory cotton sweater, gray slacks and black, comfortable flats, then carefully applied makeup, finishing off with her favorite plain gold loop earrings. She paused and then took Miss Phoebe's diamonds from the jewelry box, tucked them into her purse, then looked into the box before resolutely closing it.

With quiet, purposeful strides she went through Patrick's penthouse, pulling back the draperies and methodically checking to make certain all was ready for his arrival, just as she always did. She filled the ice bucket on the liquor tray and prepared coffee, which was usually the first thing Patrick asked for on returning.

After a final sweep of her gaze around the spacious living room, she returned to her own apartment, leaving both the connecting door to the penthouse as well as the door to the entry hall open. She tuned the bedside radio to a country station and carried a cup of coffee out to the rooftop patio to wait for Patrick. And to sweetly remember the past days with Jesse.

"Marnie?" The call came impatiently. "Marnie? Are you here?"

She stepped slowly into her living room, expecting Patrick to come through her door from the entry hall, but she heard him moving into his own penthouse and calling to her again. She entered through the connecting door and saw him toss his suit coat across the back of the couch, his briefcase onto the cushions. She caught a glimpse of Sidney's back as he disappeared down the hallway with the suitcases, and then her gaze met Patrick's.

She moved toward him, saying, "How was your flight?"

"We left Atlanta in a thunderstorm."

She came up on tiptoe and kissed him softly, quickly. Sidney reappeared; Patrick thanked him and dismissed him.

Then Marnie and Patrick were alone.

As he took off his tie and tossed it with his coat, Marnie said, "I'll get you some coffee."

She practically fled to the kitchen. While she prepared the tray, she scolded herself for her fears. She dreaded confrontation, she thought. Looking around the kitchen, she thought that it was damn hard to give all this up. *But it would be harder to stay.*

She felt Patrick's heavy gaze as she returned to set the tray on the coffee table. He was sprawled on the white couch.

"Rough trip?" she asked, making small talk.

"Yes," he answered, his eyes sharp upon her. "You didn't return my calls."

"You didn't indicate that it was necessary," she replied, sat and handed him his cup. "You simply said if I needed to reach you, I could call. I didn't need to reach you."

"I was worried about you."

She saw the truth in his face and was immediately contrite. "I'm sorry, Patrick. I just truly never considered that you would worry."

"You weren't here," he said.

She looked into his eyes. "I was with Jesse Breen."

Surprise jumped into his hazel eyes. He blinked and looked away. "I see." He raked a hand through his hair. "You were with him the entire time?"

"Yes," she said quietly and let that sit there between them for several seconds. "I will be ready to leave this afternoon, but I hope you'll give me some time, a few days at least, to get my photographs and some other things out of the apartment. I . . . I'll need to arrange for boxes and storage."

"You're leaving?" His voice and eyebrows rose in incredulity.

He was surprised? Did he want her to stay after what she'd just told him about herself and Jesse?

"Yes," she answered shakily, curiously.

"Why?" It was almost a desperate question. He plunked his cup on the glass table and leaned toward her.

A little taken aback, she said, "I just told you about myself and Jesse."

He rose and paced. "So you had an affair with this guy," he said, gesturing. "There was never any mention of fidelity in our agreement. I've had a few affairs over the years, Marnie. I don't begrudge you yours."

She was surprised again, yet she felt no pain, no sense of betrayal. Patrick's life had always been his own. "I'm glad you don't take offense," she said, somewhat sadly amused, "but that doesn't change my decision."

"So you're going off with him?" he said angrily. "You're tossing away everything I'm offering you to run off with some two-bit sheep rancher? Good Lord, Marnie!"

"No...no, I'm not." She looked away. "I'm not going off with Jesse. I'm just going."

Thick silence enveloped them.

"You're just going?"

She nodded and made herself meet his gaze, and saw clearly that he didn't understand.

"You've thought this over very carefully?" he asked. "Did you understand the contract I drew up? Do you truly understand what I'm offering you?"

"Yes. Yes, I do. I'm not ungrateful, Patrick. Your offer is...well, it's quite stunning and flattering, to say the least. But I just can't accept it. I can't go on like this. I'm sorry," she added at his sinking expression.

"Marnie," he said and sat beside her, taking her hands. "I know I've taken you for granted lately. But I do need you. I do. And I care for you."

Marnie squeezed his hand, grateful for the true emotion she heard in his voice. The telephone rang. They gazed at each other. The phone rang again. Patrick breathed deeply and answered. "Yes?"

Marnie rose and went to the window, gazed out and thought that she was surprised how little hurt she felt at all of this. She was certain now that she was doing the right thing. Oh, but she would miss that Cadillac...and all those credit cards...and doing what she wished when she wished. And she would, after all, miss Patrick. Now, right at the edge of leaving, she realized how much she cared for him.

She heard Patrick say, "Send him up." Something in his voice made her turn. His eyes were hard and speculative. "Your sheep man is on his way up."

During the quick ride up in the private, gleaming brass-and-glass elevator, Jesse wondered if Vinsand were there yet, if it had been Vinsand or Marnie the concierge had spoken to. He didn't want to cause Marnie any trouble. But he intended to speak to her, and Vinsand was of little importance to him. Marnie wouldn't have to worry about Vinsand, either, after she'd heard what Jesse had to say.

The elevator door opened, and there stood Marnie in the entry hall, just outside the penthouse double doors. Her eyes were wide, her expression a mixture of puzzlement and concern.

A movement behind her drew his attention, and he saw Vinsand in the doorway. The man's hands were tucked loosely into the pockets of his glossy dark slacks, while everything about him said he was tight as a watch spring as he gazed at Jesse with dark speculation.

"Jesse?" Marnie took a step toward him.

His heart rose as he whipped off his hat. She was glad to see him; he could tell by the upward tilt of her lips, the eagerness in her eyes. It all rushed back to him—holding her, arguing with her, kissing her goodbye.

He said, "I need to talk to you." He looked at Vinsand and added, "Privately."

Vinsand said, "You're quite presumptuous, Mr. Breen. This is my hotel. My apartment. And my woman."

"It may be your place," Jesse said, "but as for your woman, well, sir, that assumption is open for discussion." The sudden itch to punch the man in the mouth tugged at him. He didn't like the man, and that was reason enough. And he could see Vinsand felt the same.

"Patrick," Marnie said quietly. "I would like the courtesy of seeing Jesse in my apartment."

Vinsand's jawline turned to rock. Then he inclined his head and faded back into his living room. Marnie stepped quickly to the open door of her private apartment. Jesse followed and shut the door behind him. She turned and gazed at him.

"I thought you'd be well down the road toward New Mexico," she said.

He inclined his head. "I was on the road, all right. I made it almost to Weatherford before turnin' around." He studied her face. "Does he know? About us?"

She nodded somberly. "Yes," she said in a husky whisper. "I told you I wouldn't do anything behind his back."

He nodded, wondering at it all. Vinsand obviously hadn't been about to throw her out on her ear.

She waited. He licked his lips and sought the correct words.

"I don't have the money Vinsand has," he said right off and let that sit there for her to take in. "I can't offer you unlimited credit cards, or an apartment that costs thousands a month, like this setup here. But I can provide you with a nice car and a comfortable apartment. I'll get you one high up in a building like this one, with a big patio, if that's what you want. You can pick it out. Amarillo's the closest city of a size you'd like, and it's only about a two-hour drive from the ranch. I think you'd find it a real nice place to live. I'll pay for your apartment, all living expenses, and I can give you a credit card with a respectable limit."

She stared at him. "What are you sayin', Jesse?"

He stepped toward her. "I'm askin' you to come with me to Amarillo. I'll see you live well, if not as lavishly as all this—" he gestured with his hat "—and to make up for that, I'll give you something Vinsand doesn't. I'll fill up your lonely place."

"You would fill up my lonely place?" she said softly, looking downward.

He said, "I'd sure as hell try."

"While you live up at your ranch and I live in Amarillo?"

"I could easily see you several evenings during the week and most weekends. You'd have all my attention at those times, darlin'. And you could come up to the ranch anytime you might want," he thought to add, though he doubted she would want to, considering how she felt about the country.

A long moment passed in which he couldn't tell what she was thinking. He hoped that meant she was considering. Then she walked past him to the door and opened it.

"No thank you, Jesse." She was smooth and cool as a spring-fed stream. "I'm sorry for your trouble of drivin' all the way back here, but I certainly do appreciate the thought."

Somewhat amazed, he stood there. He had thought for certain that she would say yes. He had barely considered that she would say no. He'd been certain she liked him more than Vinsand. *He'd thought she might even love him.*

But now, here she was, coolly turning him away! Anger rose. "That's it? You aren't even gonna consider?"

"I did consider, and the answer is no. I do not wish to be your *mistress,* nor do I wish to live in Amarillo."

He gazed into her stubborn, angry eyes and thought how he'd been one hell of a fool. He'd thought they'd found something together. He sure as hell thought he'd given her something Vinsand couldn't. He had not believed she would choose Vinsand's money over what he could give her.

Very carefully he put on his hat, gave her a polite nod and walked out. The door closed sharply behind him. Two strides toward the elevator, and he looked up to see Vinsand in the penthouse doorway.

"Guess we can now say whose woman she is," Vinsand said with satisfaction.

Jesse paused, wondering if the man had made a lucky guess or had somehow overheard.

Vinsand gestured. "There's another door to that apartment, you know. And neither of you bothered to close it." The man gave a derisive laugh. "Marnie may have enjoyed a few days with you, old man, but she isn't fool enough to leave this setup for a back-country *sheepherder.*"

In a split second sweet fire burned through Jesse, and he figured he'd had less cause to punch a fella as he drew back and aimed his fist at Vinsand's smirking face.

The blow connected, sending Vinsand staggering back into the doorjamb. As he struggled for balance, he stared in shock at Jesse. Jesse, simmering just below boiling and trying to keep himself there, turned for the elevator. Just as he pressed his fingers on the button, he heard movement behind him. The next instant Vinsand's hand tugged at his arm, spinning him around. Vinsand threw a punch, and Jesse moved quickly enough for it to glance off his shoulder.

"I'll make mincement of you," Jesse said to the obviously slighter man.

Vinsand grinned grimly. "You may have size on me, but I'm a few years younger—and I was lightweight champion in college, so come on."

Those were encouraging words to Jesse, who never fought a man who wasn't his match. He swung and connected with Vinsand, sending him back against the wall, but Vinsand was quick on his feet—quicker than Jesse had anticipated. He came back swinging and caught Jesse in the stomach. With a flash of respect, Jesse took the punch and swung an upper cut that caught Vinsand quite neatly. The next instant Vinsand had closed in, and they went at it full-out—grappling, punching, grunting and gasping for breath. The blood pounded in Jesse's ears as he thought of Vinsand calling him *old man*. As he thought of Marnie living in the man's apartment, walking along on the man's arm, lying in the man's bed. *Damn him! Damn her!*

Again and again he swung and jabbed, his fury spewing forth like a volcano, until Marnie's voice broke through to his foggy brain.

"Stop it! Both of you!"

The next instant cold water and flowers came raining down on his head and shoulders. That succeeded in getting his attention. Blinking water from his eyes, he saw Vinsand sputtering and brushing a tiger lily stem from his face. Blood trickled from the man's mouth. Jesse looked around to see Marnie, a big vase in her hand, looming at them with fire in her eyes hot enough to melt steel.

"You are the most obnoxious, sexist, selfish, overbearing men on the face of this earth! You are . . . Oh!"

In disgust she hurled the vase to the floor. Jesse instinctively ducked the shattering glass, then looked up just in time to see her pivot and flounce back into her apartment. The door slammed.

The fire drained from him. Slowly he straightened and glanced around for his hat, without fully realizing he was doing so. He found it over beside the elevator and plopped it on his head. He pushed the elevator button, and the doors opened immediately. With a final glance he saw Vinsand propping an arm against the doorframe, breathing hard and smirking at Jesse. The doors closed, and the elevator descended. And this time Jesse had no thought of returning to her.

It was nearly two o'clock when Marnie called for a bellman to come for her luggage. It had taken her that long not only to finish her bit of packing but to get her courage in place. It was hard to leave all this, to give up a fortune. She wasn't at all proud of herself for her second thoughts.

At the last minute she took Jesse's bouquet, tossed the flowers in the trash and set the vase in the bathroom.

She was leaving, she thought as she sent the bellman on ahead of her and went to say a final word to Patrick, but she was doing it with little satisfaction and high reluctance. She supposed she was only human.

She noted several bruises on Patrick's face as she handed him an envelope containing her credit cards and the checkbook to the bank account he had opened for her and the keys to the Cadillac, which was the hardest thing to give up. She made no mention of leaving the two fur coats and all the jewelry; he would see that for himself soon enough. He frowned deeply and waved away her concern about her photographs and the few bulky things she would like to have. "Get them when you want to," he said. "I'll have someone pack the photographs and have them waiting—after a week." He reached out and rubbed her upper arms. "You might want to come back, baby."

"I might want to," she told him, "but I won't come." She smiled, and he shook his head.

"I always thought you had a level, practical head on your shoulders."

"People also have hearts, Patrick," she said. Then she added, "Did you know I loved you once?" She could say that now.

And he nodded. "I knew—and it scared the hell out of me. I...I guess I've loved you as much as I've ever loved anyone," he said, his face cracking with more emotion than she'd ever seen, sending her into his arms to hug him fiercely. He drew back and said, "What if I said we could get married?" But he was far from convincing.

She truly chuckled. "I consider you too much of a friend to do that to you."

"Do you love this sheepherder?"

"You say that like you're speaking of garbage. You've never been such a snob."

"I just don't like him."

"That's because he's as stubborn and overbearing as you are."

"And you love him."

"Yes," she said in a hoarse whisper.

"Why didn't you tell him? Why the hell didn't you go with him?"

She shot him a dry look, thinking how men could be as thick as cream soup, then kissed his cheek. "Goodbye, Patrick. Make a million this week."

"Wait!" He reached for her. "Do you have enough money? Let me give you—"

But she waved him aside. "Dear Patrick. Remember how you told me to save? Well, I did. I have almost ten thousand dollars." It amused her to see his eyes widen. "So you see, I am not quite a waif being tossed out on the street."

"Ten thousand dollars can go inside six months," he said soberly. "You don't have a car. At least let me get you a car. Let me get you a job, baby—in the hotel."

She backed away, blinking rapidly, refusing to cry. "I can't, Patrick. We have to make this clean—and I have to do this on my own."

Reluctant understanding seeped into his eyes, and his jawline tightened. "Okay, if that's the way you want it. But that door will be open to you for a few days at least, in case you come to your senses. And I'll want to hear from you—to make sure you're all right."

"I'll call. I wish . . . I hope you find someone to love, Patrick."

He shook his head, as if in despair over her fanciful ways. She smiled and turned away.

With purposeful strides she went down the hall and out to the elevator, leaving Patrick as she'd come to him, with a purse and camera bag, and Miss Phoebe's diamonds. She thought it very apt and that Miss Phoebe would love the moment for its drama.

In the lobby she began to quake, wondering whatever she was going to do. Where in the world should she go? Car dealers were closed, so it would have to be a taxi. But to where? It had been so long since she'd been out on her own.

She stood beside her bags outside the front entry, contemplating the most practical course of action and battling the growing panic, when a gray Mercedes pulled to a stop beneath the portico. It was Ogden, she realized, and Dorothy was with him.

He got out of the car and gazed at her over the hood. "Are you going somewhere, Marnie?"

"Yes," she said. "To a new life." Seeing Dorothy made her hold herself together.

Og was stunned, of course. Then Dorothy's window came down. "May we be of help, Miss Raines?" she said, her gaze moving sharply from Marnie to the luggage and back again.

"I don't think so," Marnie said smartly, "because I'm not certain where I'm going."

Dorothy opened the door and got out. "Then get in and we'll help you figure it out." She and Marnie gazed at each other for long seconds.

"Thank you, Dorothy. You are just the person I would like to have helpin' me plot the rest of my life."

She might throw away thousands of dollars, but she wasn't such a fool as to throw away an offer of friendship, however coolly made.

Dorothy amazed her by saying, in a very low voice that Ogden couldn't hear, "I'll lend you my practical knowledge, if you'll lend me your womanly expertise."

"Deal. And you're gettin' the better bargain," Marnie returned in a whisper and was rewarded by Dorothy's indignant frown.

Tears came to her eyes as she got into the back seat. She had friends. Thank you, God. She wasn't alone. Blinking, she gazed out at the sunny world and thought of Jesse driving far away. She would not cry for him nor the special time they'd spent together. She would be glad for it everyday of her life.

The first days were filled with details that gave her little time for thinking of emotions and sent her to bed each evening too exhausted to dream. She got a good deal on a ten-year-old paint-fading blue Thunderbird and found a tiny apartment above a garage just two streets away from Dorothy's house. It was amazing how quickly ten thousand dollars could shrink with these expenditures, plus car insurance and deposits on utilities and telephone and everyday needs, no matter how much she tried to conserve. Patrick had been right that ten thousand could be spent in six months. The age-old fear of being destitute grew as the days passed, and it was all Marnie could do to keep herself from running back to Patrick.

Beginning the first week, she took the job of caretaker to Hester, Dorothy's mother, two afternoons a week. It was convenient and paid enough for her to eat at least five days of the week. Hester had a viperous tongue, but Marnie set to work to mellow her. And Dorothy was sufficiently impressed with Marnie's patience and expertise. Actually, she was amazed.

"You got Mother to take a walk," she said, as if it were an impossible feat. "And to eat *oatmeal?*"

"I pointed out that old guy on television who advertises oatmeal. She thinks he's sexy, you know," Marnie said, and thought Dorothy would fall flat at the mention of her mother finding a man sexy. Marnie added righteously, "I *have* spent the better part of my life taking care of people. I know how to make them happy."

And Dorothy had actually smiled. "So you do."

She and Dorothy became good friends, though few people who heard them speaking would believe it. However, they came to greatly respect each other. When Marnie took a job at

Beaver's Camera Shop, Dorothy was so disappointed to lose her help with her mother that Marnie arranged her hours to accommodate continuing to care for Hester—besides, she needed both jobs in order to make enough to pay daily expenses and not touch any more of her savings.

After the flurry of the first two weeks, her life settled into a nice quiet and mundane routine. She usually made sandwiches—"cooked," Marnie called it—and washed her own dishes and cleaned her own apartment. It wasn't so bad—except taking out the trash. She hated taking out the trash. She missed Tacita making her morning coffee, missed going to the hairdresser once a week, missed her flowers from the florist and missed buying clothes.

It was quite a revelation to discover she had friends. She became closer to Og and Dorothy and watched their romance develop, was even a part of it in that she helped Dorothy with clothes and hair and girl stuff. And Beaver, to whom she'd been taking her film to be developed for years, was glad to have her working in his shop; he appreciated her knowledge and way with people. Even with two jobs, however, she had plenty of time to sleep or putter or take pictures. Or simply contemplate where she intended to go from here. She considered going to school to study photography, or perhaps taking up something with sales—Cadillac sales, in particular, because she would like to have one. She went on two dates, once with Beaver's brother and another time with a friend of Og's. They were nice times, and she was home by ten.

Patrick took her to dinner one evening, to the Top of the World restaurant, and it was wonderful to get dressed up in her velvet and Miss Phoebe's diamonds. She wasn't even disappointed when she discovered Patrick had an ulterior motive for the dinner date—he wanted her to plan and host a party for him to announce his acquiring the Williams Hotel Corporation. He would pay her handsomely for her services. She accepted; she wasn't going to turn down honest, hard-earned money, which she needed to pay for her photography. She had begun a collection of photographs of elderly people and children, which she thought she might try having published in a book. Everyone had to dream.

Only once did she take out and lay around her the photographs she had taken of Jesse during their days together. Afterward she packed them away, carefully tucked into an envelope to keep them safe, as she tried to do with her thoughts of him.

The weeks stretched into two months, and all in all she was happy, even content, and rather proud of herself.

Then she discovered she was pregnant.

## Chapter Twelve

It had been another tough winter, and when the first week of February had turned typically warm, melting snow and reminding everyone that spring was just around the corner, Annie laid down the law and ordered all of her Breen men, as she termed them, to show up for Sunday dinner. Always willing to please his daughter-in-law, as well as to eat of her good cooking, Jesse showed up at the appointed time at the Big House, as everyone called it these days, where all his sons, his daughter-in-law and grandson lived. He'd given the house, which had been the family home for three generations, to Matt and Annie the year before, when he'd had a new place built over near the rim rock some three miles to the west. His "little cabin," he called it, for himself alone.

Pride rolled around in Jesse's chest when he looked at his progeny sitting around the oval oak table. Matt held little Jess on his knee; the sun rose and set for Matt in that boy, just as it had for Jesse when Matt had been that age. Matt was a good father and a hell of a cattle rancher. Rory sat at Jesse's right and was talking about his latest escapade down at a horse show in Fort Worth, where he'd managed to restrain himself from getting involved in a good fracas. Oren had gone with him and was talking about the ladies he'd met there—Oren attracted women in the same manner grass did sheep, simply by being what he was. Then there was Annie. She was more beautiful than ever these days. She'd told Jesse the other day that she and Matt were working on a new baby. He'd thought to tell her that the endeavor couldn't be termed work, but he'd held his tongue. Annie was easily embarrassed about some things.

Now Annie shot Jesse an impish smile, then said to Rory, "You were just lucky you didn't get into a fight down in Fort Worth, because you didn't have your daddy there to bail you out like he did last fall in Oklahoma City."

And as Rory replied with, "You all are never gonna let me forget that indiscretion," it all came rushing back to Jesse, just like it was yesterday.

Marnie and her sky-blue eyes and pale, creamy skin shimmered up before his eyes. Her sexy smile, her sultry voice. He could even recall her scent. And he could almost feel her against him. He looked downward, lifted his coffee cup and focused on it as the sweet memories swept over him in waves. He sure hoped no one noticed.

Somehow the conversation evolved around to state fairs and which ones they were going to that year. "Are you going back to Oklahoma this year, Jesse?" Annie asked, and he thought her gaze unusually probing.

He shrugged. "I haven't made up mind about any fair this year," he said, though he'd been thinking a lot about the Oklahoma State Fair. An awful lot.

Suddenly wanting to be alone, he excused himself, kissed his grandson and Annie goodbye, touched each of his sons and went to get his coat from the kitchen alcove. He was somewhat surprised when Matt followed, grabbed his coat and said, "I'll walk out with you, Dad. Nights like this are too good to pass up."

They walked out into the ranch yard. Behind them, the windows of the house glowed yellow like the holes of a jack-o'-lantern, and above, stars were diamonds tossed on black velvet. The two of them paused side by side, their gazes making the same proud sweep over the Breen family place. For the first time Jesse noticed that his eldest son was the same height as he and had reached his full-blown build, too. His son had ripened into prime manhood.

"Dad," Matt said and pulled on his mustache the way he did when he was thinking deeply, "I guess I feel like a bull in a china shop about this, but everyone's elected me to talk to you."

Jesse frowned. "To talk to me? About what?"

"About the way you've been the past months—hardly talkin' and spending so much time alone. Mopin'."

"I like bein' alone," Jesse said, instantly planting his feet like a stubborn ram. "There's nothing to make of that. And that's not mopin'."

"I don't mean to get your back up," Matt said in a placating tone that did get Jesse's back up. "It's just that...well, Dad, you're a healthy man who's isolating himself, not only from your family but from any and all feminine companionship." And he looked pointedly at Jesse. "Ever since you came back from the Oklahoma State Fair."

"You don't know where I go every minute of the day," Jesse pointed out. He then added, "Not that I think it's any of your business, either."

"No, sir, it isn't, except that you're my father, and I love you. I guess it's safe to say you're about my best friend, too, which sometimes makes things tricky between us," he said, pulling again at his mustache. "And I've been seein' something eatin' at you." They gazed at each other for a long moment. "You seem like you're tryin' to squeeze yourself into a pair of boots that don't fit. And Annie...well, you know how she can worry."

Jesse's spirit slipped to his toes. He put his hand on Matt's shoulder. "There's nothing really wrong with me. Nothin' for any of you to worry about. I guess I'm not seemin' much like myself 'cause I don't feel much like myself. But I'm just sorting things out, son, as a person has to do sometimes."

Matt nodded with understanding, then peered at Jesse. "Rory thinks you're pining after a woman you met in Oklahoma City." He raised an eyebrow.

Jesse had to chuckle. "You all have done a lot of speculatin'
about me, now haven't you?"

"Well, you know," Matt said with a grin, "it seems that if
there's one thing that can throw a man for a loop, it's a
woman." He regarded Jesse expectantly.

"I met a nice woman," Jesse said quietly, "and I enjoyed her
company for a few great days. But I'm not pinin'. I guess what
I'm doin' is contemplating my life, which is something all of
you could spend more time doin' about your own." A man did
not care for his children to be wise with him, Jesse thought. It
went against the order of things.

Matt appeared to digest this. "Well, we just wanted you to
know we cared."

Jesse felt contrite. "Thank you, son. That's good to know.
You tell Annie not to worry about me. If it'll make her feel
better, I'll go with Rory soon on a Saturday night up to Raton."

"Somehow I don't think that's what she had in mind," Matt
said. "I think when Rory came home from Oklahoma City and
said you were enjoying time with a woman there that she envisioned you comin' home with that woman."

"She did, huh? Well, I'm sorry to disappoint her. I'll try to
do better next time." He winked and said good-night as he
stepped away.

Jesse drove home to his "little cabin" along a dark, rutted
dirt road. Alone, with country music coming from the radio,
he thought again of Marnie. She seemed to be all around him,
and he didn't think he would be surprised to find her suddenly
appear on the truck seat right there beside him.

He wondered again, as he had a million times in the past
months, if Marnie thought about him sometimes, as he thought
about her. When recalling how she'd shown him the door of her
apartment that final time, how coolly she'd spoken, he had to
doubt that she thought of him at all. But when remembering
their times of making love, he had to believe that she thought
of him. How in the hell could she forget what they'd shared?

He sure couldn't. It was with him all the time.

Would he go to the Oklahoma State Fair again that year? He
wanted to. He wanted to see her, just as he'd wanted to see her

ever since leaving her. How would it be if they saw each other
again? His mind drew up a dozen different scenarios, from the
implausible dream of running into her again to the idea of going specifically to the Vinsand Plaza Hotel and asking for her.
Would she even be there, living with Vinsand still? Would she
see him? Would the attraction still be there between them?

Was she thinking about him now, as he was thinking about
her? *Did she yearn for him, as he yearned for her?*

He did pine for her, as his son had said. Because, after all, no
matter the differences between them, he was still in love with
Marnie Raines. God help him.

*Go to see her.*

The thought dropped into his mind like a raindrop into a
wooden bucket already filled with at least an inch of the same
raindrop thoughts. He'd wanted to go back to see her ever since
he'd left. That was why he wasn't himself—because he wasn't
doing what his instincts strongly told him to do. But he kept
remembering how she'd told him she didn't want to be his mistress or live in Amarillo. Remembering how she'd shown him
the door. Remembering how much younger she was and how
she didn't like the country.

Sometime during that long return drive from Oklahoma City
months ago it had occurred to him to wonder what would have
happened if he'd asked her to marry him. He hadn't asked that.
And something inside him wanted to know what she would
have said.

*Go back and see her.*

He tried to dismiss the crazy urge all through the rest of the
night—as he greeted Ham and went into his house, encour-
aged the embers in the big stone fireplace to burn brightly, sat
with Ham at his feet and read words from a Louis L'Amour
novel and wondered what Marnie would think of his "little
cabin." As he tossed and turned in his big, lonely bed. As he
thought of Marnie. His Cadillac Woman.

Dorothy helped Marnie carry the shopping bags up the stairs
to her apartment. They had caught a good sale on maternity
clothes.

"Sit down, and I'll get you a glass of milk," Dorothy said. She kept at Marnie all the time about proper nutrition.

Marnie took off her coat and gratefully flopped onto the couch and propped her feet up on the pine trunk that served as a coffee table. Her apartment had two basic rooms: the living, kitchen, dining area, and her bedroom, with a tiny bathroom sandwiched in between. It came furnished with the basics, couch and chair, the trunk and end tables, kitchen table and chairs, bed and dresser. Marnie had made it homey with her photographs on the walls and a hodgepodge of inexpensive little things she gathered here and there to add color and warmth. She'd sewn the curtains at the windows by hand, a skill so long unused she'd been surprised she remembered. But she was discovering that a person could do anything she made up her mind to do.

She caressed her stomach. Going on five months, she wasn't showing much, but her regular clothes were no longer adequate.

Even now, with the proof before her, she could hardly believe herself pregnant. Until she had done that little test in the privacy of her own bathroom, she'd clung to the hope that her nerves had simply upset her cycle. But then, as she'd stared at that little pink dot, she'd had to admit to herself that missing her pills those two days when she'd been off with Jesse had been enough. Or, as the doctor had explained, that little sperm could have remained there for the day afterward, too, when she'd thought she didn't need to take her pills anymore. And as a result, she had amazingly, wonderfully, horribly, conceived a child.

A child. Hers and Jesse's.

"Patrick was asking about you yesterday," Dorothy said as she brought Marnie the glass of milk and a glass of juice for herself. After getting into the habit with Marnie, she called her boss Patrick to his face now, too.

"You haven't told him about...?" She pointed to her stomach.

"No. Og and I promised you," Dorothy said, as if offended. "But I still can't understand why. I know...I know. You say he'll want to help—but for the life of me, I can't see anything wrong in that. He's your friend—he cares for you. Sometimes he still says to me, 'Call...' and I know he's about to say your name, but then remembers you aren't there. And what are you going to do, Marnie? Not see him ever again, so that he won't know about the baby? That would hurt him. You know that. And what if he finds out from someone else? Sooner or later someone from the hotel is bound to catch sight of you and start to talk.''

Marnie sighed. ''I will tell him. Just not now.'' Now she intended to put it off as long as possible. ''I don't want him trackin' down after Jesse. Men go so odd when they are faced with a pregnant woman.''

''Telling Mr. Breen is something you should do yourself.'' Dorothy took on her righteous preaching voice. ''You should do that and you know it. Never mind this absurd notion you have that he'd want to marry you just because you're pregnant. I would consider it very admirable on his part. But all that aside, the man has a right to know, and the baby has a right for him to know. How are you going to take care of that baby and work?'' Her eyes filled with concern. ''How are you going to afford this alone, Marnie? You're being a prideful fool not to let anyone help you!''

''I let you help me,'' Marnie said practically.

''I'm getting worn out,'' Dorothy shot back.

''Then go home.''

Dorothy sighed. ''I do have to. Mother will be home from the senior center in about twenty minutes.'' She rose and slipped on her coat. ''Tonight for dinner, you eat a bowl of that soup Mother made you.''

Marnie held up her hand. ''I promise, Warden.'' She reached affectionately to squeeze Dorothy's hand. ''Have you decided whether or not you're gonna say yes to Og's proposal?''

Dorothy looked shy. ''No. I keep thinking how I'm five years older than he is and...''

Marnie waved away her words. ''Now look who's bein' foolish. No two people were ever more perfect for each other, and five years' difference is *nothing!*''

Dorothy smiled hopefully. ''Well, I'm thinking about it.''

"That's your problem—you think too much. You must get better at lettin' your feelings go."

"And look where that got you," Dorothy said smartly but with a fond chuckle as she went out the door.

How much Dorothy had changed, Marnie thought. She was so much more bending; she was happy. She had indeed needed some good loving to make her bloom.

As we all do, Marnie thought, rising and carrying her new maternity clothes into the bedroom and thinking that she herself had done quite a bit of changing. She spread the clothes on the bed—two sweaters and two pairs of slacks, all that she could afford right now. Gazing at the lovely blue maternity sweater, Marnie thought what a great turn her life had taken.

She was overwhelmingly happy about the baby. She truly was, even considering everything. She wasn't certain how she would pay the medical bills her insurance didn't cover, but at least she did have the insurance. And she could work for Beaver right up until she delivered, providing no complications popped up. For the eight weeks she'd be off—well, she would deal with that then. Maybe she would go to Patrick for a loan. She could do that, for the baby.

Her gaze traveled to the two stuffed bears propped against her bed pillows. Sitting, she took up the tan-and-brown one and thought how her baby had two little toys already. And she remembered when Jesse had won the bears for her.

Slowly, hesitantly, she got on her knees to dig into the bottom dresser drawer, and she pulled out the envelope containing the photographs of Jesse. *Oh, Jesse . . . oh, Jesse.* How she missed him!

Not a day passed that he didn't enter her thoughts. Such a magical time they'd had together! She knew he'd cared for her a great deal. But in the end, when he'd asked her to be only his mistress—well, that had hurt so badly. *Was that all any man was going to want from her?*

Call him if she needed anything, Jesse had told her. She imagined herself doing so and simply saying casually, "Oh, by the way, I'm going to have your baby."

She sighed. He'd made it clear he didn't want the encumbrances of marriage. He'd raised his family; she doubted he wanted to be faced with that again.

Oh, Lord. She wanted to tell him about the baby more than anything. She thought he had a right to know, like Dorothy said, and that the baby had a right for Jesse to know, just in case he wanted to be the baby's father. Marnie wanted him; she needed him. And the tears ran down her cheeks.

"A prideful fool," Dorothy had called her. Yes, perhaps she was. But after all that she had lived through, all that she had done in her life, the one thing that had become dearest to her was her pride. So many times she'd felt degraded, and she never intended to feel that way again. She could not stand for Jesse to feel obligated to her. No, she couldn't stand that.

*But, oh, Lord, how would she go through this without him!*

For long minutes she gazed at the pictures with blurred vision. Then she chose three—one of Jesse and Billy with his fair ribbon, one of Rory, and lastly, one of Jesse and herself together. She wrote Jesse's address on an envelope, inserted the three pictures and applied the stamp. Still considering whether or not to mail it, she put on her coat and carried the envelope to the mailbox sitting outside the little store on the corner of her block. She stood, like some sort of idiot, holding open the mailbox chute for about five minutes, before finally letting the envelope slide away. And immediately she wanted to grab it back. She certainly would have, if she could have figured a way to do it.

It didn't matter. He didn't have her new address. And there was little chance that he would come all the way back to Oklahoma City and go to the trouble of finding her.

Annie brought him the envelope on the eighth of February, a sunny but cold-biting day. She'd been to town for their regular every-other-day mail run.

"There's a letter there for you," she said, placing the small pile on his breakfast bar, perching on the tall stool and pouring herself a cup of coffee. "It doesn't have a return address, but it has an Oklahoma City postmark." She regarded him expectantly. "It feels like pictures."

"Why don't you just open it?" he said.

"I considered it."

He looked at the envelope. Then, because a foolish fear came over him, he flipped through the rest of the mail—the sheepmen's newsletter, the quarterly electric bill, a vet bill, a bank statement and a couple of charities wanting money. Then he picked up the envelope and handled it.

"I guess I'll go," Annie said.

"You might as well stay," he said, tearing open the flap.

He pulled out three snapshots, glanced over one of him and Billy and their fair ribbon and one of Rory in cowboy getup, and then stared at one of him and Marnie. He recalled how his arm had felt around her, how they'd laughed at Rory's clumsiness with the camera. His heart cracked wide open.

"She's lovely," Annie said, peering over his shoulder.

Jesse nodded and said huskily, "Yes . . . she is."

"No note?" Annie asked.

Jesse checked the envelope. "Nope." And suddenly everything fell into place, and he knew what he was going to do, right or wrong. He looked at Annie. "Guess I'll go down there and find out why she didn't send a note."

"Guess you should," Annie said, with a small, very pleased grin.

It was late afternoon and there was work left to be done with the sheep, so he didn't leave until the following morning. He was eager to go, but now that he'd decided, it seemed he was working in accordance with time and not against it, so he didn't fret over the delay.

As he drove through the lonely grassland of the Oklahoma Panhandle, he did a lot of considering—not doubting, because he was certain about his actions. But he did consider that he might be going off half-cocked. So she'd sent a couple of pictures? Maybe she was just being nice. Maybe she'd simply cleaned out a drawer.

However, the pictures didn't really matter; he wasn't going to see her because of them but because he had to find out what she would say if he asked her to marry him.

Now that *was* crazy. He was setting himself up to be a fool for sure. But, hell, he'd been a fool before and lived through it.

He had to see her. That was all. He had to see her, to look in her eyes, and he'd know then what he needed to know.


Jesse checked into the Vinsand Plaza Hotel and went straight to his room, where he changed into his best sport coat, his shiniest boots, his belt with a silver buckle. As he settled his finest hat on his head, he felt damn good. He felt himself again.

Taking a deep breath, he lifted the telephone receiver and punched in Marnie's number from memory. It rang and rang; her answering machine didn't pick up, and he was left feeling like a balloon pricked by a needle. He dialed the hotel operator and requested to leave a message for Miss Raines.

"I'm sorry, sir. Miss Raines no longer lives here," the operator said in a curious tone.

Jesse felt as if the earth fell away beneath his feet. "She doesn't live here?"

"No, sir."

"Do you have a forwarding address?"

"No, sir. I'm sorry."

"Does Patrick Vinsand still live here?"

"Oh, yes, sir! May I ring his office for you?"

"Please do."

The call went through, and after two rings a very precise woman's voice answered. It was a recording, announcing that he had reached Patrick Vinsand's private offices, that no one was available at the moment and to please leave a message. Jesse did and hung up. After several seconds, he got an outside line and dialed the operator. There was no listing for a Marnie Raines.

Sorely irritated, he took off his hat and stretched out on the bed to wait impatiently. And to worry. Had Marnie left town, or was her phone number simply unlisted? Where would she go? What if he couldn't find her? He *would* find her, by heaven.

After half an hour he had the operator ring Vinsand again and got the same recorded message. He slammed down the receiver and headed for the lobby, where he bought a pack of cigarettes, then headed for the desk to find out if someone could tell him if Vinsand was at least in town. The Fates were on his side, because as he was striding to the desk he saw Vinsand entering through the big glass doors.

Vinsand saw him, stopped and stared. The tall, brown-haired woman in a brown coat beside him stared, too.

Jesse approached, and Vinsand said coldly, "Mr. Breen. Forgive me, but I'm surprised to see you frequenting my hotel again. Though it is the best around, and you're certainly welcome."

"It's not your hotel that I came to see. It's Marnie," Jesse said. "But I'm told she doesn't live here anymore."

Vinsand stiffened. "That's right." He moved to go around Jesse. "If you will excuse me, my secretary and I are on our way upstairs."

Jesse stepped to block his way. "Where is she?"

Vinsand's eyes were cold and hard. "I don't think that's anything I'm obligated to tell you."

So Vinsand knew, or at least wanted Jesse to think he knew. "And what do you get by that?" Jesse said quietly. "Revenge on me—or on Marnie?" He'd guessed the man wasn't one to deliberately practice the nonsense of revenge, and he saw immediately the flicker of doubt in Vinsand's eyes.

They stared at each other for long seconds. Then Vinsand gave a reluctant sigh and motioned to the woman at his side, saying, "Write down Marnie's telephone number for him. Then she can decide if she wants to see him."

The woman immediately opened the leather notebook in her hand and scribbled, then tore away the bottom half of the paper and handed it to Jesse.

"Thank you," Jesse said to Vinsand.

Vinsand gave a curt nod and stepped around him. Jesse's gaze happened to meet that of the brown-haired woman; her eyes were sharp and intense before she passed on after Vinsand.

Eagerly Jesse looked at the paper the woman had given him. But it wasn't a telephone number. It was an address. And below it was scribbled, "after 6:00 p.m." He looked up, saw the brown-haired woman rapidly walking away. He opened his mouth to call to her, then shut it.

She'd written from memory, so she was obviously well acquainted with Marnie; Vinsand had acted as if she were. She must have had reason to give him the address; obviously she wanted him to go to Marnie instead of calling. If he'd called Marnie, there would have been a chance she would tell him that she didn't want to see him. And he had to see her. He had to look into her eyes.

With a city map he got from the concierge, Jesse found the street in twenty minutes. It wasn't hard, and it wasn't far away, and it was something of a shock. It was in an old, established, middle-class neighborhood of brick homes, narrow streets, small yards with boxwood hedges and bare mimosa trees. He pulled to the curb in front of the house number the woman had given him. The house had a wide drive leading to a garage with the same number followed by a *B*, which was obviously for the apartment above—and matched the number on the yellow piece of paper. He stared at the brick-and-white clapboard two-car garage. It was neat, with white wooden steps leading to the apartment. Wind chimes hung by the door, and the winter-bare limbs of a large tree brushed at its roof.

*Marnie lived here?*

Slowly Jesse got out of his truck and walked to the foot of the stairs. There was a small black mailbox on the wall. The name Marnie Raines was written in flowing script on a white label. Everything was quiet, and he thought how the woman had written "After 6:00 p.m." He got back in his truck and drove off to find something to occupy his time until then.


Marnie had been home for fifteen minutes, had changed into lounging pajamas—of deep blue velvet, one of her dear luxuries saved from her days with Patrick—made herself a pot of coffee and settled down to read the newspaper when the knock sounded on her door. So rarely did anyone knock, and never in the evening, that she answered with curiosity and caution. For some reason she thought of Patrick and thought that someone had told him about the baby.

Holding the newspaper in front of her stomach as if for protection, she peeked out the window. There was a man on the landing. With a cowboy hat.

Jesse? *Jesse?*

"Who is it?" she asked through the door in a husky voice.

"Marnie, it's Jesse."

Cold amazement flashed down her back, followed by a wash of heat. *Oh, heaven . . . oh, mercy. What was she to do?*

With shaking fingers, she opened the door, because she could think of nothing but to see him. And then there he was, smiling that wonderful, cocky smile. His dear, handsome, rough, precious face.

"Hello, darlin'."

"Hello, Jesse."

He whipped a bouquet of flowers from behind his back and held them toward her. Slowly she reached to take them, while still holding the newspaper in front of her. The sharp February night breezed in around her. Jesse slipped his hat from his head and motioned. "It's pretty cold to hold a conversation in the door. May I come in?"

She couldn't do anything but nod. He hadn't noticed her belly. But then, his eyes were riveted on her face, and she didn't show much, and she had a newspaper and flowers to hide behind. She kept them hovering there as, heart pounding, she moved aside to let him enter. As she closed the door, her gaze flitted across his wide shoulders, and with the memory of his strong arms, she had to stifle the urge to throw herself into them. His hair was shaggy, in need of cutting, and his skin was somewhat paler. But those eyes were as striking as ever. How mangificent he looked—enough to set any woman's heart to beating right out of her chest. And he'd come. He'd found her. *Oh, but how embarrassed she was!* She suddenly couldn't bear for him to know about the baby. She couldn't stand to have him feel obligated, and the Jesse she knew would most definitely feel responsible.

Jesse looked at her, saw her hair was longer and her face seemed even more creamy than he'd remembered. She was every bit as beautiful as he'd recalled. If he'd had a doubt about how he felt about her, it was certainly washed all away as he gazed into her glistening blue eyes.

"Come in," she said, her lips trembling into a smile. "I'll put these in water." She turned and rounded the breakfast bar in a tiny kitchen area.

Jesse glanced around, seeing a room as homey as the apartment she'd had at the hotel, even if sparsely furnished with cheap furniture. Some, certainly not all, of her photographs were on the wall. Past the kitchenette area was a little alcove and doors that obviously led to the bedroom and bath.

Marnie brought a vase from a cabinet, filled it with water. Jesse moved to the end of the bar. "I got your pictures," he said.

"You did?" She cast him a quick, furtive glance.

"Why didn't you send a note? Why didn't you tell me your new address?"

"I don't know.... I didn't think it would matter. They were just pictures I thought you might want."

He searched her profile and found her strangely distant, unreadable. "I did. Thank you for sendin' 'em."

"How did you find me?" she asked.

"Patrick—actually his secretary." He moved closer, inhaled her scent.

"Oh." She kept her gaze on the flowers. "So, what brings you to OKC?"

"Now what do you think brought me?"

"I don't know. There isn't a fair goin' on that I know of— oh, I did hear there was a horse show at the fairgrounds."

Tentatively, wondering what her reaction would be, Jesse reached out and cupped her chin, turned her face so he could look into her eyes. They were deep, deep blue. He rubbed his thumb over her soft cheek and saw a flickering in her eyes.

"I know you were pretty mad at me back last September— and that you're pretty good at grudges. But haven't you forgiven me enough for a hug?"

She shook her head uncertainly. "I wasn't..."

But he slipped his hand to the back of her neck and urged her toward him. Then she was in his arms and holding him as he held her. Jesse squeezed his eyes closed and gave thanks and held on to her, inhaled her scent, savored the feel of her tinier, tender body.

He moved his lips to her mouth and kissed her, and she responded with unmistakable desire. When they broke the kiss, he continued to hold her, to run his hands over her. He pulled back to gaze into her eyes.

"Now what do you think brought me to town?"

"A good time?" She raised a saucy eyebrow. And there was a dark shadow in her blue eyes.

He draped his arms loosely around her waist and gazed at her. In the space of a second it rushed at him in rapid impressions—how she'd felt against him just then, her thicker waist beneath his hands, the way she moved—that built into one big realization.

Was she *pregnant?*

Even while he was telling himself the idea was crazy, he stepped back and looked downward. She went to turn, but he took her arm. She froze, didn't look at him. And he knew, as if her thoughts had spoken directly to his.

"Are you . . . ?" As he spoke he placed a hand on her abdomen and felt.

*Oh, Lord. She was! She was pregnant.*

His breath left him, and the realization washed over him as it only could over a man who'd planted and watched three children grow inside his wife. Dropping his hand from her, he stepped backward, as if from a blow. It was a blow—a hell of a blow!

Their eyes met. Hers were sassy and with a spark of defensiveness.

"Surprise," she said.

He breathed deeply and propped his buttocks on the chair back. "It is that, gal." So now he knew why she wasn't with Vinsand anymore.

She rounded the small breakfast bar. "I'm sorry to throw a hitch in your plans for a good time in the city, Jesse."

Barely hearing her, he swallowed and gazed at her belly. He imagined the fetus snuggled inside. Small, only a few months formed, but human.

"Damn Vinsand," he ground out. What kind of a man got a woman pregnant and then abandoned her? "Isn't he gonna acknowledge the baby? Provide for it at all?"

"Patrick has been very generous to me," she said and threw away the florist's paper.

"But he won't marry you—and he couldn't allow you to be anywhere around him!" He gestured at her surroundings with his hat. "This sure as hell isn't the Vinsand Plaza Hotel, or anything near it." No wonder that brown-haired woman had given him the address. She'd wanted him to see what was what.

Watching him, Marnie was torn. He obviously thought she'd gotten pregnant after their weekend; that he could be the father hadn't even occurred to him. She wanted so much to tell him—but what would happen then? If he thought Patrick should marry her, he would no doubt think he himself should certainly do that.

And maybe it didn't occur to him that he could be the father because he didn't want to be the father.

"Don't take on so, Jesse," she said. "I'm just fine. And Patrick hasn't abandoned me. He speaks with me on a regular basis, and if I need anything I only have to call." Some of which was even true. "This was my choice. All of it. I want to build a life for myself and my child. I had savings from my allowance from Patrick, and I have a job now. I'm makin' it on my own."

"A job?" He frowned. "Doin' what?"

"I work in a camera shop, and I like it very much. I've been thinking of going to school, and I will, when I figure out exactly what for."

"You won't have much time for that and work and a baby."

"I'll work it in. Lots of women do."

He gazed at her for a long moment. "I asked you back last September to go with me to Amarillo. You said then you didn't want to be my mistress, that you didn't want to live in Amarillo. What would you say to marryin' me and livin' with me at my ranch?"

Time and her heart seemed to stop. She gazed into his intense, beautiful luminous eyes.

"It'd be a good place to raise a kid," he said gruffly.

Overwhelmed, she looked away. "You are somethin', Jesse Breen, that's for sure." He would do that, even thinking the baby belonged to another man. Blinking, she met his gaze. "I thank you for the gesture, Jesse, but there is no need for you to feel responsible for me," she said, forcing herself to speak as normally as possible. "I'm a big girl, and I can take care of myself and a child quite well."

"You're gonna need help," he said. "And I speak from experience—I've raised three, remember?"

"Oh, yes, I remember. And I seem to recall you sayin' that you didn't feel up to marryin' again, to givin' all that such a relationship takes. Now you come waltzin' in here and find out I'm pregnant, and like the good guy in the white hat, you think you'll do me the favor of marryin' me to take care of me. To make it all right. I don't need that—I don't need your pity."

"It's not pity!" he said, frowning and raising his voice. "I came down here to OKC for the express purpose of askin' you to marry me. A man can change his mind, you know."

She looked at him and didn't believe a word of what he said. "You changed your mind when you saw me with this belly."

He frowned and jutted his chin. "If that was so—and I say *if*—why do you make it sound like a sin? What's so wrong with wantin' to help you? I care about you, damn it! I *love* you."

He'd said it now, popped it out, and he steeled himself for her reaction. He saw immediately that she didn't believe him.

"You don't have to feel sorry for me. I don't need that!" She turned and strode from him.

"Where in the hell do you get that nonsense? I just said I love you."

"You feel some crazy sense of obligation. Well, don't, Jesse. I'm not your burden to bear."

"No, you're not a burden. I *want* to help take care of you and the baby."

"Well, I don't want you to. I don't need you to." And her face crumpled. "Oh, good grief! I'm gonna throw up. Go away! I don't want you to see me!" She turned and ran from the room.

Jesse strode quickly after her, but the bathroom door was shut in his face.

"It doesn't matter what you look like, Marnie," he said through the door. "It's natural for you to do things like throw up in your condition. Besides, you aren't the beautiful mistress on display anymore."

"Shut up, Jesse," came her muffled reply. "I haven't thrown up since I got pregnant. I *don't* throw up, and I don't let people see me when I look like hell. Ooooh!"

"I may not have as much money as Vinsand," he said, "but I know about this stuff. I can help."

"Go away! *Please* . . . just for now."

He fumed helplessly. He considered breaking down the door but restrained himself. Finally he said, "I'll go for now. But I'll be back. And in the meantime, you think about what I said. I want to marry you, Marnie."

## Chapter Thirteen

When Jesse got back to his hotel room, he opened the pack of cigarettes he'd bought earlier and lit one.

*Marnie, pregnant.* It was hard to take in.

Well, he'd asked her to marry him and had gotten her answer. But he'd been so thrown about the baby that he hadn't paid a whole lot of attention to reading her eyes. His strongest impression was of her doing her best to skitter away from him. Of her hiding from him. Of her distrust.

He picked up the telephone and had the operator ring Vinsand's penthouse, only to get that stupid recording again. He dialed the operator once more and told her to leave a message for Vinsand to call Jesse Breen as soon as possible. Then he stretched out on the bed, propped on two of those lousy fiber-filled pillows, and smoked his cigarette, turning everything over in his mind. It was a jumble, to say the least.

He didn't buy what Marnie had said about leaving here on her own. She liked luxurious amenities too much to leave here. After all, she'd refused his offer of putting her up in Amarillo—and he considered that his offer hadn't been a bad one.

And no way could he imagine her voluntarily giving up her Cadillac for the old clunker he'd seen parked in her drive.

Any way he figured it, it added up to Marnie getting pregnant, refusing to abort the baby and Vinsand giving her the heave-ho. Vinsand wouldn't have wanted her hanging on his arm with a big belly in plain sight; it wouldn't be at all the correct image for him. And no doubt he would have been at a loss with a woman who might cry or throw up or look like hell when she felt like hell. A man like Vinsand would be at a loss with a woman who showed herself to be human.

Jesse couldn't quite understand why in the world Marnie had gotten her back up about his proposal of marriage, though. Pride had a lot to do with it, he guessed. And she was probably still hoping Vinsand would marry her, he thought sadly. That was hard to face. He'd thought, after what they'd shared, that she'd cared for him. Maybe even loved him. He was usually good at judging such things, but he guessed every man had his weak spot.

Maybe if he told her that he wasn't some poor rancher but quite a well-to-do one. Not in Vinsand's league, but with all Jesse had, he did add up to millionaire status. He sighed. He doubted that it would matter to her—she had to know he wasn't terribly poor after his offer to set her up in Amarillo. Besides, he lived simply, didn't use his money for show or excess and couldn't be anything other than what he was—a rough, earthy man, more at home on the range than in a fancy penthouse.

He mused and looked at it from every angle and came up with only one conclusion, and that was that he wasn't leaving until he had something settled about Marnie. He loved her, and he would see her secure, one way or the other.

Jesse arrived in Vinsand's apartment the following morning to find the man having breakfast on his rooftop. The white cloth-covered table with its pristine china, crystal glasses, all the costly surroundings, raised his ire.

"How'd you get up here?" Vinsand asked, rising.

"I remembered the numbers to punch. I *have* been brought up in that elevator twice."

"You're a sharp man."

"You got it, and I want some answers."

The dark-haired maid hovered nervously to the side. Vinsand glanced at her and said, "It's okay, Tacita. Please leave us alone." After she'd left, he said to Jesse, "I got your messages, and I was going to call you. Please join me and we'll discuss whatever you wish—or would you rather go at it with fists again? I'm perfectly willing to sink down to your level, Breen." He looked defiantly at Jesse.

"What I want," Jesse said, being as cool as the man before him, "is to know your exact intentions toward Marnie and the baby."

Vinsand stilled, and his eyes narrowed. "What?"

"What is your intention concernin' the baby? Marnie says she's the one who's chosen to go it alone, but I don't believe it. I think you didn't care to have her around because she certainly wasn't the perfect picture of a mistress any longer."

"What baby?"

Jesse watched the man's face go white as potato soup and heard the crackling in his voice and was suddenly presented with the possibility that the man knew nothing about the baby.

He couldn't quite believe it. "Are you tellin' me you didn't know that Marnie's pregnant?"

Vinsand shook his head and, clearly dazed, lowered himself into the chair. His face was pasty and drawn. "I had no idea."

Jesse tossed his hat onto the table, took the other chair and raked his hand through his hair. Now this was sure one giant wrinkle in things. *What in hell was going on here?*

Vinsand said, "What's the matter? Disappointed to discover I'm not the slime you think I am?"

Jesse cut his eyes at him. "I'm not convinced of that yet. How could you *not* know? Haven't you been seein' her? She said she talks to you regularly. And if it wasn't because of the baby...why isn't Marnie here with you?"

"She isn't here because she left me," Vinsand answered harshly. "And I have talked to her—just last Friday, on the phone." He frowned. "I haven't *seen* her in...two months, I guess." He peered intently at Jesse. "She told you she was pregnant with *my* child?"

That made Jesse think. He gazed into Vinsand's eyes, and a prickling began on the back of his neck. He recalled putting his hand to her belly.

"How far along is she?" Vinsand asked quietly.

"Close to four months, I'd guess." Jesse's thoughts jumped to the time in the hay barn.

Vinsand gave a dry laugh and shook his head. "Breen, you surprise me." He cast Jesse a long and amused look. "I had a vasectomy five years ago, when I realized how...*attached* Marnie was becoming to me. I was afraid she would do something foolish, like get pregnant in order to get me to marry her. And I never told her, because I couldn't see that it would do anything but upset her. Not too honorable, perhaps, but wise, because, you see, I know myself very well. I not only intend never to marry again, no matter how fond I grow of a woman, as I have of Marnie, but I don't intend to have a child."

As he spoke, the word *vasectomy* echoed in Jesse's mind. It was like a giant neon sign flashing on and off.

Vinsand said, "I know that vasectomies aren't foolproof, but the chances of that baby being mine are slim." He paused, stared at Jesse. "If you want to know the father of Marnie's baby, I suggest you go look in the mirror. I haven't even slept with Marnie in at least six months—but you, sir, have. And I'd say she was closer to five months' pregnant—count them up yourself."

Jesse felt like a herd of buffalo had just run over him. Twice.

Vinsand smiled at him. "Hello, Papa."

*The baby was his? Marnie was carrying his baby?* He'd gotten her pregnant? He hadn't used anything, but she'd said she was on the Pill. Still, his Gina had been on the Pill when she'd conceived their little girl that they'd lost.

*He'd produced a child again—at his age!* A sweet, indefinable feeling swept over him. Male pride—foolish, wonderful, grateful. A kid. Would it be a boy or a girl? He thought of the girl Gina had lost. He wished it would be a girl. Then he wondered why Marnie hadn't told him.

Vinsand was speaking. Jesse focused on him. "What?"

"I said that I think it's my turn to ask you what you're going to do. After all, no matter what you may think, I, too, care about Marnie's welfare."

"I asked her to marry me, but she said no. It's you she wants." His anger grew. She should have told him about the baby, damn her! He'd had a right to know. It was his baby, too!

Vinsand gave him a withering look. "For all your rugged charm and posturing, which no doubt attract women like flies, you don't know that much about them."

"I understand them a sight more than most men," Jesse said, bristling at the pip-squeak who thought he knew more.

"Yes, but love distorts vision, makes a person blind," Vinsand said dryly. "Marnie's in love with you. She told me so back last September when she left. *That* is why she left here. Not because I got angry over her little fling with you. I considered that of small consequence. I wanted her to stay."

"She told you she loved me?" *Had she actually said that to this man?*

Vinsand wisely inclined his head, and Jesse had a sinking feeling as he thought of how he'd driven off and left her here. She'd been wanting him as much as he wanted her.

"But I offered to—" he began, then broke off. He had offered her an ongoing affair, not marriage.

"Exactly," Vinsand said, as if reading his mind.

He and Vinsand gazed at each other for long seconds. Then Jesse reached for his hat and stood. He could discuss this all day long with Vinsand, could get Ogden's opinion, too, because he was Marnie's friend, and maybe ask that brown-haired woman what she knew of it all. But the only one who could truly tell him how she felt and what she wanted was Marnie herself. And by damn, he had a few things to say to her about not telling him about the baby. *His* baby.

"Thank you," he said to Vinsand.

"I'll expect to be told what Marnie's plans are," Vinsand said. "No matter what you may think of me, I do care for her and I won't allow her to want for anything."

"She won't," Jesse said firmly. "I'll see to it." He wouldn't have Vinsand taking care of the woman he loved or his child—even if Marnie refused to marry him.

He took several strides away, then turned back. "I understand Marnie works at some camera shop. Could you tell me where?" It was galling to ask this man for any kind of help.

Vinsand clearly enjoyed it. "Beaver's—west on Reno, just past MacArthur."

Jesse waved his hat as thanks, then left, eager to be away from the man and his fancy, cold penthouse. Eager to go to Marnie. Impatient to confront her.

Marnie had been shaky all morning, thinking of Jesse and expecting him to show up, dreading it and fearful that he wouldn't all at the same time. If he didn't contact her again, she would have to contact him. She would have to tell him about his child. There was no way around it. She should have done it when she'd first found out; waiting had done nothing but make it harder. Now she would have to try to explain why she hadn't told him, and she wasn't certain of all her reasons, just that they added up to one giant fear.

He'd asked her to marry him. She kept recalling that. And he'd said he loved her. It could have been simply a moment of weakness, of pity for her, she thought. He could already have left town, for all she knew.

She was showing a customer a camera when Jesse walked through the door.

She dropped the lens cap, and it rolled across the glass-top counter to the floor, then across the tiles to Jesse's feet. He picked it up. His movements as he stepped forward and handed it to her were smooth, as tightly controlled as a powerful cat. He flashed her that charming grin, yet sparks shone in his luminous blue eyes.

"Thank you," she managed, staring at him. She felt his searing energy.

"You're more than welcome, ma'am," he said with a deliberate drawl.

Calling up all her genteel training, Marnie returned to her customer, explaining about the camera's capabilities while not really aware of what she said. She was too busy glancing at Jesse, feeling his gaze on her. On her belly. He'd no doubt had time to think about things and had some pretty good suspicions. Of course, they could only be suspicions.

When the customer asked to see another camera, she had to grit her teeth to keep from screaming at him. A small, pinched-faced man with fish eyes, he'd seen four already and was the sort to have her bringing out every camera and every accessory in the shop just so he could handle them and deliberate but never make up his mind. Jesse hovered nearby, appearing to browse. Across the shop, Beaver waited on a young couple.

After what seemed an eternity, Jesse came up beside the fish-eyed man. "Excuse me, sir, but could you do your ponderin on these cameras by yourself—I need to talk to the lady."

"Jesse . . ." Marnie said in a hissing whisper. "This is my customer."

"He doesn't need you to go over all this stuff again."

"It's my job, Jesse," she said, her temper rising. He was the most overbearing man!

"Yeah—I *am* the customer," the fish-eyed man put in.

At which Jesse and Marnie both gave him a hot glare. Jesse loomed over him. "I wish to speak to the lady."

The little man seemed to shrink. "I think I'll look in this case over here," he said, pointing and moving away.

"You just cost me a commission," Marnie said accusingly.

"I'll buy the camera—here, this one. Wrap it up."

"There's no need, thank you." She turned her back to him and concentrated on returning boxes to the shelf with shaking hands.

The next thing she heard was Jesse's voice announcing "This beautiful young lady is gonna have my baby."

She whirled around. *Oh, Lord, he knew!* He stood gazing at her. His eyes were bright. Beaver was staring at her, as were the two people he was waiting on. The fish-eyed man's mouth was hanging open.

Jesse smiled brilliantly. "I've come to plead my case to get her to marry me. And I'm prepared to do it here and now, if have to, and I hope you all will be my cheering section."

Marnie, heart racing, gazed at him, unable to believe he was doing this, astounded by what he'd said. From Beaver and his customers came applause.

Jesse stepped closer and said softly, intently, "Come with me. Let's talk." His eyes glittered; he wasn't going to take no for an answer. She had the feeling he was about to lift her up and carry her out.

She took a deep breath and glanced at Beaver, who waved her away. She grabbed her coat and put it on as she came around the glass counter. Jesse held out his hand, and she took it. His grip was hard. Applause came again, even from the little fish-eyed man, as they went out the door.

Tears blurred Marnie's eyes. *He knew. Of course he wanted to marry her. She was carrying his child. And she hadn't told him—that was inexcusable.* All her arguments dissolved at that one overwhelming thought. No matter whether he truly loved her or not, she loved him, and she loved the child she carried. She would not deny either one of them their rightful relationship.

She stopped at the passenger door of his red truck and turned to him, "Jesse . . ."

"Not now," he said tersely and opened the door. "Wait until we get to where I want to take you." He was definitely angry.

He helped her up into the seat, reached across to take the seat belt and fasten it around her. He laid his hand on her belly for a long second, then shut the door. She watched him walk around the hood, his shoulders straight and strong, his movement a self-confident saunter.

He didn't say where he was taking her; she didn't ask. Her heart swelled when he turned into the road leading to the fairgrounds. Somehow she had known.

He drove through the tall, open gates and out onto the blacktopped area that during fair time was filled with the midway game booths and the colorful, giant metal rides, going up and down and round and round. Now, beneath a bright winter sun, all was quiet, empty. Jesse stopped the truck, turned off the ignition. Memories of their time at the fair tumbled over themselves inside her.

He turned to her, and his gaze was hurt and accusing. "I had a nice talk with Patrick this mornin'." He paused. "It turns out that he had a vasectomy a number of years back."

"A vasectomy?" She was stunned; he'd never told her.

"Yes, ma'am. So there's no way he could be the culprit." And he waited, staring at her.

"There's no way anyway," she said in a soft whisper. "Patrick and I hadn't been together for over a month before you and I...had our weekend. And I left him that Sunday afternoon."

"Why didn't you tell me, Marnie? Just as soon as you found out? That baby is part *mine*. By damn, gal, were you *never* gonna tell me?"

Marnie struggled to hold back her damnable tears. "I wanted to tell you. I mean, it came as a great shock to me, too, you know. And I did think you should know. I was going to tell you. I really was." She sucked in a shaky breath. "But I knew this would be your reaction. You'd feel so damn *responsible*." She gestured helplessly. "You'd be the hero in the white hat coming to rescue the woman in distress, the woman you'd gotten pregnant, so you'd do the proper thing and marry her. Oh, Lord!" The tears welled up and spilled over. "I'm sorry for not tellin' you, Jesse. I am. I just didn't know what to do. You'd made it plain you didn't want to be married again." She stopped, sniffed and wiped at her tears with her clenched fist. "You asked me to be your *mistress*, damn you! If you cared for me, if you *loved* me, why didn't you ask me to marry you? Because I belonged to Patrick? Because I was only good enough to be a mistress—never a wife?"

He pulled a handkerchief from his coat, took her chin and began wiping her cheeks. "Why don't you ever have any tissues? A woman who cries like you do should carry a wad of them."

Sniff, sniff. "I have them in my purse—back at Beaver's."

He dabbed at her nose, saying, "I didn't ask you to marry me because I didn't think you'd want to marry a man sixteen years older than you—nor to go live in the country with him. And at that time, I still didn't want to get married," he admitted gruffly as he drew back his hand.

"You don't have to marry me to be a father to your child, Jesse. I won't keep the baby from you. I wouldn't do that."

He sat back and gazed at her. "I'd made up my mind to ask you to marry me before I ever knew you were pregnant. Askin' you to marry me was the sole reason for my coming to OKC."

She searched his face, wanting to believe.

"I love you," he said. "If you'll recall, I told you that last night."

"You didn't tell me until after you'd seen I was pregnant," she said.

"It just turned out that way. And there's nothin' shameful in a man feelin' obligation toward a child he's fathered. That's a good and honorable way to feel. It doesn't take away from the love I feel for you—if anything, it makes it more."

She gazed at her coat while fear welled and churned inside her. "Jesse, I love you." Her voice came out a hoarse whisper, and she couldn't look at him. "I think you are the finest man I've ever known. But I don't want to ever be put in a position of dependin' on someone again. I just *can't*."

He sat there, hearing what she didn't say—that she loved him but was afraid to trust. Afraid to believe, because her experience with love had always brought her heartache, and she couldn't stand any more of that.

"So what are you gonna do?" he asked quietly. She turned her head to him, and he captured her gaze. "Are you gonna struggle along alone, tryin' to raise a child and keep a roof over both your heads? What if you get sick? What about sending the child to college?"

He paused, then said, "I want to marry you, Marnie. I can give you and the baby a good home. I can give that baby every material thing she could need or want. And it is my right to do that, for you as well as the baby. But even more, I love you, darlin'. I *need* you. I feel alive and kickin' and that all of life is worth livin' when I'm with you. I feel a purpose with you. And I'm askin' you to give *us* a chance. I know you'd be riskin' your heart again, but, darlin', a person can't keep their heart locked away from hurt and still live. It's just the way life is. If you turn away from feelings, you begin to die. I found that out the hard way."

They gazed at each other, and the emotion built. Jesse slowly reached out to cup her chin, to rub his work-roughened thumb over her cheek. He watched the tears well into her eyes and saw the protective wall begin to crumble within her. When he leaned toward her, she met him. Her lips were warm and hungry on his, and he lost himself in her, sealed her to him.

At last he lifted his head, gazed down at her and saw the love light shining in her eyes. He saw what he'd been looking for.

"Ah, darlin'." He stroked her cheek. "What you do for me."

"I love you, Jesse." She felt as if she were breaking out of some cold, hard shell of fear and disbelief. *"Oh, God, I love you."*

He smiled tenderly and kissed her again, causing her blood to boil and her hairs to tingle. And for long minutes, as they kissed and slipped their hands beneath their coats to touch each other, nothing else mattered except the love they shared.


They were married that afternoon at a marriage chapel that Dorothy arranged. After hearing of their marriage plans, Dorothy had taken over all the arrangements.

Marnie wore an ivory satin and lace dress she'd hurriedly bought—she'd refused to be married in anything old, and she'd also ignored the exorbitant prices and had bought shoes to match, too, because she intended to be a beautiful bride to Jesse. Besides, she told her shaky confidence, she only intended to get married once. As Dorothy handed Marnie flowers to weave into her hair, she reminded her that she wasn't young enough to be getting married too many more times. Marnie wore Miss Phoebe's diamonds, too, though they were a little showy. However, Jesse appeared to love them on her.

Dorothy and Ogden stood up as witnesses, and Patrick came, too, standing far back with his hands slipped casually in the pockets of his dark slacks. Marnie held Jesse's hand the entire time. He appeared so calm, she had the urge to kick him.

"I know what I'm doin'," he told her, "so why should I be nervous?"

And to that Marnie said, "I shall do everything I can to make you the happiest man on earth." She was wise enough to know she had in Jesse the greatest of blessings.

He winked. "And you're just the gal to do that."

Marnie went through the ceremony in something of a daze. She could barely get her words out, couldn't quit staring at the carved gold band Jesse slipped onto her finger and was somewhat surprised when the minister pronounced them man and wife. Jesse kissed her lightly.

Marnie turned and tossed her bouquet to Dorothy. Og was the first to hug and kiss her, with amazing enthusiasm and a reddening face. When Dorothy hugged her, she was surprised to see tears in Dorothy's eyes. And then Patrick was before her.

"I get to kiss the bride," he said and swept her into his arms, kissing her deeply, with all of his practiced expertise. When he finally let her go, Marnie saw him send Jesse a wicked wink. "Don't begrudge me a last time, ol' man."

Dorothy had thought of everything—a photographer, the best champagne the Vinsand Plaza Hotel had to offer, which was a gift from Patrick, and sparkling confetti to toss at Marnie and Jesse when they left the chapel.

Laughing, holding tight to each other's hands, they burst out into the bright February sunlight. Halfway down the steps, Marnie stopped still.

Jesse's truck was nowhere in sight. There, on the concrete parking lot at the foot of the steps, sat a gleaming white Cadillac Allanté convertible, with its black top up and in place. A red ribbon fluttered from its side-view mirror.

She looked at Jesse, and he grinned. "Happy weddin', darlin'," he said, pulling a key from his pocket.

Her breath left her. "But, Jesse . . ." She didn't understand. How could he afford this? Did he feel he had to do this? That he would have to give her the life Patrick had, in order for her to be happy?

He tucked the key into her hand, than dangled another. "I get to drive, though. Come on." Giving her no more time to think, he hurried her down the steps and into the car.

Dorothy followed and bent beside the window. "Thank you," she said in a soft and quiet voice, her eyes intense. "Thank you for everything."

Marnie grasped her hand. "Thank *you*. Oh . . ." She pushed up to touch her cheek to that of the other woman. "We'll be back for your wedding."

Dorothy smiled through her tears. "April second. Og and I set the date on our way here. You know—it's catching." She stepped back, waving. Marnie's heart squeezed as she returned the wave.

And then Jesse drove them away.

She turned to look back at the three people she was breaking from. She looked longest at Patrick standing off to the side. Alone, as always, by his own choice.

Jesse took her hand and smiled at her, and emotion washed over her. She thought of how she was his wife, he was her husband and they were going to have a baby. And they loved each other. And this was something she had chosen.

They spent the night in Amarillo and by midmorning the following day were cruising down the blacktopped highway that snaked through the grassland of northeastern New Mexico. The sun was high and bright, and a spring breeze blew, and Jesse was a man bringing home his new wife. He knew winter wasn't over quite yet, but it seemed Mother Nature was smiling on them, giving them her blessing in the promise of spring. He felt as if he had a whole life ahead of him again, and that it was much richer now because he had the wisdom from so many lessons learned in his youth. He knew to value the present for all it was worth.

Beside him, Marnie looked fresh and eager, and nervous, too. "I've never been this far west," she said. "It's so different. So . . . so . . . *big*. And open. The sky looks bigger."

"That's because it is, darlin'."

She smiled at him and slipped her hand into his. She'd been exhausted the night before, and Jesse had refused to make love to her. He'd been concerned that she not overdo. Now that he had her for his own, he certainly didn't want to take a chance of losing her. He'd lain with her cradled in his arms, kissed her softly and told her to go to sleep.

"But, Jesse," she'd breathed into his neck and moved seductively against him, "it's our wedding night."

And man, had he wanted her, so very badly, even as he'd caressed her belly and whispered, "There's time ahead, darlin'. We have to think of our little one. You need rest."

He thought now that there were always secrets even between people in love, because he couldn't find words to tell her that he wanted it to be on his own territory when he took her to him again.

As they drove through Wings, he pointed out the post office, and Kelly's Tavern and Lemonade Parlor, and Cobb's Drugstore. Jada was sweeping the steps of the drugstore. He waved to her, and she dropped her broom. Over at Shatto's Garage and Fuel, Shatto and Kelly were sitting in the sun. Jesse slowed enough to call to them, and they gawked; then Shatto waved his dingy baseball cap in the air and yelled, "Ooo-weee!"

Marnie laughed and said, "Oh, Jesse, where have you brought me to?" She didn't seem too sorry.

They neared the ranch, and he found himself as eager as a nine year old wanting to impress the new teacher. "Our ranch begins here." He pointed.

She cast him a shadowy smile and said, "I hope your family isn't angry that we didn't wait for them so they could see you married." She'd said that at least half a dozen times since they'd left Oklahoma City.

"They understand," he told her. "They'll throw us a party."

"You really did tell them about the baby? You did?" She put her hand on her belly.

"I did. I told Matt, and he'll tell the others." He smiled at her. "He was happy for us."

"They might not like you bringing a woman home after so long a time."

"They will. They'll love you."

"You didn't have to buy me this Cadillac, Jesse. I don't need *things*. I have you now. And what about your truck?"

"Darlin', I told you, the truck will be delivered tomorrow to the ranch. And I *wanted* to buy this car for you. It makes me happy."

"But it's so much money!"

And he laughed. "Yeah, it was a bit."

"Your family will think I'm some spendthrift who'll spend you into poverty."

"No... Oren will be after you to borrow your car."

They'd had a similar conversation a number of times during the trip. Jesse knew buying her the car had been a childish, showy thing to do. If pressed, he would have had to admit he'd done it for himself more than for her. He enjoyed sweeping her off her feet—and sticking it to Vinsand that he could buy Marnie anything Vinsand could, or just about.

"Here we are," Jesse said and turned into the long road that led to the Big House. He took her hand, and she gripped his tightly. He pulled to a stop in the ranch yard behind Matt's pickup truck. Marnie stared at the house, then at him.

"Oh, Jesse. It's lovely! I had no idea."

And he was a proud man.

Before he'd opened the door for Marnie, his family came streaming out of the house.

"Hi, Dad!"

"Welcome home!"

"Pa... Pa... Pa..." This from little Jess in Matt's arms.

Annie was the first to hug him and whisper in his ear. "Congratulations."

And then they were all standing there, looking at each other. Jesse put his arm around Marnie. "This is the whole brood," he said, smiling at her. He looked at his sons, his daughter-in-law, his grandson. "This is Marnie, my wife."

There were immediate welcoming smiles and hellos from everyone, and Annie reached out for Marnie's hand. "I'm so glad for another woman in this family."

They all went inside and sat around the big oak table for coffee and cake. Annie spoke of the party she was planning and asked Marnie to go shopping with her. Matt and Rory took it upon themselves to tell her a few tales about Jesse that Jesse would just as soon had remained quiet. Oren, on discovering Marnie's interest in photography, showed her photos he'd taken and his darkroom setup. He also managed to squeeze in a request to take the Cadillac out for a spin. And little Jess, after fifteen minutes, slipped up to hang on her knee and get chocolate all over her skirt.

And then Annie said shyly, "I have a dress, one Jesse bought me when I was pregnant with little Jess. I think it'd look beautiful on you. I'll get it out tomorrow for you to try."

"I'll bring Oren's cradle from the barn this afternoon," Rory threw in eagerly. Then, glancing at Jesse, he said, "Tomorrow. I'll get it tomorrow."

"Friday will be soon enough," Jesse said with a meaningful look as he pushed back his chair and stood. He gazed at his wife and saw the happy light in her eyes. "I think it's time Marnie and I went home," he said.

Her eyes popped wide. "You don't live here, Jesse?"

He shook his head. "*We* don't live here. Our place is a little cabin about three miles west."

His gut tightened as they neared his place. For the first time he became nervous. Like a young teen wanting to impress his sweetheart, he thought, chuckling inwardly at himself.

"This is the long way in," he explained, watching her face for signs of disappointment. For signs of happy tears, which so far she hadn't shed, and that was making him uneasy. When Marnie didn't cry, he had to worry about her. "There's another road that is only a quarter of a mile from the paved road."

"I don't mind, Jesse. Anywhere you are is fine."

"Well, we can get to Raton in about forty minutes—thirty, if we have to. Raton isn't Oklahoma City, but it is a nice town. And I can take you down to Amarillo or up to Colorado Springs often."

She just smiled. "I imagine that would be nice."

And then they topped the hill, and his "little cabin" came into view. "There it is—home."

With growing pleasure he watched amazed admiration bloom across her face. "Jesse Breen! You said it was a 'little cabin.' I thought it was some rustic *shack!*"

"We call it the Little Cabin to distinguish it from the Big House. And it is made of logs." He pulled to a stop atop the brick-paved drive in front of the double garage, then came around and took her hand as she got out of the car.

He led her up the wooden steps and across the wide veranda that wrapped around three sides of the house. Ham ran up to greet her, and she bent to happily pet him. Then Jesse swept her up into his arms and carried, her, both of them laughing, across the threshold into the house he had designed himself. With Ham trailing behind, Jesse showed her the tall-ceilinged living room with its big rock fireplace, the kitchen with its spacious eating area, the sunroom with hot tub, the attic bedroom, and lastly, the master bedroom, with its fireplace and private veranda and the enormous clear skylight situated directly over the bed and angled to catch winter and summer sunlight from morning to afternoon and to enable star-watching from inside.

He watched her move around the room, tilt her head and look up at the skylight, touch the rocks of the fireplace. "We'll go to Amarillo this week, and you can replace whatever furniture you want—except my chair by the fireplace there," he told her, enjoying the wonder on her face. "I've got that chair so it fits my behind." It was then he noticed the ice bucket with the bottle sticking out of it and two champagne glasses sitting on the table beside his chair.

There was a note. "Congratulations, Marnie and Dad—love Matt and Annie."

Jesse stood there staring at the note, recalling when Matt and Annie had married and filling with emotion.

"Oh, Jesse," Marnie said at his elbow. "Your family... they are so special. They've been so kind to me."

He looked over to see tears glistening in her eyes and smiled. "Of course. I told you they would love you."

She sniffed, then fixed him with a pointed gaze. "There must be a lot more money in sheep than I ever realized."

He chuckled. "There's a lot more money in sheep than most people realize... but I've also made my fair share on cattle, and I do have a few oil wells over in Texas and did quite well during the boom some ten years back. Of course, there's still gas comin' out of a couple of my wells, and I've been awfully lucky with some stock investments. I guess it's safe to say that I'm far from poor," he said quietly. "And you and our child won't ever have to worry again. You're my wife, and what's mine is yours."

She turned away. "Oh, Jesse." She buried her face in her hands.

"What's wrong, darlin'?" He quickly stepped beside her, took her hands from her face and grinned at her. "Are you upset that I'm not some poor sheepherder?"

She smacked his chest. "Jesse Breen! You never said anything!"

"I never said I was poor. Did I act poor? Would a poor man have suggested settin' you up in an apartment in Amarillo?"

"If you know what's good for you, you won't ever mention that again. And no, I didn't think you were poor. I just thought you were...well, I thought you were a good, hardworkin' man. I never thought...this." She gestured helplessly at the room and again turned from him.

"I *am* a hardworkin' man. A man can't make money if he isn't," he teased, then reached for her and pulled her into his arms. "Are you disappointed?"

She gazed shyly at him from beneath her eyelashes.

"Come on—let's hear it. Don't be shy. Which credit card do you want first?"

"Jesse, I love you. You havin' money can't make me love you more." And her expression grew very sad. "I feel that I have so little to offer you."

"Oh, no, darlin'—you're offerin' me the world. We both know that money doesn't necessarily add up to riches, don't we? And in that knowledge is where our riches lie—though I'm not a whit sorry for havin' money. I've been poor and I've been rich—and rich is better, isn't it?" He grinned cajolingly.

A faintly sad smile tilted her lips. "Yes, it is," she whispered.

"Well, gal, it gives me the biggest hoot to give you things." He kissed her neck and ran his hands all over her, feeling the curve of her back, the swell of her breasts, the blossom of her belly. A woman in his life again. A woman to love and be loved by. A woman to touch all he wanted. Everything inside him that was man cried out, *Thank you, Lord!*

And Marnie said in a husky voice, "If that's the lay of your heart, *darlin'*, what I want most in the whole world is—" she pulled away to look him in the eye "—for you to fill up my lonely place. And to let me fill yours. I would give up all the credit cards in the world for us to do that forever and ever."

Gazing down into her deep blue eyes, he saw the heat grow. Then he cupped her pale delicate cheeks with his dark, work-roughened hands and kissed her with all that was in him, with all the love and desire and manly need pulsing through his veins.

When they broke apart, he backed up and began unbutton-ing his shirt. She smiled up at him, then shyly lowered her eyes and turned her back to him and slowly, seductively, lifted her sweater over her head. Jesse sat in the chair, took off his boots and the rest of his clothes, all the while watching her remove each piece of hers with erotic slowness until she stood there in nothing more than her alabaster skin. She looked over her shoulder at him when she'd finished.

Truly a man living his dream, he reached for her, swept her up into his arms and carried her to the bed, where he laid her upon the colorful Indian Paint quilt.

Her blue eyes widened, and she gave a giggling sigh as she sank into the softness of an old-fashioned feather mattress. Then those blue eyes danced with delight as she looked at the sunlight around her and the bright blue sky through the sky-light above.

"Jesse, it's like bein' outside!" she said in breathless won-der.

"That's the idea, darlin'. The beauty of outside—without the bugs. How do you like that?"

"Oh, Jesse . . ."

He covered her lips in a kiss that began tenderly and turned fiery. And again Jesse found reason to be grateful for his years of experience, for he knew how to make love to a pregnant woman. He knew the tender and sensitive portions of her swelling body, the areas to treat with extreme care and the areas that sent her moaning wildly with desire. And he knew how to lead her to discover his sensitive areas, too.

He touched her, savored her, pleasured her. She touched him, savored him, pleasured him. The sunlight fell in beams that caressed their bodies. Jesse felt it upon his back, tasted it upon her warm velvet skin, saw it gleam copper upon her hair. It glowed all around them until it seemed to become part of them, until it seemed they glowed, too. And when they met in love it was if they rode the sunbeams right up to the heavens.

The sun moved far to the west of their skylight, and they remained in bed. Marnie snuggled against Jesse beneath the quilt and ran her hand over his hard chest. She couldn't believe it had all really happened. That she was lying against the man she loved, listened to his breathing, after sharing an incredible experience with him. She couldn't believe that she loved Jesse and he loved her back and they were going to have a baby and live in this wonderful house by his wonderful family.

She wanted to hold time still—forever. The idea struck her, and she moved to get out of the bed.

Jesse grabbed her. "Where are you goin'?"

"To get my camera. Wait here. Don't move." She hurriedly slipped into his shirt and ran out to the car, grabbed her camera bag and ran back to the bedroom.

"What are you doin'?" Jesse asked.

"I'm gonna get our picture. Now, stay right there." Quickly she grabbed books from a shelf and stacked them on the trunk at the foot of the bed until she had the right height. She adjusted the camera and set the switch, tore off Jesse's shirt and jumped back in bed beside him, jerking the quilt up over her naked body. "Kiss me."

They kissed, laughing, and the camera flashed.

"There," Marnie said with satisfaction. "I'll frame that and put it on our dresser, and when we have fights or things go wrong, it will remind us of this time." She wasn't so foolish as to think every minute of every day was going to remain as magical as this moment. She gazed at him. "It will remind us of the love we share."

Jesse put his hand to her belly. "We'll have a live reminder in her," he said. "She'll be our incentive to keep our love alive."

"Her? You're so certain we have a girl?"

Her heart squeezed at the pensive expression that came over his face. "Regina lost the last child she and I made. It was a girl."

Marnie gazed at him. "Then if this is a girl, we'll name her Regina."

He grabbed her and pressed her to his chest. "I love you, darlin'."

"I love you, Jesse."

Something fluttered inside her. Marnie held her breath and felt it again. She rolled aside and put Jesse's hand to her belly. Lightly, the kick came once more.

"It's a girl, Jesse. That's a girl kick."

\*     \*     \*     \*     \*

*Silhouette Special Edition*

# There's Another Breen Man on the Horizon!

For those of you who fell in love with *all* the Breen men in Curtiss Ann Matlock's ANNIE IN THE MORNING (SE#695), here's some good news: Jesse Breen, the father of the whole clan, is about to get his own story. August brings LAST OF THE GOOD GUYS, a tantalizing tale of love on a collision course. Marnie Raines and Jesse are perfect for each other—though it takes them a little while to discover the truth of that. Don't miss their story—only from Silhouette Special Edition.

---

## Silhouette Special Edition®

### Linda Lael Miller

Beyond the Threshold

## Two stories linked
## by centuries, and by love....

### *There and Now*

The story of Elisabeth McCartney, a woman looking for a love she can't
find in the 1990s. Only with the mystery of her Aunt Verity's necklace
can she discover her true love—Dr. Jonathan Fortner, a country doctor
in Washington—in 1892....

*There and Now*, #754, available in July 1992.

### *Here and Then*

Desperate to find her cousin, Elisabeth, Rue Claridge searched for her in
this century . . . and the last. She found Elisabeth, all right. And also
found U.S. Marshal Farley Haynes—a nineteenth-century man with a
vision for the future....

*Here and Then*, #762, available in August 1992.

---